"Finn, I don't know how much you overheard tonight." Kelly ran a finger along the rim of her mug, her eyes following the movement. She was obviously embarrassed, but he gave her credit for starting a conversation he'd been struggling to begin.

"Don't worry about it. Neely was out of line and I get you responded with the first thing that came to mind."

Kelly took a sip of her coffee and finally, finally looked him in the eyes.

"I told the truth."

Finn froze, his mug halfway to his mouth. What did she mean? He put the mug down on the counter, careful not to slosh the hot liquid.

"About having been married and not wanting to go down the same road again?" Hell, he couldn't even understand why people got married anymore anyway. Too many ended in divorce and he'd seen too many of his friends, his family, torn apart by the pain it caused.

Kelly nodded. "And wanting you for your body."

The Devil's Invention

by

Gina Leuci

The Devil's Invention

Cover Art by *Diana Carlile*

The Wild Rose Press, Inc.
PO Box 708
Adams Basin, NY 14410-0708
Visit us at www.thewildrosepress.com

Publishing History
First Champagne Rose Edition, 2015
Print ISBN 978-1-62830-840-2
Digital ISBN 978-1-62830-841-9

Published in the United States of America

Dedication

To my husband.
It's easy to write a happy ever after
when we are living it.
Thank you for encouraging me to live my dreams.

Chapter One

Kelly grasped the branch in fear. The earth rotated below her like an obnoxious amusement ride. She'd tried to be brave. She had only climbed the tree to save her nine-year old daughter from falling. Now her hands were clammy. She couldn't breathe. And there was no way she could rescue Olivia when she needed someone to rescue her.

It was all Jeff's fault, of course. If he hadn't called to cancel his visit with his children, again, then Olivia wouldn't have run off.

"Mommy, what are we going to do?"

Kelly tried to focus her spinning vision on her beautiful, emotional, stubborn daughter. She gave what she hoped was a convincing smile. "I'll figure it out."

Damn that man. He'd promised his daughters he'd be here this time. Instead, when he called, she had heard the ruffle of bed sheets and giggles from his latest airheaded slut. Jeff had cheated on her throughout their eight-year marriage; did he have to cheat his own kids out of time with him, too? Bastard!

Now she was picking up the pieces of a broken heart. Olivia's, not hers. She was over him. Completely. She'd long since moved past resentment and into absolute disgust with the man. And it didn't excuse the fact his actions today had put their daughter in danger.

When Olivia handed the phone to her after Jeff's

fabricated reason to cancel his visit, Kelly saw the look on the young girl's face. It was the 'I need to cry but I'm not going to let anyone see me' look. She'd recognized it immediately because she'd lived that life herself at Olivia's age.

As a matter of fact, it had been twenty years ago when her own mother had moved them here to Rocky Point when she'd divorced her father. Twenty years ago when her mother said her father wasn't coming to visit her again. Twenty years ago when she'd done the same thing Olivia had done: hidden in the high branches of the oak tree beside the house.

It was twenty years since she had fallen from this very tree and broken her arm.

Of course, Olivia knew this tree was forbidden, but she'd climbed it anyway. And when she'd tried to come down and almost slipped, Kelly had had no choice but to climb right up to rescue her daughter. Then she had done the one thing she told her daughter not to do: she looked down.

Now who was going to save them?

For a bright Saturday morning in mid-April, there didn't seem to be a single neighbor anywhere in sight. No one planting in the early spring soil. No lawns being mowed. No children playing in their back yards with doting parents by their sides. There was no one outside at all. This was not a typical Saturday in Rocky Point, New Hampshire.

It was just her and Olivia, stuck in a tree, and her four-year old, Hannah, standing in the fenced in yard, looking up at them silently while sucking on her thumb. What were they going to do?

Olivia's arms wrapped around her like a lifeline

and yet Kelly felt anything but her daughter's savior. Her heart thudded against her chest in a fast staccato; it's beat drowning out all rational thought. She could feel the start of a panic attack beginning. It had been two years since her last one, but she knew the signs. If she let it take complete control, she could actually pass out and that was not a good solution while perched fifteen feet in the air.

Breathe. She had to concentrate on breathing so she could think. There had to be a way down. A ladder would be good right about now.

A ladder. Firefighters had ladders. It would be humiliating, but it was better than falling.

"Hannah? Honey?" Kelly's stomach heaved as she opened her eyes and glanced at her youngest daughter, so far away on the ground. Hannah now sat on the wet grass, looking even tinier from Kelly's elevated position. "Do you remember what to do in an emergency?"

The thumb came out as Hannah answered her mother. "Dial 911, then the fire trucks come."

Kelly's slick hands slid on the branch as she shifted slightly. "Right. Well, Hannah, this is an emergency. I need you to go inside and call."

When her youngest daughter walked casually into the house, Kelly prayed something didn't distract the four-year old from her mission. Hannah was a good girl, but often needed to be reminded of a task several times before accomplishing it. Hopefully, this would not be one of those times.

Perhaps it was hearing the plan to call for help, but Olivia became calmer. Her tears stopped their flow and her grip loosened around Kelly's waist. As the nine-year old began to relax, Kelly felt her own panic rising. Her chest constricted. Her breath became shallow and breathing more difficult.

"Are you okay, Mommy?"

Kelly felt the hysterics bubbling as she held onto the branch in a death grip while her daughter continued to hold onto her waist.

"Now what do we do?" Olivia hiccupped.

Kelly leaned her head back against the tree trunk and kept her eyes tightly closed. She'd been grasping the tree branch above her head with such a fierce grip, she wondered if her fingers would ever be able to unclench again. But her daughter needed her; needed reassurance. She could hardly tell Olivia her doubts help would arrive anytime soon. It took all her effort to answer in a soothing tone. "We wait and hope Hannah gives the right information to the operator."

It seemed like forever before she heard the sirens, although she knew realistically it was only minutes. A wave of relief hit Kelly hard enough she blinked back tears. She opened her eyes reluctantly. With the advent of the big red trucks with the flashing lights and blaring sirens came the nosy neighbors who had been nowhere to be found moments before. The irony of it didn't escape Kelly.

The engine stopped in front of the house and the firefighters emptied from the truck in a blur of protective clothing and black helmets. One firefighter strutted to her front door while Olivia yelled to get the attention of the three others.

She knew they were spotted when she saw one of the men point toward them. She couldn't hear what they were saying over the rush of noise in her ears.

Focus. Kelly. You can do this.

They were carrying a ladder now. They opened the gate.

Breathe in. Breathe out.

They propped and secured the ladder against the trunk of the tree while Hannah came back outside holding the hand of a firefighter.

Kelly felt nausea well in her stomach from looking down. She tried to become one with the tree as she closed her eyes once again.

"We've got two kids stuck up there." The voice was deep, and filled with exasperation. Okay, so tree rescues weren't on the top of the list for fun ways to fill their days. "Where are their parents?"

"She said her mother was outside."

Ah, sweet Hannah of little words. Yes, Mommy is outside. You could have told the man where.

Kelly prepared herself for humiliation and opened her mouth. "Her mother is outside. She's stuck in the tree."

She couldn't open her eyes to see their reactions, but figured the men were finding this humorous. She heard the snickers from her neighbors as a few more showed up to see the commotion.

The creak of the ladder as one of the firefighters started to ascend was a dull sound behind the freight train in her head. Only as she sensed the man close by did Kelly force herself to look.

She'd met firefighters before. They'd strolled through her house to inspect it for safety for the daycare she ran. She'd been comfortable with those men. They'd smiled at her, and shook her hand. She'd welcomed them into her home for their input on creating a safe place for the children she minded.

This man, though, had on his oversized fire coat and wore his black leather helmet with the bright yellow reflectors high on his head. The chinstrap to the helmet hung loosely on a firm square jaw and the man's nose was long and straight. From her vantage point, she couldn't see into his deep-set eyes shaded by the helmet, which was okay by her. She really didn't need to see any more judgment about her tree mishap than she'd already heard from her perch. And if the pinched mouth was any indication, she knew at least one person on her block didn't find this situation funny.

Kelly moved her head slowly toward Olivia. Big mistake! Her intention had been to tell her daughter to trust the nice firefighter, but when her gaze swept downwards, the only thought in her brain was the distance between where she sat and the hard surface of her yard. All assurances disappeared. With eyes clamped shut, Kelly began a silent mantra: *It's okay. Olivia will be safe.*

Despite the harsh look on the firefighter's face, his voice was kinder than she'd imagined as he introduced himself.

"I'm Lieutenant Finnigan. What's your name?"

"Olivia. But my mom calls me Livvy."

There was no fear in Olivia's voice, which reassured Kelly her daughter was now more interested in all the hoopla her antics had produced rather than afraid of actually falling. Kelly listened to the firefighter with only half an ear while she tried to find an internal happy place in order to push her own fear aside.

"It's nice to meet you, Livvy." His voice continued

in a soft, soothing tone. He was speaking to her daughter, but the voice called to her. "I'm going to help you down, but I need you to listen to me and do exactly what I tell you."

Kelly felt a new sensation in her stomach that had nothing to do with fear or nausea. As the man directed her daughter on maneuvering along the branch, Kelly felt her own nerves calming, if ever so slightly.

"That's it, Livvy. I've got you. Now bring your foot around to the ladder."

As much as she wanted to watch her daughter reach the safety of the ground, Kelly kept her eyes closed and listened as step by step, the lieutenant talked Olivia down the ladder. She heard a cheer from her neighbors, which she took to mean her daughter had reached safety and Kelly breathed a sigh of relief.

In no time, she heard the creak of the ladder and knew the firefighter had climbed back up beside her again. What was his name? Finnigan. She'd have to thank him for saving her daughter. Kelly opened her eyes and smiled weakly, but her relief was short-lived.

"You're the mother?" His voice was as cold as his glance as he took in her faded jeans and oversized T-shirt she had donned for her Saturday morning house cleaning. "I expect kids to be climbing trees and getting stuck, but parents should have a little more common sense."

Kelly fumed. How dare the man? How dare he judge her? He didn't know her. He didn't know what had transpired this morning. In another time, another place, she'd have let the man have it with all the wrath of a mother protecting her offspring. At the moment, however, she couldn't breathe, let alone get more than a clipped few words out of her mouth. "I'd bet a month's salary you don't have kids. Are you going to lecture me, or are you going to help me down?"

With a slight harrumph, the lecture stopped and the instructions began. "Like I did with your daughter, we are going to swing you around between me and the ladder. First, I want you to let go with your right hand and take mine."

Kelly's chest tightened at the thought. Suddenly the branch seemed sturdy enough to hold her all day, and the thick, rough bark of the tree became more inviting than moving. Her arm felt like lead as she slowly lifted it from the branch. She didn't think she'd swung her arm out enough to reach his, but somehow he had hold of her hand. His hand seemed huge around hers. Large. Warm. Safe.

"Shit, lady, your fingers are like ice."

Kelly gave a half-hysterical laugh as she turned her face to look at her rescuer. Within a fraction of an instant, the judgment clouding his eyes disappeared and a warmth of understanding passed between them. His harsh tone switched to compassion.

"This is what we are going to do, ah," the lieutenant's voice stumbled. "What's your name?"

While her hands perspired, her mouth had become dry as cotton. "K-K-Kelly."

"Kelly." He nodded and the large leather helmet he wore glinted in the sunlight. "Okay, Kelly, you are going to look right into my eyes as we get you onto this ladder. Look in my eyes, and listen to my voice. Got that?"

Violet. His eyes were violet. She'd never seen eyes that color before. They reminded her of a watercolor she'd once seen of the ocean sky during a thunderstorm. Instantly, Kelly recognized an inner strength to this man who rivaled a fierce summer storm. She could trust him to get her down. He wouldn't let her fall. She tightened her hand in his and began to move.

She followed the sound of his voice, moving inch by inch, exactly as he told her, until she had to turn from him and found herself staring at the metal rungs of the ladder.

The shortness of breath returned. Her slick hands slid on the metal, and yet she knew she would not fall. The man behind her seemed enormous. Even standing two steps below, she felt him at her back. He smelled of smoke and something all male. Kelly's head swam with the scent of him. Her body turned from icy fear to melting at the heat emanating from his body. His gentle voice guided her down, step by step. His strong arms, moving inches below hers, were a solid wall of safety.

"Almost there."

If she let go, he'd catch her. What would it be like to be carried in those muscular arms? To have his voice slide over her skin like a wispy fog? She felt a tug within her stomach.

"Stay with me, Kelly. One step at a time."

Kelly felt another round of hysterics building inside. This time it wasn't from the dizzying height. It wasn't from humiliation. She hated to admit it, but as scared as she was, she dimly recognized the feelings washing over her. Attraction. She was attracted to the man who called himself Lieutenant Finnigan.

So what if his violet eyes had entranced her and his musky, smoky scent filled her nostrils? It was ridiculous, really. Nothing more than an adrenaline rush.

"You're doing fine. I've got you."

Huh! Wouldn't that be nice? To be safe within those arms? When was the last time she'd felt protected?

As her feet came in contact with the firmness of the ground, Kelly allowed blackness to swallow her as she passed out.

****

Finn stared at the woman who went limp in his arms. Kelly. She was tiny, barely taller than her daughter he'd helped down the tree seconds before. She was a lightweight, too, he noticed as he lifted her in his arms.

"Hey, Probie," he turned to the newest firefighter in training on his shift. Although the kid had a name, while he was on probation and wearing the orange shield on his helmet, he was known as just probie. "Get the jump kit."

The grass was still damp from the rain the night before, so Finn carried the tiny woman to the walkway by her front door and placed her gently on the cement.

"Is my mommy going to be okay?" a little voice asked.

He glanced over as Firefighter Rawlings squatted down to the youngest girl's level to reassure her. There was no doubt the little one was Kelly's daughter, with the same blond hair and anxious blue eyes.

The older child didn't appear as concerned. She hadn't stopped talking since her feet hit the ground and she continued to prattle on as she found a place to sit on the front steps. "… And, like, mom told me she was, like, afraid of heights and stuff but I never really believed her, you know? But, like, I guess she really is. When mom painted the house last year, she had Uncle Mark paint the higher places. We call him Uncle Mark, but he's not really. He's actually Maddie's brother and she's like mom's best friend and all.

"I guess this is my fault. My dad was supposed to pick us up for a visit but he called to say he had to work. They're divorced, you know. Anyway, I got really mad and climbed the tree. Mom came up after me when I almost fell. You should have seen her. I didn't know she could climb like that."

Finn wondered if Livvy had taken a single breath during her ramblings. He tried to tune her out while he placed his fingers on Kelly's wrist to find her pulse. He didn't know what to make of this woman. This mother. Was she brave, climbing the tree to help her daughter? Or was it plain stupidity?

It couldn't be easy, raising two girls alone. Of course, with his dad's schedule as a firefighter, his mom had often claimed she'd felt like a single mother.

Her pulse was steady. He was vaguely aware of Rawlings ushering the girls to check out the engine as the Probie returned with the first aid kit.

Finn focused on the job. Opening the kit. Locating the packet. Breaking the seal. It was all routine. He didn't have to think about it. Or shouldn't have to. But he did. He mentally reviewed each step so he wouldn't keep staring at the woman on the ground.

Maybe from a distance Kelly looked like just another kid in the tree, but up close, she was all woman. Trim waist, slightly flared hips, tits high and firm beneath the oversized shirt. Add the nicely rounded ass that had been in his face as she'd climbed down the ladder in front of him plus those blue eyes pleading with him to help her and…Hell's fire! He'd have to be a saint not to find her attractive.

And his crew would testify he was no saint.

Kelly's nose wrinkled as he waved the smelling salts beneath it. Even her nose was tiny, Finn noticed, with a slight lift at the end. Slowly her eyelids opened and he was awarded the view of her sapphire eyes.

"Welcome back."

He could almost read her mind while watching the emotions cross her face. The 'what happened?' as her eyes opened. Then the frantic search for her children and immediate relief as she spotted them. Finally the awareness as she remembered why there were firefighters and neighbors in her yard.

She sat up. Too quickly, he assumed, when her hand grabbed his.

"Easy there," Finn put a steadying arm around her shoulders. With Kelly sitting and him kneeling beside her, the touch brought them close enough to almost be an embrace.

His senses seemed to be in hyper-awareness. Her hands were warmer now than in the tree. Her shirt smelled of fabric softener and her skin held a scent of citrus. The wet grass glistened beside them and the morning sun had finally gathered strength and baked him in his bunker coat. His helmet felt like a fifty-pound weight on his head and yet he didn't have the wherewithal to take it off. To do so, he'd have to let go of Kelly. He chose to keep it on.

Keeping Kelly in his arms had nothing to do with making sure she was no longer dizzy. He couldn't take his eyes off her face. Her skin was the color of butterscotch; her lips were a ripe peach.

If he hadn't been working… If his crew weren't here…

Damn, but he wanted to kiss her.

Aww, hell. What was he thinking? She wasn't his type. His type was, hmmm, the leggy brunette public defender, or the saucy redheaded phlebotomist, even the blond stripper who'd… *Shit*. Okay, maybe he didn't really have a type, they were all fair game.

Except *mothers*. He didn't do mothers. Mothers meant kids and kids meant responsibilities and commitment. But if he continued to be this close to this particular woman, he would do something stupid. Like ask her out.

He gave the woman a flirtatious grin. "Now, I have to admit you are the first woman to actually fall at my feet. If this is your way of getting me to ask you out, it just might work."

The beautiful eyes widened. Shock? Embarrassment? Whatever she felt, it was enough for her to release her grip on his hand, although his arm still supported her at her shoulders.

"*Oh, God.*"

"It's a little early, don't you think?" Finn winked. "Most women I date don't use that particular phrase until, hmmm, at least after we've kissed."

A spark of blue fire glistened in her eyes and bright spots of pink infused her cheeks. With a few short words, Kelly had changed from a *damsel in distress* to *I am woman, hear me roar*.

"You can take your hand off me. I'm fine."

While Finn casually pulled his hand off her shoulder, he made a point to slide his glance across her body. "You certainly are."

The blue eyes sparkled with suppressed fury and the ripe mouth opened to respond in kind, but then the youngest child, the one who was the mirror image of her mother, suddenly materialized beside him to plop herself onto her mother's lap.

Kelly wrapped her arms around the girl and kissed the child's temple. He watched as she instantly became soft and compliant although the glare in her eyes warned him to back off.

Yeah, the woman screamed commitment. Any man who wanted a piece of her would have to be ready to accept the whole package. That wasn't him.

"Smitty, come take the report." Finn grabbed the first aid kit and rushed to put it away.

What the hell had happened to him? What he had said bordered on sexual harassment. He had to be crazy. He'd watched a mother kiss her child and wished those lips were on him instead.

As the engine pulled away from the house ten minutes later, Finn couldn't get the woman out of his mind. Yep, he had to be crazy. Certifiable, even.

Although he'd first assumed she'd been another kid stuck in the tree, when he'd gotten to her level he'd seen the differences. But it had been her eyes, those deep pools of bottomless blue that had communicated to him. She'd trusted him.

Sure, people put their trust in firefighters all the time. It was part of the job. They expected them to show up and save their house from a fire, rescue their pet, or pump life back into their husbands who'd had a heart attack. So why did those particular eyes call to him in a more primitive way?

"Hey, Finn," Rawlings said from the driver's seat beside him, "there's a house for you."

The truck had made a few turns and Finn turned his eyes to the small, cape-style house with the picket fence and a 'For Sale' sign out front.

It wasn't bad. Needed some paint and the grass mowed. And he did need a place to live now that his sister and her family were back from overseas. As the truck continued past, Finn saw a familiar oak tree located on the street directly behind the empty house. If he bought the place, he'd be close to a blue-eyed lady who seemed to be firmly imprinted on his mind. For the life of him, he couldn't figure out why that thought alone didn't scare him?

Chapter Two

April showers, and there had been several, had truly brought May flowers, as well as plenty of warm days. Spring had fully blossomed and Kelly liked to have her daycare kids spend as much time outdoors as possible. She handed young Noah a plastic trowel to dig up weeds in her flower garden and took a moment to look over her other charges.

She could hear Piper telling more ghost stories to Demetri and Hannah. Emma and Callie were having their turns on the swings while Brayden, Billy, and Lachlan drove their toy cars through a sand castle.

With nine of her usual ten children making a cacophony of noise on Tuesday morning, it didn't surprise Kelly she never heard the moving truck arrive at the house behind hers. A barking dog and the *whoop whoop* of her charges, informed her someone had finally bought the Belanger home.

"Cool, a dog," Noah cried, jumping up and running toward the back fence. Hannah, on the other hand, tackled her mother before she had a chance to stand.

Hannah's eyes were wide with a mix of fear and excitement. Never having spent much time around animals, Hannah currently had a fascination of desperately wanting a pet, especially of the canine variety, and still having apprehension when confronted with the animal.

Kelly squatted in front of her daughter with a bright smile. "If they have a dog, maybe they have children, too. Won't it be fun to make new friends?"

"And we could use the gate?"

Kelly glanced over to the far corner of the fenced-in yard where her grandfather had installed a gate years before in order to visit his friend and neighbor living behind him. With her grandfather living in Florida most of the year, as well as the death of Mr. Belanger six months before, the gate had been locked and unused for some time.

"Yes, I suppose we would be able to use the gate."

Hannah seemed satisfied and moved away to join the other preschoolers, but not before Kelly saw Hannah's thumb slip between her lips.

Secretly, Kelly also hoped the new neighbors were friendly. It could mean the difference between watching each other's kids or putting up a new stretch of fencing with no passageway through to the other side.

Kelly looked over to see her two employees, Susan and Heather, keeping sharp eyes glued to the children who climbed to the platform of the swing set in order to get a good look at the dog on the opposite side of the fence. Their squeals of laughter kept the dog barking continuously.

"Guinness! Quiet, boy." The order was sharp, but not mean and Kelly found herself smiling as she made her way to the fence. If she stood on a lawn chair, she'd be able to peek her head over and introduce herself to her new neighbor.

"Well, what have we got here?" She heard what she classified as amusement in the deep male voice. "Guinness, my boy, I think you have a yard full of potential playmates back here."

"Is he a friendly dog?"

Kelly was impressed her normally shy Hannah had asked the question.

"Guinness is very friendly. He loves to play and he likes children, too." The man's voice was gentle and smooth as he responded. There was something vaguely familiar about it that Kelly couldn't quite place.

She grabbed a plastic lawn chair and propped it against the back fence as the kids from her daycare peppered the new neighbor with questions.

"Do you have any kids?"

"What's your name?"

"Can we play with your dog today?"

"My brother says dogs like to lick their balls."

The last comment from Demetri had the kids laughing. Time for another chat with Demetri's mom.

Kelly stood on the chair and looked into the yard behind the fence. She saw the animal that had first caught the children's attention: a black Labrador. She gave the man credit for a perfect pet name, as its coat was as black as the stout with the same name.

Yet, the animal that warranted her attention was of the two-legged kind.

He was tall. The fence was six-feet high and the man didn't have to strain to look up at the kids on her side. At her height—five-two and three quarters, thank you very much—she was a little jealous of anyone who didn't have to stand tippy-toed on a chair in order to have a conversation with a neighbor.

With the man standing at an angle to talk to the kids, Kelly was awarded a profile view of Male Species Extraordinaire. He had a deep carpet of black, wavy hair trimmed to perfection. His arms bulged against the blue T-shirt and his denim jeans were worn to the point where they hugged his butt and legs. And he certainly had a nice butt.

There was something about him. He seemed familiar although Kelly was sure she'd never met him before. The man was, well, as her grandmother used to say, *Male with a capital MmmMmm!*

Kelly sighed with appreciation of the view. He'd yet to notice her, his attention still on answering the abundance of questions the kids were asking. So Kelly looked.

The large dog strained against his collar in order to meet and greet his potential new playmates, but the long, lean fingers that held him back were firm, yet gentle. The man had an easy camaraderie with kids and animals. A definite plus in her book.

And those fingers holding the dog's collar were bare of a band of gold.

Sorry, Hannah, Kelly mused, *there might not be any playmates for you, but for mommy, on the other hand...* Kelly mentally shook her head. *Get a hold of yourself, Kel. You are not in the market for another man in your life.*

Kelly noticed a slight tremor in her stomach as the man turned to face her. He looked vaguely familiar. Kelly could not quite brush off the feeling of déjà vu as she swiped her soil-encrusted hand against her thigh before extending it over the fence.

"Hello there, neighbor. I'm Kelly Reisland."

"Yes, I know." The man strode over and grasped her hand in a large paw that seemed to swallow her own. From the rough palm touching hers to the tanned forearms, she knew this man spent time outdoors and wasn't afraid to work. He had a slightly lopsided smile which she found endearing. Yep, this man oozed sexuality.

Kelly silently cursed the on-looking preschoolers, and wondered if she had dirt on her face. For a first impression, she knew she wasn't at her best, but surely a smile and charm could make up for a messy appearance. Plus, the fence hid the worst of her "business" attire.

The sight of a man caused her insides to do flip-flops. Pure and simple lust. It had been a while, but she recognized the signs. As he shook her hand, she gave him a warm and welcoming smile while he introduced himself.

"The name's Finn. We've met before."

"We have?" It took her a moment, only a moment. His eyes. They were a rare shade of violet. The smile froze on her face. Oh, heavens! He was the firefighter who had saved her from the tree last month.

Kelly quickly pulled her hand from his and felt herself stumble on the flimsy lawn chair. She grabbed at the fence and stopped herself from overturning the chair and tumbling to the ground.

"Careful, there," the man's voice was tinged with humor. "Wouldn't want you falling at my feet a second time."

Heat scorched her face as embarrassment washed over her. *Conceited jerk.* She should have known he was too good to be true. "You have nothing to worry about. I usually keep my feet well-planted on the ground."

"Good. I like stable women."

"Hey, Finn." A voice calling from the front yard saved Kelly from spewing the sharp retort burning on her tongue. "You going to hump some of this furniture or should we make a sculpture of the junk on your front lawn?"

Finn tipped an imaginary hat at Kelly. "Gotta go. Good help is hard to find these days. Guinness, here boy. We'll get you set up inside so you don't bark all day long."

With a final yelp, the dog seemed to say goodbye to the kids and followed his master back around to the front of the house. Kelly jumped down from the chair to discover Susan and Heather staring at her with raised eyebrows and telltale expressions on their faces.

Kelly ignored them and instead gathered the kids together for snack time. As she closed the sliding glass door behind her, one thought raced through her mind: it was time for a new fence.

****

"Maddie, you will never believe what happened today." Kelly paced her living room as she spoke into the phone to her best friend. It was nearly ten, but she knew she wouldn't sleep until she talked to someone about her new neighbor.

"Your mother showed up on your doorstep with yet another potential husband?"

"Oh, dear God! What a horrible thing to say." Kelly shuddered at the mere mention of her mother. "Do you remember me telling you about the firefighter who rescued me and Livvy from the Oak tree last month?"

"You mean the one who flirted with you?"

"Aggh! He has an ego the size of New York.

Maddie, he moved into the Belanger house."

"The house behind you? Really?"

"I hear your smirk, Maddie. It's not funny." Kelly heard the buzzer to her dryer and headed into her laundry room. "He's still an arrogant jerk and now I'll have to buy new fencing to get rid of the gate between our yards."

"What does he look like?"

Sexy.

Kelly opened the blinds to the window and stared out into the darkness of her backyard and the shadowy outline of the house behind hers. "He's not bad, but that's the point. He knows it."

"Okay, Kel, tell me what happened today."

"We heard a dog barking. I stood on a plastic chair to see over the fence and introduce myself and when the chair tipped," *(Okay, maybe it didn't tip so much as I was shocked when I recognized him, but Maddie doesn't need to know that),* "he made a comment about me falling at his feet again. Madison Leigh Carlisle, are you laughing at me?"

"No. Of course not. I have a slight cold. I almost sneezed."

"You know me, Maddie, I'm not the type to lose my balance. I passed out last month because of my fear of heights. I had a panic attack, that's all." *Those violet eyes and wide shoulders had nothing to do with it. Nothing!* "It's not the first time I passed out during a panic attack."

"Yeah, well, you know my theory on that particular situation."

Kelly finished folding the clothes and walked into her dark kitchen, not bothering to turn on the lights. "I know, you think Jeff caused those attacks, but I don't see how. Besides, it's been two years since my last attack."

"Ah, huh, and you were still married to Jeff at the time. Coincidence?"

"Jeff wasn't around last month, though."

With the silence, Kelly could almost picture her friend biting her tongue. "So now a cute firefighter has moved into the house next door?"

"He's not cute, Maddie. He's drop-dead gorgeous. And he's conceited, to boot."

"And…?"

Kelly sighed. Didn't she get it? "He hates me, Maddie. He basically told me I was a bad mother because I climbed a tree."

"Are you a bad mother?"

"Of course I'm not! You know I would do absolutely anything for my girls."

"Which is exactly what you did. You faced your greatest fear and climbed a tree in order to protect your child. I bet a certain firefighter may have realized that once he got over his initial judgment of you."

Kelly gave a harrumph of despair. "Yeah, I faced my fear and the fear won. Great first impression."

"And then you nearly fell at his feet a second time?"

Yup, Maddie was laughing at her again. Why had she called her tonight?

"Hold on, Kel."

Maddie's voice became muffled, as though she held the phone to her chest, while she talked to someone on her end.

"Hi, Bryan. I'm talking to Kelly. No, everything's

fine. She has a gorgeous new neighbor and is pretending she doesn't think he's sexy."

"That's not true, Maddie," Kelly nearly screamed into the phone. "Yes, he's good looking, but he doesn't like me. He probably thinks I'm an incompetent mother and a klutz, to boot."

Maddie's burst of laughter caused Kelly to see how ridiculous she sounded.

"The words 'Klutz' and 'Kelly' are far from synonymous," her friend assured. "You've always moved with grace whether you were running the ten-K at school or out on the dance floor. I can't wait to meet this Adonis to see why you've suddenly developed two left feet. Forget the tree incident. Start fresh with the guy. Bake him cookies or something. Then, when the girls are with their father, tell him you find him enormously sexy and jump his bones."

Kelly tripped over a kitchen chair in the darkened room.

"Madison!"

"What? You and Jules gave me the same advice last year and look at me now? In love and having great sex."

Kelly ignored the sound of lips engaging on the other side of the phone.

"That's just it, Maddie. I've already been with the beautiful, strong, alpha-male type and I got burned. I don't want to travel down that road again." She plopped down in the chair before she caused any further injury. "It bothers me his type is what turns me on. Maddie, do you think I can find a boring, oh, I don't know, podiatrist or something, who will turn my bones to mush, or am I doomed to a life of wanting men I should never have?"

"Kel, you kill me sometimes. Take control. Just sleep with the guy. You don't have to marry him."

Those words haunted Kelly an hour later as she checked on her girls before heading to bed. She'd done the marriage thing before and it hadn't worked out. She had no intention of walking the matrimonial path again. And it wasn't like she hadn't had sex since her divorce two years ago. She had. Twice. Neither time had caused her any heartbreak, nor were they anything to write home about.

But something about this Finn guy drew her to him. He was strong, but she'd been married to strong. He was sexy, but Jeff had turned a lot of heads too. There was no denying her attraction to him, but Kelly had a feeling getting tangled with her neighbor was asking for trouble.

Chapter Three

The next day it rained. Not a drenching, wind-tossing type of day, but one of those humid, mostly sunny days with light scattered showers making everything outside wet enough for Kelly to keep the kids inside.

She knew Finn was home. She saw him working outside when she went to Hannah's room to get the Chutes and Ladder's game to bring down to the daycare room.

He had a friend with him, helping him move a doghouse to the corner of the yard. Finn's damp shirt clung to his chest and Kelly wondered if he had a six-pack underneath his clothes. His friend must have said something funny, because Finn suddenly laughed. He appeared more carefree today, such a different man than the "oh-so-serious, how dare you climb a tree" man who had judged her a month ago.

She must have moved in the window. One moment Finn was laughing and the next he stared up at her as she looked down at him.

Kelly's heart stopped for a moment as their eyes met and time stood still. Then Finn gave a salute and turned his back on her. Damn the arrogant men of the world!

The day passed slowly for Kelly even though she packed it with activities for the kids. She organized a game of hide and seek, helped put together a racetrack circling the entire room, and even arranged for art time with all the kids drawing or painting at their own little easels. By the time the last child left with their parent, she was as tired and dirty as her charges.

Despite the activities of the day, her mind returned repeatedly to a pair of mocking purple eyes. She was infatuated with her new neighbor but she didn't understand why. He was just another good-looking man who probably played the field. But she was a single mother who'd been too busy running her business to have any kind of social life. Why did her sex drive have to kick into gear for a man who was too handsome for his own good?

Maddie had a point, though. It wasn't like she planned on marrying the guy. What would the guy think if she jumped the fence for a little night of tango?

Kelly shook off her wayward thoughts. She had a six-foot fence, seriously, how often would she actually see the guy? Maybe the out-of-sight, out-of-mind philosophy would work.

Yet, when she closed her eyes at night, her brain had plans for her that had nothing to do with sleep.

She was in a man's bedroom with large, dark mahogany furniture that, despite its size, didn't fill the room. A fire roared in a huge stone fireplace. An abundance of candles flickered throughout the room: long tapered candles, thick, three-wick candles, even candles in sconces above the headboard.

She watched herself in the dream, propped up in the middle of the king-sized bed, devoid of the feminine touches of throw pillows. She wore a black bustier, which lifted her breasts to overflowing. The panties were little more than a scrap but they emphasized her butt, which she worked so hard to keep firm.

Even in sleep, Kelly knew she looked hot. But it couldn't compare with how she felt when the door to the room opened and in walked her neighbor in full uniform. From the dark leather helmet to the heavy boots on his feet, he exuded an aura of power, of heat, of sex.

"I heard there was a fire needed tending to," he drawled as he sauntered over to stand at the foot of the bed.

Finn's eyes gleamed as they devoured her near naked body before meeting hers with obvious approval.

In slow motion, he began stripping from his uniform. First the helmet, then the long, heavy coat. One red suspender, then the other. The t-shirt and pants were discarded with haste and Kelly was awarded the view of gleaming muscles and the fullness of the male anatomy that could douse the flames consuming her.

Kelly woke in a sweat. Her body on fire with sexual need. Her breasts were full and she had to squeeze her legs together to stem the ache between them.

What was going on with her? She had never had a dream so vivid before. And could the dream be any cornier? A firefighter dousing the flames? Come on! Be a little more original.

She'd never been one to obsess over a man she'd just met. Okay, so it was the second time they'd met, but still. It was unlikely they would have any kind of relationship.

She was a single mother with two children. She ran

a daycare, so there were always young eyes and ears around to distract and interfere. Besides, the man thought of her as a joke, nothing more than a woman stupid enough to climb a tree while she had a severe phobia about heights. It wasn't exactly a recipe for romance.

The clock barely touched on the five o'clock hour, but she knew sleep would continue to elude her. Kelly swung her legs out of bed and made her way in the dark down the stairs to the kitchen. She put a single light on over the stove and set the kettle on to boil for tea.

As she grabbed a mug and a soothing chamomile tea bag, Kelly had to admit her firefighter neighbor was nice looking, but was he really fantasy material?

Sure, he had a nice looking body he obviously kept in good shape. His face was handsome enough with a slightly chiseled but firm chin, giving him a rugged, manly look. His hair was thick, black, with a slight wave, and dark full eyebrows. He also had beautiful eyes calling a person to stare into their amethyst depths.

When he'd glared at her up in the tree, she'd seen a brooding, serious side that seemed to fit with his dark, almost exotic looks. Yet, during the past two days, she'd seen him relaxed and full of amusement. Almost flirty. Charming, even, in the overly confident way he had. She supposed he was also aware of his assets. That would explain why he was so cocky.

She must have a thing for men who knew they looked good. Her husband had been that way. Jeff had looked amazing out on the football field, with those wide shoulder pads and the tight white pants curving around his ass. All the girls in high school had wanted him, but he'd picked her. Kelly had been the star female athlete back then, breaking a couple of the school's records in track, and even bringing back a state championship.

But after she and Jeff had married, Kelly realized her husband wasn't the type to give up being the center of attention—female attention, at least. And when Kelly had had the nerve to divorce the conceited Peter-Pan-Wannabe, she'd vowed off any man who was too beautiful to be faithful.

But tell that to her over-active, fantasy-driven mind. If her dream was any indication, Kelly had one serious infatuation with a man she would never have.

With the steaming mug of soothing tea in hand, Kelly moved to the glass sliders and stared out into the darkness beyond. The moon and the streetlights within the neighborhood, gave the yard a hazy glow, allowing Kelly a view of the shadowy formation of her fence and the house beyond it. She saw a glow of light from behind a window shade and Kelly wondered if that was Finn's bedroom. She saw the silhouette of him moving around the room and wondered what had him up at such an early hour.

****

Finn stepped into the cold shower at the ungodly hour of four-fifty-five. He'd had this amazing dream about his tiny blonde neighbor that woke him with a total boner.

Shit. The dream had seemed so real. He'd been up at his friend's ski cabin in North Conway, with a roaring fire and way too many candles burning in the bedroom. But the heat had all been in the bed. Sweet Kelly Reisland had been sprawled on the covers wearing a little black number that fit her body like a glove, showing off all of her lovely curves.

He'd been wearing his gear, which surprised the hell out of him, because he'd never understood the appeal of the heavy, smoke-soaked coat and pants as a turn-on for women. But, hey, his subconscious must have decided this woman liked it.

In his dream, Kelly's hair had been unpinned from its usual braid, and he'd discovered her head was a mass of riotous, blonde curls. He'd gotten hot wondering if the hair on another part of her body was as light and springy.

Shit. Finn pressed his hands against the stall and let the cold-water splash against the back of his neck. What was it about Kelly that made his mind conjure such vivid thoughts of sizzling sex?

She wasn't even his type. He liked them tall, independent, and not looking for a commitment. Kelly Reisland reeked of family. He would not get involved with a woman with kids. It wasn't like he hated kids. Hell, he loved his nieces and nephews; even Guinness loved being around little ones. But being a favorite uncle was a lot different than being responsible for how the kid turned out in life.

He turned the water off and reached for the towel he'd dug out of a box for the shower he'd taken the night before.

She probably hated him, anyway. He'd been a total ass to her when she'd woken the day he'd rescued her. But he had caught her checking him out the day he'd moved in. Before she knew who he was, of course. Once she'd recognized him, he'd become a leper in her eyes.

Finn leaned against the sink and gazed at his

reflection in the mirror. He was thirty-two and single. Some would say it was time to settle down. His younger sister, Kathleen, had certainly said it enough times. But she was young, in love, and had a sparkly diamond on her finger.

Unlike his love-entranced sister, he wasn't looking for happily-ever-after bullshit. It didn't exist.

He hastily dried off and tossed the damp towel on the floor. He padded naked to his bedroom, carefully stepping over Guinness who couldn't be bothered to lift his head off the floor at this ungodly hour.

He went to the window and peeked behind the shade at the house behind his, silhouetted in the pre-morning glow. Which window was hers? What did her bedroom look like? Was it all pink and feminine? Or was she a no-nonsense type of woman who kept her bedroom neat and tidy. Did she have a king-sized bed with lots of frilly pillows?

He thought back to his dream with Kelly waiting for him on a bed, with those wild, untamed curls, and felt himself harden all over again.

Then he saw her. She was awake. She stood by the kitchen window washing dishes in the sink.

"Aww, hell." The shower had done nothing for him. He went to his bureau and pulled out running shorts and a T-shirt. Maybe a long run would cool him down.

Chapter Four

"Damn the man! What does he want from me?" Jeff Reisland pushed Alicia away from where she knelt, quickly zipped his pants, and began pacing his office.

"My guess is money, babe." Alicia stood, wiping the corners of her mouth with bright red tipped fingers.

"Oh, you think?" Jeff's sarcasm seemed to be lost on Alicia as he watched her stroll to the chair where he'd tossed her pocketbook when she'd come into his office to say goodbye for the night. "I said I'd get his money for him, but it will take a little time."

"Can't you take out a second mortgage on this place?"

Jeff sighed. *This place* was his garage. He was an auto mechanic, but he specialized in high-end foreign cars. Cars that cost as much to repair as they did to buy. He catered only to clientele who spent their days on the golf course and nights socializing with the elite members of the Rocky Point Country Club.

His garage was as upscale as the very same country club. The dirty, oil-stained shop was hidden in the back lot never to be seen by his clients. Instead, when the owner of Jaguars or Porsches or Maserati's walked into his place, they entered into a showroom and were treated as royalty. From being served famous renowned coffee, to being attended to by his front-end staff who wore suits instead of grime-covered overalls, before they were given a choice of either a rental for the day or chauffer service from his fleet of limousines.

Jeff had taken his father's simple, average auto shop—a shop his rich grandfather had given to *his* son who had wanted to "tinker" with cars in his spare time—and created his pride and joy. But it had taken money, a lot of money.

"I've already taken a second mortgage out." Jeff stared out the glass wall of his office into the darkened showroom, closed for the night. "And sold a couple cars, and had a car 'stolen' and 'damaged' to get the insurance money."

He'd paid half of what he owed and gambled the rest, hoping to make a profit. That hadn't worked out as he'd planned. He'd been on a losing streak for the past two years.

"It's too bad the rich bitch divorced you."

"Kelly isn't rich. Her miserly grandfather has tight reigns on his money." Jeff watched as Alicia reapplied color to the lips that had just done a full-service job to his lower anatomy. Alicia had always known how to please him. Of course, they'd started practicing on each other at the tender age of fourteen in the equipment room of the school's gymnasium. And she was as much of a sexual deviant as he was. Anytime, anywhere, anyway.

He looked at her now. Alicia Jones was as different from his former wife as anyone could be. She may have been around the same height as Kelly but Alicia had hair as black as night and curves she knew how to accentuate with the form-fitting sweaters and tight skirts she wore.

Alicia was stacked and gorgeous. Even though

they'd been doing the nasty together for thirteen years, Alicia came from the wrong side of the tracks. She was good enough to hire as his secretary, but he could never marry her.

But, man oh man, could he bang her. He remembered the night Kelly's grandparents had hosted an engagement party for them. Both their families and friends were gathered downstairs, while Jeff snuck Alicia inside, up the stairs, and into Kelly's room. They'd done it on the prim and proper Kelly's bed while his fiancée had been entertaining his parents.

"Of course, if you had custody of the little brats, she'd have to pay you child support, not the other way around."

The words drifted through the fog of his memories.

"What did you say?"

Alicia gave him a satisfied smile and pulled her shoulders back, thrusting her breasts forward. She knew he'd been looking at her. She sauntered toward him, her hips swaying as she teetered on her pencil-thin heels.

"Child support. If you had custody, she'd be paying you."

Jeff shook his head. "Come on, you know judges rule in favor of the mother."

Alicia ran her hands across his chest. He could almost see the wheels turning in her deliciously twisted mind. "But if you could prove she's an unfit mother…"

Her fingers unbuttoned his shirt and she scraped her nails lightly down his chest eliciting a moan from him. "And I'm sure it wouldn't take much for little Miss Perfect to start having panic attacks again." She pushed his shirt down his arms and leaned forward to suck on his nipple, causing a deep moan to escape.

"Yeah, but then I'd be responsible for the kids, needing to take them to doctors and after school activities." Jeff reasoned, but Alicia had planted a seed.

"It won't be so bad." Alicia grabbed his hands and put them on her full breasts, and he happily obliged her silent request. "The oldest is in school most of the day and Kelly runs a daycare with staff. You can make a stipulation she can have her visits with the kids during working hours when her staff is available. They call it *supervised visitation*."

Oh, yeah. He could see it now. If he had custody of the kids, Kelly would do anything to get them back. Anything.

Including remarrying him.

Plus, Kelly's grandfather wouldn't live forever. Accidents happened. And when they did, Kelly—and subsequently he—would be in line for a very substantial inheritance.

"Alicia, I love you," Jeff grinned before stripping Alicia's clothes off and rewarding her for her clever plan.

Chapter Five

"Watcha doin'?"

Finn laid down the handful of eight-foot timbers and turned toward the voice at the fence line. Kelly's oldest, Olivia, sat on top of the monkey bars of the swing set. He'd been in the house a week, but this was the first time he'd seen her.

"Well, hello there, Olivia. You're out early."

"I've got school soon. I like to be called Livvy."

"Then Livvy it is." Finn gave a wink as he walked closer. "I know how you feel. My name is Shawn, but my friends call me Finn. You can, too, if you'd like."

Olivia worried her lip for a moment before speaking again. "I'm, like, not really supposed to talk to strangers, and I don't think my mom would want me to, like, call you by your first name. She'd say it wasn't polite."

"And your mom is right about both things." Finn cringed as Olivia twisted around on the monkey bars until her feet hung off the side as she faced him. Obviously, this child had no problems with heights. "You should never talk to strangers, but you and I are neighbors now and will see a lot of each other. And we've met before. As for my name, why don't we compromise so you don't get in trouble with your mom? How about you call me Mr. Finn?"

Olivia's feet kicked the air and Shawn prayed he

wouldn't have to jump the fence for another rescue. "Cool. So, Mr. Finn, watcha doin' with all the wood?"

"I thought I'd build a bigger deck to make room for my grill and table and chairs."

Olivia looked over at the deck that was more of a platform from the kitchen door down into the yard. He'd already torn down the railings and stairs. "I guess it would be nice. Mr. Belanger kept his grill in, like, the middle of the yard. Mommy said it was because a long time ago he used to keep it on the deck but it almost caught the house on fire 'cause it was, like, too close, or somethin'."

Finn heard the slam of a car door and barking seconds before Guinness came barreling toward him. He braced and allowed the Labrador to stand and place his paws on his shoulders. The man who followed the dog carried two Dunkin Donuts cups in his hands.

"Livvy, this is my dog, Guinness, and my brother, Tom." He put Guinness to the ground and took the coffee from his brother. "And so you don't get in trouble with your mom, you can call him Detective Tom. He's a cop."

"Sweet. Can I play with your dog sometime?"

"I'm sure Guinness would like that. We'll talk to your mom and make plans."

"Livvy, let's go." Finn heard Kelly's voice and wished the fence between the yards was chain link instead of the six-foot high vinyl that certainly did its job with privacy. He wondered what she wore and if her hair was in the thick braid, she always seemed to have it in.

Olivia rolled her eyes. "Gotta go or mom will freak. Bye." She scooted back, grabbed the side of the bars, and flipped over backwards and out of sight.

"Cute kid."

Finn took a long sip of the hot drink and nodded at his brother. "Mm,hmmm. But I think she gives her mother a run for her money."

"Comes with the territory. Lisa got in a fight at school on Friday."

"No shit? What is she now? Nine? Ten?" Finn pushed thoughts of his neighbor aside and took a long look at his sibling. Tom was only four years older, but looked tired. Old. His hair had more gray in it than even a year before. His eyes were sunken and his shoulders slumped. "The divorce hasn't been easy on any of you."

"She's ten. The kids are taking it real hard. Lisa yells at everyone and barely talks to me when she's with me. Tommy on the other hand, is trying to get everyone to stop arguing with each other. He's become this little people pleaser. I fucked up, Shawn."

It was hard watching his big brother fall apart. Tom had always been strong and in control. When their mother died, Finn followed his brother's example and hadn't cried. They'd been the ones to hold the family together. They'd taken turns dragging their father out of one bar or another; they'd been the shoulders for their two sisters to cry on. They'd lectured Kate, their younger sister, to stay in school when she wanted to quit and help support their father.

Tom had been stoic through it all. But when Bethany left him a year ago and filed for divorce, Tom ceased to be the rock he'd always been.

"Don't be so hard on yourself. Bethany knew what the job entailed when she married you. It's not as if you screwed around on her, did you?"

"Hell no. Being a cop's wife, or a firefighter's wife, ain't easy, you know that. Bethany couldn't deal with it anymore. I guess I'd rather the divorce than what Ma did."

Finn noticed the slight quiver in his brother's voice when he mentioned their mother. Shit, he really was wound tight.

"Ah, Tom," Finn fiddled with the lid of his coffee as he tried to find the right words. He didn't want to offend his brother. "You haven't, well…you know…I mean, like dad, you haven't …"

He watched as Tom's eyes narrowed then widened with realization. "Fuck No! Aw, hell, little brother. Other than the first weekend when Bethany left, I haven't gotten drunk. I won't be like the old man and live in the bottle, as tempting as it is some days."

Finn decided to change the subject. Their father was a sore subject for all four of the siblings. "Thanks for taking Guinness for me yesterday." He'd ended up with overtime, which meant working thirty-eight hours straight. He didn't mind the extra shift, but he only had an hour between shifts to let Guinness out.

"No problem. I picked Tommy up after school and we took the dog to the park for a while. It worked out fine this time, but you might want to make nice with a neighbor in case I can't take him the next time."

A picture of Kelly and her two girls running around his yard with his dog flashed through his head. He could hear the dog barking, and the girls laughing as if it were actually happening. Kelly tackled Hannah to the ground and they rolled, getting dirty in the process, while Guinness joined in the romp, licking their faces.

"Earth to Shawn. Where'd you go?"

The picture disappeared as Finn realized his brother stood in front of him waving his hand back and forth.

"Huh?"

"Huh?" Tom repeated. "Who were you daydreaming about?"

"No one." But he couldn't resist looking toward the back fence.

"What? Did you meet a neighbor already?" Tom looked to him and then to the white fence and his eyes widened.

"Whoa. Do you have a thing for that kid's mother?"

"No!"

"Yes." Tom glanced at the fence again. "Let me guess, single mom with wide eyes and the '*Oh, please, mister strong, single, firefighter, could you come over and check my house for any fire hazards.*' I bet you've been over there every day since you moved in."

"It's not like that at all. As a matter of fact, she hates me."

Aw, hell. His brother was grinning his own special grin. Finn had never been able to keep a secret from Tom, and by trying to explain Kelly to Tom was like throwing a bone to Guinness. He would grab on and not let go. Damn, damn, damn.

"Are we going to stand here all day, or are you going to help me build a deck?" Finn started toward the front of the house but he caught his brother making faces at him. It was going to be a long day.

They made it nearly ninety minutes before the topic came up again. At around nine-thirty in the morning, Finn heard the whoop and holler of several kids as they raced around the yard behind the fence. It took all of thirty seconds of the kids releasing their pent-up energy before Tom put down his tape measure.

"Holy shit. How many kids does she have?"

"Shh! Watch your language, they'll hear you." Finn looked up and waved at the two boys who had climbed onto the swing set platform. "Kelly runs a daycare."

The silence was deafening. He turned to look at his brother only to find him staring at him, mouth open.

"What?"

Tom shook his head at him. "I need to get something out of the truck."

Finn watched his brother disappear behind the house shaking his head and muttering something that sounded strangely like, "This can't be good."

****

The brothers worked well together. Once they'd discussed the details of the deck plan, they measured, cut, and nailed with easy camaraderie. By late afternoon, they had the frame built and started laying the floorboards.

When he heard a car door slam, Finn didn't think much of it. When his older sister, Shannon, walked into his yard with her fourteen-year-old daughter, Trisha, in tow, Finn groaned. Both Shannon and Trisha had plastic bags filled with groceries. One look at Tom and Finn knew his brother had called in reinforcements.

"Bastard!" Shawn muttered for his brother's ears before putting down his hammer and turning to his sister with a smile.

"Hey, Shannon, Trish, what brings you here?"

"I knew my two favorite brothers were working

hard and I thought I could provide some sustenance for you."

"With the amount of food you brought, it looks like you could feed an army." The answer he dreaded came.

"Oh, Luke and Simon are on their way to pick up Lisa and Tommy. Kate and Bill will be here after work."

Surprise, surprise. Practically the whole family. The only two not mentioned were their father, who was usually too drunk to participate in any family activities, and Shannon's husband.

"How's Devon?"

Pain flashed across Shannon's face before she pasted a nonchalant smile. "Oh, he had physical therapy today and needed to rest."

Finn took the lie in stride and instead grabbed the bags from his sister's hands. "Here, let me get those. Trisha, watch your step around those boards."

While he and his niece emptied the grocery bags, Finn watched his brother and sister talk outside. When Shannon glanced at the white fence separating his yard from his very sexy neighbor's, he silently seethed. When he saw Shannon grab the ladder and head toward said fence, Finn raced to the glass doors and yanked it open.

Too late.

"Hello over there," Shannon called.

"Hi." Kelly's voice answered hesitantly.

"It's so nice to meet you," Shannon practically hung over the fence as she spoke. "I'm Shawn's sister, Shannon, and we're having the family over tonight for a barbeque. When I found out Shawn had already met one of his neighbors I had to invite you to join us tonight."

"Oh, umm, thank you, but—"

"I heard you run a daycare out of your home. How nice." Shannon interrupted Kelly. "I have three kids, all teenagers now, and I know how exhausting it is to have so many children running around. I imagine it's tough to send all those kids home and then get supper going at night and cleaned up before your children have to go to bed."

"It's not too bad." Finn heard Kelly. She'd try to make excuses, but knew his sister. Kelly didn't stand a chance.

"Either way, you won't have to worry about it tonight. You and your girls have to join us. I feel so much better knowing my brother has started to make friends in this neighborhood.

"Yes, but …"

"Then it's settled. Do you like wine? I've got a couple bottles chilling inside. Between my three kids and our brother Tom's two, your girls will have plenty of kids to play with, and you and I can put our feet up and get to know one another."

As Finn watched his sister climb down the ladder, he didn't know whether to laugh at the thought Kelly was coming over, or cry, knowing there was a very good chance meeting his family could cause Kelly to stay far, far away from him.

Chapter Six

"Good grief, Hannah, you look like you plopped your face in a bowl of chocolate."

Kelly glanced at the clock as she grabbed a cloth to wash her daughter's face. It was after six. She hated being late. As she knelt in front of her youngest daughter, Olivia walked into the room.

"Your shirt is dirty, you need to change."

"But we're going to be outside. What's the big deal?"

"Mommy said to change your shirt," Hannah butted in.

"Shut …" Olivia closed her mouth as Kelly threw her a warning glance. She turned and ran upstairs.

Kelly prayed Olivia would be quick as she stood and brushed a wayward curl away from Hannah's face. The child's hair never stayed in a ponytail for long.

She squirted a dab of lotion on her hands and rubbed it in as she paced in front of the sliding glass doors. Why was she doing this? Why had she agreed to go to a barbeque at *that* man's house? He didn't even like her.

Olivia ran into the room. She stopped in front of her mother, standing at attention and threw her hand up in a salute. "Olivia Reisland, reporting for inspection, ma'am."

Kelly rolled her eyes and silently prayed for

patience. She ran a daycare full of precocious children, but when her own child was fresh, it took all her willpower not to lose her temper.

Then Kelly saw what her daughter wore and bit her cheek to keep from laughing. Olivia had put on a pair of black Capri pants and a red and white striped top. It wasn't the outfit she found humorous. What brought the smile to her face was Olivia's clothes were almost an exact match to her own white capri's and red top.

Her nervousness waning, Kelly grabbed the store-bought fruit platter she'd sent Susan to buy for her earlier.

"Let's go, you imp."

"Wait, Mommy."

Kelly stopped as Hannah ran over to the hook holding all their keys. She stood on her toes and grabbed the single key with the blue tip. The key to the gate in the fence.

As they approached the gate at the back of the yard, Kelly handed the fruit platter to Olivia and took the key from Hannah.

The gate swung inward and Kelly was greeted with a view of a perfect family scene. The dog ran wildly between a throng of children tossing a Frisbee back and forth. Finn staffed the grill in the middle of the yard, a beer in his hand while another man stood beside him making comments about the way the burgers were being cooked, and the woman who'd called herself Shannon placed a bowl of macaroni salad onto a long folding table, which had been set up in the yard.

Normalcy. It hit Kelly with a calming peace that had her reconsidering her arrogant neighbor as one who actually appreciated family. She'd take this opportunity to get to know Finn a little better. Maybe she'd discover he'd been having a bad day when she'd been stuck in the tree. Maybe he'd discover she wasn't the klutz she'd been both times he'd talked to her.

Kelly caught Finn's eye as he spotted the trio invading his property. She thought she caught a glimpse of a smile directed at her before she saw his eyes widen.

"Guinness. No!"

The chaos that happened transpired in slow motion. The Frisbee soared over her head. Guinness took a flying leap as he tried to catch the disc. Hannah screamed in terror as the dog came toward them and hurdled herself into her mother's arms. Olivia turned to run away from the oncoming canine only to barrel into her mother. The three humans and one dog went down in a jumble of arms and legs with the fruit platter sailing in the air. It was comedic movie madness as the contents spilled around them with a splat.

Kelly groaned. So much for new impressions. She should go home now. She couldn't deal with another stupid comment about falling at that man's feet again.

The look on her children's faces stopped Kelly in her tracks.

Hannah still clung to her, fear evident as she stared at Guinness who stood with his head hanging forlornly, almost as though he were waiting to be admonished. Olivia sat up with wide eyes and an expression almost matching the dogs.

"I'm sorry, Mommy," she whispered, her lip trembling. The water works were only a harsh word away. Kelly took a deep, calming breath. Her children needed her to be calm and make this night okay for them. They'd been excited to come, despite her own embarrassment, she could and would reassure her kids.

"Olivia, honey, it's okay. It was an accident."

Finn kneeled down beside them and Kelly immediately tensed for some comment about her clumsiness. Instead, she heard the smooth voice that had talked Olivia down from the tree.

"Is anyone hurt?"

Kelly shook her head. "No, I think we are all okay. Sorry about the food, though."

Olivia turned toward their neighbor and nearly burst into tears. "I'm really sorry. I guess we have to go home now because Mommy says we should never go to someone's house empty-handed and now I've ruined everything."

"But you didn't show up empty-handed, Livvy, and it's not your fault my dog crashed into you."

Finn helped Olivia to her feet. "Besides, I want you to meet my niece, Lisa. She's ten." The girl in question stepped closer as introductions were made. She was tall for her age with dark brown hair swinging past her shoulders. "I bet the two of you will be great friends."

With her oldest reassured and moving away with her new friend, Kelly sat on the ground with Hannah clinging to her because the dog was only a few feet away. Finn picked up on the situation instantly and was back on his knees talking softly to the four-year old before Kelly could speak.

"He's big, isn't he?"

Hannah nodded.

"It's okay to be afraid but can I tell you a secret? Guinness loves kids. He's very gentle and even protective." Guinness nudged his nose against Hannah's leg, saying hello.

Finn motioned for Hannah to come to him and she slid easily off her mother's lap and into his arms. "When you meet a new dog, he needs to get used to your scent. The best way to do this is to hold your hand out, palm down, and let him smell your hand."

Finn put his hand out to Guinness as an example and Hannah followed suit. The dog sniffed her hand, then his tongue licked her fingers causing Hannah to giggle before she reached out to pet the soft black fur of the dog.

Kelly stood up and watched as her neighbor gently helped her daughter overcome her fear of dogs. It was such a simple thing. Something Jeff would never have taken the time to do. Kelly felt a wave of something unidentifiable wash over her. She pushed away her previous judgments of the man and allowed this one moment to take over.

Hannah was shy and didn't go to strangers easily, yet she'd crawled into Finn's arms as though she'd known him all her life. Sure, the girl had spoken with him over the fence but that was different than actually trusting him to protect her from the large animal.

Finn was a natural with the child. Perhaps it was his voice, which was the perfect pitch to ease Hannah's fears; or maybe because he was such a big man and could easily pick Hannah up out of the way of the dog. *Or because he smelled of charcoal and something so male and inviting.*

Kelly shook her head to clear it. Okay, then. She had it bad. Her neighbor was sexy, there was no denying it. Even in a pair of jeans and a blue T-shirt with Rocky Point Fire Department emblazoned on the back, the man exuded sexuality.

"I take it you're okay, too?" The voice was deeper than Finn's but oddly familiar. Kelly finally allowed herself to look around and met the eyes of the man beside her. She welcomed the distraction. This man was even bigger, if at all possible. Maybe not taller, Kelly surmised, but certainly bigger in the chest and shoulders. His hair was lighter but the eyes were the same shade of violet. Even without introductions, Kelly knew the man was Finn's brother.

"I'm Tom."

"Kelly." Kelly grasped the hand he extended.

"Why don't you come and meet the rest of the family."

Leaving her youngest in capable hands, Kelly allowed herself to be escorted away, to meet Shannon who now manned the grill.

"Hello there, neighbor," Shannon welcomed her with a large smile. "Sorry about the chaos, it's pretty typical in this family."

Kelly was taken aback at the apology. "Oh, well. I was about to apologize myself. It seems disaster is following my daughters and me these days and your brother seems to be around to witness them, too. I'm afraid I haven't made the best of impressions."

"Oh, nonsense," Shannon motioned for Tom to take over at the grill. She wiped her hands on a dishcloth hanging on a hook. "Why don't you come inside with me? I need to check on the salad my sister is supposed to be putting together."

"Be careful on the deck," Tom called out. "We've nailed the boards down on each end but they still need more support."

Kelly followed Shannon into the kitchen. Shannon

took one look at the array of salad makings left unattended on the counter and turned to Kelly with exasperation. "Would you excuse me a moment?"

Shannon disappeared down a hallway. A few seconds later Kelly heard the older woman's admonishing tone. "Kathleen Faith Finnigan! I don't care if you two are engaged to be married, we have guests and impressionable children on the premises."

Kelly grinned at the immediate impression that came to mind and decided to help out. Kelly had the salad almost complete by the time Shannon reappeared in the kitchen, a younger woman following closely on her heels.

Kathleen's face was flushed—whether from her sister's scolding or from a quick make out session with the blond weightlifter who entered a moment later, it was hard to tell. But the scarlet color that flooded her already red face when she saw Kelly was all embarrassment.

Weightlifter wasn't nearly as fazed. He grabbed his would-be lover around the waist only to be rebuked when she slapped his hands and pushed him away.

The girl did have manners, though. "Hi. Sorry, I didn't realize you'd arrived already."

Kelly took pity on her and put out a hand. "That's okay. I'm Kelly Reisland."

"Kate. And this is Bill." She used her head to point at the man behind her. "Umm, we're getting married in September."

Shannon rolled her eyes. "If either one of the brothers caught you instead of me, you'd be before a Justice of the Peace tomorrow instead of the church wedding you're planning. Take the condiments and paper plates outside. And behave yourselves."

Kelly stared wistfully after the couple who were obviously very much in love. She figured Kate to be slightly younger than her own age of twenty-seven, but she felt so much older. With a divorce and two kids under her belt, being so carefree seemed a lifetime ago.

Then Finn stepped into the house and Kelly's mind scattered. She turned to the counter to finish chopping the tomato.

"Anything I can help with?"

Damn. What a voice! Kelly concentrated on her task, determined not to be distracted and cut her fingers.

Shannon had her hands full with a plate of corn on the cob. "I'm all set here, Shawn. See if Kelly needs any help."

Finn slid the screen door closed behind his sister and turned to her.

When there had been four people in the kitchen moments before, the room seemed large enough, but suddenly the walls closed in. Which was silly, of course. There were no blinds on the slider doors and the screen allowed plenty of noise and light to permeate from outside.

She couldn't ignore him forever, and God knew she couldn't cut the tomato any more or it would be a mess of red slop.

Kelly mixed the salad together and finally turned toward her host while wiping her hands on a paper towel. He leaned against the wall, a bottle of Guinness in his hand and a hangdog expression on his face.

"Thanks for coming over tonight." Well, goodness, he almost sounded shy. She decided to make good with her resolution to start over.

"Thank you for helping Hannah out there. You've got a way with kids."

Finn lifted his beer in acknowledgement and took a long sip. His eyes never left Kelly's, though, and neither moved from their self-appointed corners of the kitchen.

Kelly couldn't stand the silence. "I know we started off on the wrong foot with each other, but I'm hoping we can make amends and be friendly neighbors."

Darkness flickered in Finn's eyes, but he masked it as he finally moved across the room toward her and held out his hand.

"Then by all means, let's start over. I'm Shawn Finnigan. My friends call me Finn."

Kelly slipped her hand into his and her heart thudded loudly in her chest. The boyish grin he flashed dazzled her. His violet-colored eyes were bright beneath the dark eyebrows.

She'd witnessed him mad. She'd seen him arrogant and even flirtatious. This, though, was downright sincere and it nearly took her breath away.

Madison's words flashed through her mind. *Tell him you want to jump his bones.* She didn't think she was quite ready to be that friendly of a neighbor. Yet.

"Kelly Reisland." It came out softly, almost a whisper of sound, not nearly the assertive, controlled woman she wanted to appear.

"It's a pleasure meeting you, neighbor. Would you like to meet the rest of my family?"

****

Finn stepped out of the kitchen into the early evening haze. He took Kelly's hand, ostensibly to guide her across the decking to solid ground, but he knew better.

From the moment Kelly Reisland had tumbled to the ground with her two children, he'd realized, mother or not, he was crazy-attracted to his accident-prone neighbor.

When he ran to her side, he wanted to laugh and kiss the worry from Kelly's face. If he'd touched her, he probably would have startled them both with his intensity. So he'd done the only thing he could do, he ignored her and concentrated on calming her children.

Olivia had been easily distracted and the other children had gathered her into their fold. Hannah had surprised him, though, with her easy trust, moving into his arms as he introduced her to his large, black Labrador. He'd helped the young child but had been very aware as Kelly stood and moved away.

He'd taken his time with the young girl so he could get his emotions under control. He'd been with a lot of women. Probably more than he should have over the years. All had one thing in common, though: they'd been single and not wanting commitments. And if those women had started looking for something more than the occasional date and a bout of sex, he'd sent them packing and moved on.

So what was he going to do about this attraction he felt for Kelly? She was a complication he hadn't planned on. Her curvaceous body enamored him. Her blond curls, which escaped her thick braid and pinged around her forehead, taunted him to touch the strands. Her face was devoid of make-up, but she'd taken the time to put some kind of pink gloss on her ever-full lips.

And her hands were baby soft.

When she'd placed them against his own rough palms, he'd wanted to take her hands and rub them against his face. How did she get them so smooth and soft? Was the rest of her body as soft?

Aw, hell. He had to stop this train of thought. Kelly was a mother. Mothers meant commitment. He was a firefighter. Firefighters and commitments didn't work. He knew this. He lived this. Kelly Reisland could only be a neighbor to him.

As they stepped off the deck onto the firm ground, Finn slowly released her hand, but after she gently placed the bowl of salad onto the folding table holding all the other food items, Finn gave into temptation and touched her again. He placed a gentle hand on her back as he pointed out his nieces and nephews.

"Shannon has three kids, Lucas, Simon, and Trisha, and then there are Tom's kids, Lisa and Tommy. And you met my sister, Kathleen and her fiancé, Bill."

As he took another slow sip of his beer, he realized once again, he'd been lacking in manners.

"Would you like a drink?"

"Um, sure."

She sounded as nervous as he felt. Maybe it was a good thing. He'd been a jerk the first time they'd met and he wanted to change her opinion of him. Having family surrounding them, giving him a bit of a buffer, perhaps she'd see a better side of him.

He opened the cooler as Shannon announced the food was ready and Kelly excused herself to help Hannah fix a plate and get her children settled.

Maternal to the core. He could tell that about her. Much like his sister, Shannon.

The two women were a lot alike. He stood back and watched as Kelly and Shannon performed the mother dance: a perfect choreography of preparing plates, ensuring drinks and napkins were taken, and getting their kids completely settled before they even thought about their own needs.

They sat down on the ground next to each other and began talking like old friends. They were both mothers and he'd bet great ones as well. It was like they instinctively knew the best thing to say to their kids, when and how to ease their fears. They'd do anything to help make their children's lives better. Safer.

Like climb a tree when they were afraid of heights.

Damn! He really did owe Kelly an apology.

Tom popped open another can of Sam's Summer Ale as he came to stand beside him.

"She's all mother, through and through."

His brother's words were an echo of his own thoughts, so Finn only grunted as he turned to load his burger with A-1 sauce.

"Single mom. Two little girls. She's gotta be on the make."

Finn didn't think so, but he couldn't find his voice to deny it. So his brother kept talking.

"I mean, she's cute enough, with a body that could probably run a marathon, but I bet she's the type who is very needy."

Like mom.

He knew where Tom was going with this. Shit. He looked at Kelly and thought the same thing.

"She's just a neighbor, Tom. Nothing more."

But he couldn't meet his brother's eyes when he said the words and he moved to sit on the grass across from Kelly. He had patio furniture picked out, but hadn't bought it yet. Of course, he hadn't realized he'd be hosting a cookout quite this soon after moving, but it didn't look like anyone minded lawn seats. He tuned in to what his new neighbor was saying to his sister.

"Oh, I grew up in that house. It was my grandparents' home and they raised me. After my divorce, Grandpa Joe helped put on the addition so I could start the daycare."

"How many kids do you watch?" Shannon knew how to get people to talk.

Kelly leaned over to wipe Hannah's mouth with a napkin. Once her mother had turned back, Hannah took a piece of her hamburger and fed it to Guinness who seemed to have become the young child's best friend.

"I have ten full-time right now," Kelly explained, "but in September four of them will begin Kindergarten."

"Ten kids around the house on a daily basis." Tom had decided to sit next to him and continue being the voice of…reason? Insanity? "Even if you did want to date her, when would she find the time?"

"I'm not dating her, Tom." Finn gritted. "She doesn't even like me."

"What made you decide to open the daycare in the first place?" Shannon prodded.

"Well, I always wanted to work with kids. I got married right out of high school and my grandparents took care of Livvy while I earned my degree in early childhood education. I got pregnant with Hannah right around the time my grandmother got sick. So I spent most of my days at the house, taking care of Olivia and my grandmother." Her face softened as she spoke of her grandparents. "My grandfather suggested the idea and even drew the plans for the addition."

There was a flash of something dark in her blue eyes, but it passed as quickly as the shrug of her tiny shoulders.

"After Grandmama passed away, Grandpa moved me and the girls into the house. I got my divorce and started my business." Finn saw a beam of pride tug at Kelly's luscious pink lips. "I'm almost in my third year and love every minute of it."

"Maybe I'm wrong."

The low comment from his brother had Finn looking away from the object of his fascination. "Hmmm? What?"

"She might not be as delicate as she looks."

"What does that mean?" The abrupt change in his brother's voice bewildered Finn. "First you tell me she's needy, now you say she's not delicate. What the hell are you getting at?"

Chapter Seven

Kelly enjoyed herself. Finn's family was warm and welcoming. The kids played well together and Hannah had become attached to the dog quickly.

She'd witnessed a different side to her neighbor. He was full of life and laughter with her and his family. Every time he spoke, every time he let his sultry smile tip his lips, she felt a quiver inside.

She didn't know how she felt about it. It was easier to push those feelings aside when she thought of 'Shawn, my friends call me Finn, Finnigan' as an arrogant, woman-hating, self-centered man. After watching him interact with her girls, his siblings, and nieces and nephews, Kelly couldn't deny the growing attraction.

Who wouldn't find the man down right gorgeous?

But it was almost nine and time to get her girls home. "Livvy, time to go."

"Aw, mom."

Kelly rolled her eyes at Shannon who gave a chuckle at the typical child response.

"There's school tomorrow and you are already up past your bedtime," Kelly reasoned. "Where did Hannah disappear to?"

Finn touched her shoulder, sending a tingle down her arm as he stood beside her. He pointed toward the doghouse. Hannah was curled up, sound asleep, her head resting against the animal's soft fur. Guinness had a paw resting protectively across the young child's arms.

"Oh, wow," Kelly gazed lovingly at her youngest. "It's hard to believe she was afraid of the dog when we first arrived."

"Would you like me to carry her home for you?"

The question caught Kelly off guard and she bit back the immediate 'no' that sprung to her lips. She'd been taking care of her girls alone for so long she didn't know how to respond. Would it be so bad to have a helping hand?

"Thank you. That would be nice."

Kelly watched as Finn lifted Hannah in his arms as though she weighed no more than a pillow. Olivia stopped her complaining and walked beside them, talking as usual, about anything and everything that came to mind.

Kelly opened the gate and stepped into her yard. It was odd having a man beside her again. A man holding her child in his arms. A man who made her heart flip with his caring manner.

Okay, not *just* with a caring manner. The way his shirt clung to his chest and his jeans hugged his lower half might also be part of the reason she felt an overwhelming need to touch him.

He'd carried her once, too. Sure, she'd passed out and didn't remember a second of it, but it didn't stop her imagination from kicking into overdrive. There was no denying Shawn Finnigan had muscles, and it would be nice to be swept off her feet, literally, as he carried her up to bed, laid her gently upon the covers and

Kelly was breathless as she opened the sliders into

the kitchen and led Finn into the main part of her home.

"I'll take her upstairs. I'll be right back." Kelly couldn't look at him in case he read her thoughts. She slid her arms under her daughter, but all she noticed were the strong muscles of Finn's arms flex as he shifted Hannah over to her.

"Upstairs, Livvy."

She glanced at her daughter who looked up at their neighbor with awe. Kelly sighed. Olivia so wanted a father figure in her life.

"See ya, Mr. Finn. I had fun tonight."

"I'm glad, kiddo. We'll do it again, soon."

Kelly climbed the stairs as fast as she could while carrying the heavy weight of a limp four-year old. *We'll do it again, soon.* Did he mean it? Or was he only being neighborly. After all, it had been his sister who'd invited them, not him.

Hannah barely stirred as Kelly stripped off the child's clothes and slipped a Tinker Bell nightgown on over her head. She stopped by Olivia's room and reminded her to brush her teeth, gave her a kiss and headed back down the stairs.

Finn waited in the kitchen, leaning against the counter. Large. Imposing. Incredibly sexy.

Just sleep with the man!

Maddie's words came at her in a rush. Damn her. There was nothing she wanted to do more at the moment than jump the man's bones. But she was a mother with children upstairs and she would never do anything improper with her girls in the house.

She gave Finn an appreciative smile. "Thank you for inviting us over. We had a wonderful time."

He smiled the smile that sent the butterflies

scattering in her stomach. "My pleasure. I owe you an apology."

He pushed away from the counter moving closer to her in the confines of her kitchen. "I was rude to you when we first met. I hope you can forgive me and we can be friends."

He stood close. The scent of fresh air and charcoal clung to him and sent her senses spinning. She felt dizzy with desire. God, it had been so long since she'd felt this way. Too long since she'd craved a man's touch.

She lifted her head to look up at Finn and saw something indefinable in his eyes. Was he going to kiss her? Time stood still as they stared at each other. Should she kiss him? Should she say something? Anything?

He stepped toward her and Kelly breathed in the crisp clean scent of outdoors. His eyes were hooded. Kelly's eyelids fluttered closed as his mouth captured hers. His kiss was tentative at first, testing her response. He gave her lower lip a nibble and Kelly felt the tug permeate to her toes.

Oh, he tasted so heavenly. She had wanted this since the day he moved in. What harm could one kiss do?

Kelly lifted to the balls of her feet and pressed into him, deepening the touch. Finn's tongue found entry and Kelly drank him in. His arms wrapped around her, pulling her to her toes and Kelly melted into the hard warmth of his chest.

When he pulled away, Kelly's heart beat fast. She forced her eyes open and stared up at the dark purple depths that proved he was just as affected by their kiss.

And she hadn't a clue as to what to say to him.

Kelly saw a shift in Finn's gaze as his eyes cleared to their brilliant lavender hue. He took a step back and gave a little salute.

"Good night, neighbor. See ya over the fence."

Kelly watched as Finn trotted across the grass and exited through the gate between their yards. She lifted her hand to run a finger over lips still tingling from their kiss.

"Yes," Kelly whispered. "See ya."

Chapter Eight

"What the hell are you doing here?" When Kelly's doorbell rang at seven thirty in the morning the last person she'd expected to see was her ex-husband.

"I brought you coffee." And the last thing she'd expected was to see him oozing charm and holding out a Dunkin Donuts coffee cup while he took a long sip from a matching one in his other hand.

When she stood staring at him with no response, Jeff Reisland took matters into his own hands, typical of him anyway, and brushed past her into the entryway.

"You came here to bring me coffee?" Kelly couldn't seem to think clearly this morning. She'd spent the night reliving a bone-melting, heart-stopping kiss from her sexy guy-next-door, the last thing she needed was to be faced with the man who'd fathered her two children.

So what if she'd half-hoped to see Finn at the door? Maybe he'd decided their kiss was worth asking her out on a date. God knows she'd spent the night fantasizing about running her hands through his dark hair and across his strong, muscular chest.

But, no, instead it was Jeff at her door. Sure, he was good looking, and there was no denying the boyish charm he exuded. He wore faded denim jeans and a golf shirt sporting the logo of Rocky Point's exclusive country club. His smile had melted many women's hearts, hers included once upon a time, but Kelly was immune to his wily ways.

"Well, not exactly," Jeff gave her the sheepish grin he'd perfected and used whenever he wanted something. Kelly mentally braced herself for Jeff to ask for a favor, or for money, or to tell her he wasn't going to pay child support again.

"I've been neglecting the kids and canceling visits lately and I thought maybe I could drive Livvy to school today, spend a little time with her."

Huh? He wanted time with the kids? Kelly blinked back the shock. "Oh." This didn't feel right.

"Do I have time to take the girls out to breakfast first? Where are they?" Jeff walked over to the stairs and looked up. "Are they awake?"

Kelly shifted from one foot to the other. She still gripped the front door, unable to grasp the concept of Jeff as the doting father missing his children.

"Why?" She knew her voice dripped with suspicion, but she didn't care.

Then Olivia walked into the upstairs hall and spotted her father. With a cry of glee, she bolted down the stairs. Jeff shoved a coffee cup into Kelly's hands as he gathered his daughter into his arms.

"Daddy, Daddy. What are you doing here?"

"I thought I'd take you and Hannah Banana out for breakfast and take you to school."

Kelly felt a twinge of remorse for her suspicions as she saw the two embrace. Livvy missed her father terribly and was the most hurt when he cancelled visits. Having him show up unexpectedly for a visit was irritating, but if she said no to him taking the girls out, Livvy would be devastated.

Kelly unconsciously opened the tab of the cup and sipped at the sweetened coffee. Aw, hell, when she was Livvy's age, she'd wished for nothing more than to have her father show up at the door once, just once, for an unexpected visit. She couldn't say no.

Kelly heaved a resigned sigh. "I'll get Hannah ready."

****

Kelly couldn't sit still. She'd been a jumble of nerves since Jeff had left with the girls. She couldn't figure out what had prompted him to take the girls out. Jeff didn't do anything unless he benefited. He was selfish.

Yet he'd been nothing but jovial when he'd dropped Hannah off ninety minutes later, having already taken Livvy to school. More surprising, he'd left without asking for a favor. Kelly still couldn't figure out what Jeff was up to.

The kids in her daycare ran around outside with Susan and Heather doting on them. Kelly remained inside to clean up from lunch. But she'd gone from washing the table to pulling out the vacuum to suck up the crumbs on the floor, to washing the dishes rather than stacking them in the dishwasher.

As though Jeff wasn't enough to keep her mind busy, there was the little matter of Finn (hmm, she kind of liked his nickname) and the kiss they'd shared. Before his sister had invited her over for the cookout, Kelly could have sworn her neighbor didn't like her. She had to admit, other than lusting after his hunkish body, she hadn't been a fan of him, either.

Last night though, she'd seen a side of him that had stopped her in her jaded tracks. Finn was sensitive and fun and had a close-knit family who seemed to gravitate toward him.

He'd been kind to Livvy when he'd rescued her from the tree, and the way he'd been with Hannah and the dog showed Kelly he was great with kids.

And holy smokes! The man could kiss.

Kelly put the last dish in the drainer, dried her hands with the dishtowel, and soothed her dishpan hands with cucumber-scented lotion.

What was she thinking? She didn't need another man around to screw up her life. She'd worked hard to get her degree and start her daycare. She was independent now. She may find Finn sexy, but she'd felt that way about Jeff at one time and look what it had cost her.

She'd had to go to school in secret while her grandparents watched Livvy, and then she'd been dependent on her grandfather as she'd gone through her divorce and started her business.

Why would she even think about another man in terms of whether he was good with kids?

Kelly felt jittery, like she had too much energy. Maybe if she went out and started a game of Rover, Red Rover with the kids, she'd feel better.

****

Jeff leaned against the counter at the pharmacy and waited while Ken Lear, the pharmacist, reviewed the side effects of a medication with an elderly woman. Once the wrinkled, mentally dense, blue-haired biddy headed toward the exit, Ken turned his attention back to him.

"So, did you do it?"

"Of course," Jeff fiddled with vitamins lining the

counter, not really looking at them, but he was bored. "Ritalin in her coffee. You are a brilliant man. She was full of excess energy when I got back."

"And you're sure she didn't suspect anything?"

Jeff paused to give his friend a hard stare. "Ken, during the eight years of my marriage Kelly never suspected any of the times I slipped her a mickey. She was more surprised by my being there today to see the kids without having another agenda. That alone was enough to send her into a neurotic spiral. The drug enhanced the effect. I also crushed half the bottle of the Ritalin and when she went upstairs to get the girls ready, I mixed the stuff into her can of coffee. Now she'll be feeling jumpy all the time and won't associate it only when I show up."

Ken began filling a phone order as they talked. "So when are you going back?"

"I dunno." Jeff paced, thankful the store was quiet. "I have to wait at least a few days. I don't want to show up too often, too soon. Then again, the girls let slip Kelly has made friends with some new dude who moved in next-door or something. Has a dog."

"You think he'll be a problem?"

Jeff stopped striding back and forth and stared off into space as he gave it some thought. Would the neighbor be a problem? Would the guy want to be around a woman who doubted her own sanity? Would he want to be around a woman who was prone to anxiety attacks and became weepy after?

Probably not. But Jeff knew how to handle Kelly in those situations. Hell, he'd been around to 'save' her every time. She needed him.

So what if he was the one who'd produced the

anxiety attacks in the first place. When Kelly Stanick Reisland began having new panic attacks, he would be available to rescue her from herself once again.

"No, the neighbor won't be a problem."

Chapter Nine

The firehouse was quiet, which usually meant trouble, as far as Finn was concerned. After the Saturday morning housework had been done, he'd escaped into the day room with his study material for the Captain's exam. He'd expected most of the crew to be in the room, either watching television or to start a game of poker. But only Jack Rawlings sat in a recliner, a James Patterson novel in hand.

It was too quiet. The calm before the storm, as they say. Either all hell was going to let loose within the city or the guys were going to get restless and release their steam indoors.

Somehow, he preferred a riotous city. As three of the firefighters entered the room, he knew his wish would not be granted.

"Hey, Finn, did you hear what the probie did?"

Finn looked up from his recliner to see Reggie Buckland and Terry Shapiro pulling a soaking wet Pete Clarkson toward his chair. Jack Rawlings, after twenty years on the job, shook his head and continued reading his novel.

Finn put down his book and sat up. "Well, it looks like he got wet again." Soaking a new firefighter was a favorite pastime of the duty crew. Most of the new recruits he knew couldn't wait until their nine-month probationary period was over so they could actually arrive at work with only one spare change of clothes instead of the two or three they needed now.

"Walk into another bucket of water, Clarkson?" Finn asked in good humor.

"Yes, sir," Pete replied sheepishly.

"He broke the cardinal rule, Finn," Shapiro nearly whined. "The probie here went and bought his girl some bling."

The smile left Finn's face as he glared at Pete Clarkson. "Bling? What kind of bling are we talking about, Probie? Is it a charm necklace with a little heart on it or are we talking the serious, sparkling bling bling which leads to the dreaded 'M' word?"

Pete stared at him with a blank stare and Finn could tell the kid didn't know if the crew was joking with him or not. Shit. When it came to marriage, he didn't joke with the guys.

Finn shook his head in despair. "Okay, kid. Time for confession. Come tell Father Finn all your sins."

Reggie pulled a chair around so Shapiro could push the drenched man into it.

"Probie, probie, probie, it's time for us old guys to fill you in on a few things. See, when you grow up in the fire service like I did," Finn began, "you learn early that marriage and firefighters don't mix. Dating is cool. Living together ain't bad for a while. Everything is fine until you put a ring on their finger and then, BAM!"

Finn slammed his hand down on the table beside him, punctuating his words with the sound, and startling Pete. But he continued. "They go and start to get all smothering. You catch a fire a half hour before shift change and she won't understand. All she'll care about is you weren't there for the home cooked meal she prepared, or that you missed Pete Junior's little league game."

Finn knew his voice was intense, yet he couldn't help it. A little blond neighbor's face kept popping in his mind and he needed to push it aside. Quickly.

"The hours are rough. You work your two days and two nights, but then you get called up for overtime and you don't see your spouse for four days straight. Then, when you do finally get home, instead of letting you sleep she'll slap a chore list so long on you you'll start to resent her as much as she resents you. It's a pure recipe for disaster."

Pete shook his head and water dripped off his head onto his nose before landing with a plop onto the floor. "Shelly's not like that, though."

Shapiro put a hand onto Pete's shoulder. "I thought the very same thing with both of my marriages, and I still ended up divorced with attachments on my pension. If it ain't the schedule, it's worrying about the dangers of the job."

Pete turned toward Rawlings. "What about you, Jack? How long have you been married?"

Rawlings lifted a hand to say he wasn't getting involved and continued to read. Finn silently blessed the man who'd defied the odds and remained married for nearly twenty-two years now. "Listen closely. Don't put the ring on her finger. Live together for a little while if you have to. I guarantee within two years, she's going to discover how much she hates your job."

"Lunch in five," Smitty called from the kitchen. "What's going on? Did the probie get in trouble?"

"Nah! He thinks he's gonna get married," Reggie relayed.

"Shit, kid. Listen to what Father Finn has to say. He's the master at loving them and leaving them before the noose gets tightened around his neck. The broads don't really care for all those holidays and anniversaries they have to spend alone."

Finn gave Pete a reprieve. "Go get some dry clothes. And for goodness sake, will you get the floor mopped? It looks like you pissed your pants over here."

Lunch was a raucous affair. Pete showed up in dry clothes, but the rest of the crew had heard the news and continued to needle him about the trials of married life. Finn could tell the kid was starting to get a little riled.

"Ah, come on." Pete was trying hard to look at the positives. "The schedule is actually kind of cool, what with the four days off between shifts."

"Yeah, but the pay sucks, so you either have to fill those days with a second job or work your ass off on overtime shifts to pay for your mortgage and car payments."

"And your kids will hate you for all those holidays, birthdays, and school plays you'll miss."

Pete looked around the room at the crew of six casually talking about all the reasons why to hate their job. "So, why do we do this job?"

"Because we get to run into burning buildings while everyone else is running out, dumb ass!" Reggie explained.

"Hell, yeah!" Smitty joined in. "There is nothing like the rush you get with the roar of a fire in your ears, smoke black as midnight and thick as cotton candy surrounding you, but you know you can beat the devil-monster back into his grave. The thrill seeps into your blood and there is no going back."

Finn looked at Jack Rawlings who remained quiet. Jack was the one in six on this crew who believed in the sanctity of marriage. Even looking at the entire department, there were more single or divorced firefighters than those who were married; and of those married, many complained about the difficulties.

The house lights came on and all the guys stopped to listen as the dispatch tones rang through the station.

"Engine three. A.L.S.-four. Medical emergency, White Birch Mall at the food court for a patient experiencing chest pains. Engine three. A.L.S.-four. Medical emergency, White Birch Mall at the food court for a patient experiencing chest pains. Time out is twelve-seventeen hours."

The sound of chairs scraping back filled the room as Finn, Jack, Terry and Pete headed toward the tub room and got into the engine.

Finn grabbed the microphone and pressed the button. "Engine Three's on."

"Engine three on, twelve-nineteen."

Saturday at the mall, during lunch, equaled crowds. The details registered as mall security waved them over to a middle-aged, overweight man sprawled in one of the chairs near the entrance.

Terry and the probie began patient assessment, while Finn listened to the security officer and watched as the ambulance pulled up outside the doors.

Within minutes they turned the patient over to the paramedics and Finn prepared to go in service when he heard her voice.

"No, you will stand right here. He's working."

Finn turned toward the sound and wondered why he hadn't seen her before.

Kelly sat at one of the round tables in the food court; the remains of lunch stacked on the tray. Hannah knelt on her chair munching on a French fry while Livvy stood behind her mother, obviously debating the pros and cons of disobeying her mom's orders to come say hi to him.

Finn decided to save Livvy from being grounded and strolled over to them.

"Hi, Mr. Finn," Olivia called out as he approached.

"Hello, Livvy. Hi Hannah." Hannah greeted him by standing up in her chair and lunging herself into his arms. He gave her a big squeeze and looked down at Kelly, still sitting in the chair.

"Hi, Finn."

Her voice was quiet. Shy, almost. Was she thinking about their kiss from the other night? 'Cause he sure as hell was. He hadn't stopped thinking about their kiss, or the fact he wanted, no craved, another taste.

"Hey, Kelly." Okay. He'd said hi. His crew stood by the entrance, waiting for him. He needed to go. "Would you and the girls like to grab a pizza later?"

Kelly's eyes widened in response. Aw, hell. Had he read her wrong? Was she not interested in him?

"Yeah. Okay. Sounds nice."

Finn felt an unexpected surge of pleasure at her response, while a silent, but forceful 'yesss!' swamped his brain. He was going to see Kelly again. Tonight.

"I get off at six. I'll pick you up at seven."

He put Hannah back down in her chair, gave Olivia a brush of her hair, and headed toward the exit.

He actually made it out the mall doors before his crew started on him.

"Hey, Finn, who's the new girlfriend?"

"She looked familiar. Do we know her?"

He brushed off the comments. "Give me a break, guys. She's just my neighbor. Nobody special."

Yeah. Kelly Reisland was *just* a neighbor. A new friend. They were *just* having pizza—with her two daughters.

And if he was lucky, maybe, just maybe, he'd get to kiss his nobody-special-neighbor again tonight.

Chapter Ten

Finn didn't take them to any pizza place; he took them to TiTo's, the best pizza in the city. Tito's Family Pizza and Restaurant opened in nineteen eighty by Louis and Carmella Giabaldi and was named after their two grandchildren: Tina and Tony, and was now proudly owned and operated by Tina and her husband.

The Giabaldi family had set out to create the pizza shop to be a warm, welcoming place for the entire family, and had included a small alcove with a few pinball machines. Over the years, the restaurant had expanded and Tina had turned the twenty-five table pizza shop into a ninety table restaurant with a game room to include the old pinball machines, as well as several ski ball and arcade games.

TiTo's was the hot spot of the town; always crowded with teenagers in the game room, and families in the restaurant. And with it conveniently located directly across the street from the police station, it was also one of the safest from crime or gang fights.

Olivia and Hannah actually behaved, to Kelly's relief, despite their excitement to going to their favorite restaurant with their new neighbor.

Kelly found she enjoyed listening to Finn as he relegated them with humorous stories of life at the firehouse.

"Here I am, the new guy, eager to please, and they

told me it was time for rescue training."

Kelly took a bite of her ham and pineapple pizza. Finn was animated as he talked and her girls were entranced. Okay, she was too. Kelly watched the grin curve Finn's lips, the sparkle of laughter in his eyes, and his broad shoulders straining at the seams of his shirt.

The man had a voice that called to her in a primitive way. Her daughters were with them and Finn talked to all of them, but she knew he spoke to her.

Tonight was a very casual, 'let's get to know each other' dinner.

"I emptied out my pockets, took off my watch, and lay down on the floor. It seemed like training at the time. I believed it, at least. The crew back-boarded me. Put me in the Stokes—the rescue basket. Strapped me in. Made sure I couldn't move."

He closed his eyes briefly, shaking his head at the memory. Kelly waited with bated breath, wanting to know what happened next.

"Then they filled the Stokes basket with water, carried me outside and propped me upside down against the fence and left me there to be the amusement of every car driving past."

Kelly put her hand to her mouth, trying not to laugh at the mental image. Her children on the other hand, roared with laughter.

"That is sooo funny, Mr. Finn," Hannah exaggerated, earning a smile from the man sitting across from her.

"Yeah," Olivia could not let Hannah have any attention, "How long did they leave you there?"

Finn gave an equally brilliant smile to the girl

sitting beside him. Although the attention was on her girls, Kelly felt warm and tingly inside.

"Only for a few minutes. It seemed longer, though."

The evening was almost surreal to Kelly. The four of them, sitting together, laughing, talking, eating together, from the outside, it would look like they were a family out for an enjoyable evening together.

It had never been like this with Jeff.

Jeff refused to go to places like this: bright, casual, family-friendly. No. When they'd gone out they went to the country club or they'd head into Boston to restaurants requiring proper dress and dinner jackets.

And a babysitter at home for the kids. Usually, Lily, the eighteen-year old who'd he pay with a hundred dollar bill and a quickie in the back of his car before driving her home.

"I have some quarters in my pocket begging to be used by a couple of young ladies who have been very good at waiting."

Kelly pushed the thoughts of her ex-husband aside and smiled gratefully at the man who'd captured her young girls' hearts—and tugged at hers.

"Do you mind if I take Livvy and Hannah over to play ski ball?"

Kelly laughed at the expectant look Finn gave her, one mirroring the hopeful glances from her two girls.

"Go. Have fun. I'll clean up the table and join you in a minute."

"Yay!" her girls chorused as they both stood and grabbed Finn's hands as they weaved their way past the tables into the game room at the far end.

Kelly moved the remaining half of cheese pizza

onto the tray holding what was left of the Hawaiian and gathered the paper plates filled with the crusts her daughters never ate, and piled them onto the now empty tray. She walked over to the can and slid the trash into the container and put the tray on top.

As she turned, she nearly crashed into a woman who came up behind her.

"Oh, I'm sorry," Kelly excused herself, not really paying attention.

"He won't stay, you know."

The cold, bitter voice stopped Kelly in her tracks and she looked up.

The woman was beautiful. Blonde and blue-eyed, like herself, but that's where the similarities ended. This woman was tall, with luscious curves men craved. She wore jeans that hugged her hips and double tank tops showing off her large breasts and skinny waist.

"What did you say?"

"Finn. He won't stay. He doesn't believe in marriage or commitment. I should know."

Kelly was taken aback by the resentment in the woman's voice and demeanor and stood silently as the girl filled her in on Finn and his preferences.

"Finn's a player. He swoops in with all his charm. Treats you like a princess. Lavishes you with his attention. Then the minute he thinks you might be expecting a ring on your finger, he drops you faster than you can blink."

"I see." Kelly managed to muster. The woman painted a picture that reminded her all too much of her ex-husband. She should have known Finn was too good to be true.

The woman tossed her perfectly straight hair as she

continued. "Finn is married to his job and won't let any woman get close. It's all a game to him."

It was probably the truth, but Kelly wasn't about to let this obviously scorned woman think she won by cornering her while Finn entertained her children. No. This woman was out for revenge and Kelly wasn't going to be used as a pawn.

Kelly pasted on a silky smile, looked the woman up and down, and lied through her teeth. Maybe.

"Then I guess Finn has nothing to worry about. I've already been married and have no intention of treading those waters again. I'm only interested in Finn for his oh, so hot body."

When Kelly saw the self-satisfied grin cross the woman's face, she knew she was in trouble.

"Hiya, Finn," she said, looking behind Kelly.

Kelly gulped. *Please don't let him be behind me. Please tell me he didn't hear me.*

"Get lost, Neely."

She knew that voice. And she had become familiar with this particular tone. It was the one he'd used toward her when he'd had to rescue her from a tree.

Yep, Shawn Finnigan was not happy.

Kelly turned toward him, prepared for his wrath. Though it was hardly her fault one of his ex-bimbos had targeted her. Besides, if this Neely had told the truth, Finn should be happy she wasn't looking for another opportunity at marriage.

"I'm sorry."

With two words, Kelly felt ambushed. "What?"

"What Neely said, what she did, I apologize. It was rude of her."

"You're apologizing for the actions of a woman

you're no longer dating?"

Kelly allowed Finn to move her back a few steps as another customer stepped by them to empty their pizza tray. She stood in the corner, looking up at a man who'd been accused of charming and seducing women before leaving them high and dry. A man very much like the one she'd married and divorced. Yet she found herself easily taken with this one.

She knew the truth, now, regardless of how the news had been broken to her. Shawn Finnigan was nothing more than a handsome man and a good kisser. Probably a great lover.

Stop it. She would not be susceptible to his kind ways. She would not allow her children to get attached to a man who would only be a mere shadow of time in their lives.

Her children. Oh, my God. He'd left her children alone.

"Where's Livvy and Hannah?" Kelly tried to push past the wall that was Shawn, fear surpassing the attraction which had overcome her reasoning moments before.

But he held her back by her arm.

"Whoa. It's okay. They are with someone they called Aunt Maddie. They were introducing me to her boyfriend and his daughter, Casey, when I spotted Neely bothering you."

They were with Maddie. They were okay. Finn hadn't abandoned them. The adrenaline rush left her body as quickly as it came, causing Kelly to lean heavily against the wall.

"I'm sorry, Kelly." Finn leaned an arm against the wall beside her. "This evening didn't turn out quite as

I'd planned."

Kelly sighed. "I'm sorry, too." He looked sad, almost resigned, much like she felt. "I think I'd like to go home now."

****

The ride home would have been quiet if it weren't for the two girls in the back seat of his pick-up. He was thankful for their banter and encouraged them to sing songs on the fifteen-minute ride home.

The longest fifteen minutes ever.

The evening had started off on the right track. He'd had a great time with Kelly and her girls. They'd laughed. He had teased Livvy about her aversion to the cooked pineapple on his pizza. Hannah had sung him a song.

All the while, he had watched the super springy curl that had escaped Kelly's braid and bounced around her face every time she moved. He'd so wanted to reach over and twirl the strand around his finger, to release the rest of her hair and finally see the curls around her face.

He'd also hoped to have a repeat of their kiss from the previous Wednesday.

Then Neely had come along and ruined the day. He hadn't heard what she'd said to Kelly; though he'd figured the gist by the answer Kelly gave.

She only wanted him for his body.

He wondered if it were true or her way of getting rid of a pesky nuisance such as Neely. He half hoped she wasn't lying because he'd been having some very lustful thoughts about Kelly Reisland, pretty much since the day she'd fainted in his arms.

But the only way he'd have a chance with Kelly

was if there were no expectations of something more. Sex with no commitments. That was how he lived. He doubted Kelly had the same philosophy.

He'd have to push his lustful thoughts of his beautiful neighbor far away. He needed to think of Kelly as a neighbor. A friend. Nothing more.

He pulled up in front of Kelly's house and put his truck into park. Jumping out, he opened Kelly's door before she'd gathered her bag. As she stepped onto the sidewalk, she looked up at him.

"Thank you."

Two words, that's all. Yet, he heard so much more. He knew she was being polite, thanking him for the dinner. Yet he also recognized the wall she'd lifted between them, shutting him out.

He should be thankful. He should walk away from Kelly and her girls, away from what they represented, away from the life he'd avoided. He didn't need a wife and kids. He didn't want that kind of heartache.

And yet...

"Kelly, can we talk?"

She turned her face from him. Maybe it was to ensure her girls climbed out of his truck safely, but he didn't think so. She was avoiding him, trying to come up with an excuse to say no.

"I need to get the girls ready for bed."

Though he'd been expecting the excuse, Finn was suddenly filled with a sense of loss. Maybe he and Kelly were not meant to be lovers, though the one brief kiss they'd shared tempted him to try again. Still, for some inexplicable reason, he wanted Kelly Reisland as his friend.

He touched her arm until she finally looked back at

him. She looked tired, resigned. He did not want to walk away tonight with Neely's words hanging in the air between them.

"Please."

Her eyes closed, almost as though she were gathering strength to say yes—or was it no—to his pleading. Finn held his breath as he waited, and when she opened her eyes and nodded her head, relief swamped him.

"I'll make us coffee."

He followed her as she opened the front door and watched as the girls automatically kicked off their shoes and placed them into a bin beside the door.

"It's late, girls. I want you both to go directly upstairs and change for bed. Hannah, make sure you go potty. I'll be up in a few minutes to help with your teeth. Livvy, remember, you have Cara's birthday party tomorrow, so no reading under the covers all night."

As Kelly talked to her girls, Finn took a moment to take in the furniture of the living room to his right. It had obviously belonged to her grandparents. The style was Victorian, trimmed with dark wood. Although the back of the furniture showed the floral design to the fabric, the cushions had been recovered in a thick material. Kelly's attempt at protecting the sofa from the wear and tear, and more likely drink spills.

Other than the furniture, the rest of the room showed children were present. Two beanbag chairs, a PlayStation, a checkerboard on the coffee table, and a wicker basket in the corner filled to overflowing with various toys. Yes, children lived here, and yet the room was spotless. Not a speck of dust. The rug recently vacuumed.

He'd noticed the same about her kitchen, too, when he'd carried Hannah home on Wednesday. His neighbor was a neat freak. Interesting.

Once Livvy and Hannah disappeared at the top of the stairs, Kelly motioned him to follow her down the hall into the kitchen. Finn figured this room had been left exactly as Kelly's grandmother had designed it. It was cute, yellow, with strawberries stenciled as a border along the wall, but somehow it didn't seem to fit Kelly's personality.

He didn't know what her personality was yet, but he'd bet a month's paycheck this wasn't it. Kelly either didn't want to change the rooms that reminded her of her grandmother or, being a single mother, she couldn't afford the luxury.

Finn leaned against the counter as Kelly opened a pantry door and pulled out a container of coffee. From the lower cabinet she located the coffee brewer and plugged it into the wall.

"Do you drink this often?"

Kelly looked startled. It was the first either had spoken to each other since entering the house. "Occasionally. Why?"

Finn shrugged. "In my house, the coffee pot sits on the counter and runs pretty much all day. If I could drink the stuff intravenously, I would."

Kelly smiled. Not the carefree smile she'd shared with him at the restaurant, but enough to show she was starting to relax again.

"I used to be the same way but when my grandmother got sick, she switched to drinking tea, so I did, too. It stuck. I only make coffee when I have company. It's a nice change."

There was a *kaboom* from upstairs followed by a wail. Kelly bolted toward the stairs before Livvy yelled down.

"Mom! Hannah pulled her drawer out of her bureau onto her toe."

Finn mentally winced at the image. Kelly would be a few minutes. He placed the filter in its compartment, filled it with the grounds, and poured in the water. Within seconds, the brown liquid dripped into the pot below and the sweet aroma filled the room.

The kitchen was spacious, probably twice the size of his. He walked around, peeking into what he expected to be a dining room. Instead, he discovered an office as meticulously organized as the rest of the house. Her desktop held a computer, phone and calendar, a file cabinet with baskets on top, neatly labeled: incoming, outgoing, household, daycare, other, and not a speck of dust to be found.

He walked down three stairs to the garage that had been converted to the daycare area. Finn saw where Kelly's money went. The room was bright and colorful and divided into sections, using bookcases and various toys as the dividing walls.

Beanbags, oversized pillows, and posters advertising books welcomed the early reader. Another section with easels and bins holding crayons and paints held court on a tiled section of flooring. Storage bins throughout the room contained labels with both words and pictures for the kids to put away cars, action figures and various other toys.

The walls held pictures of animals in one section, the alphabet in another. There were even planets and rocket ships hanging from the ceiling.

He turned as he sensed, more than heard, Kelly enter the kitchen again. "This is nice. I'd want to come here every day if I were a kid. How's Hannah?"

Kelly shrugged. "She's fine. I think it scared her more than anything else. Livvy offered to read her a story, so she's cuddled in with her big sister. At her age, sometimes all it takes is a little distraction."

The coffee pot let off a shrill beep and Finn moved back into the kitchen as Kelly poured the steaming liquid into huge diner mugs. She placed cream and sugar onto the table and he watched as she added both to hers.

He, on the other hand, preferred it strong and black. He took a sip. He had asked Kelly if he could talk to her, yet he wasn't sure what to say. *Hey, Kelly, did you mean what you said back at the restaurant? That you only wanted me for my body? 'Cause it's okay with me.* He didn't think that would go over well.

"Finn, I don't know how much you overheard tonight." Kelly ran a finger along the rim of her mug, her eyes following the movement. She was obviously embarrassed, but he gave her credit for starting a conversation he'd been struggling to begin.

"Don't worry about it. Neely was out of line and I get you responded with the first thing that came to mind."

Kelly took a sip of her coffee and finally, finally looked him in the eyes.

"I told the truth."

Finn froze, his mug halfway to his mouth. What did she mean? He put the mug down on the counter, careful not to slosh the hot liquid.

"About having been married and not wanting to go

down the same road again?" Hell, he couldn't even understand why people got married anymore anyway. Too many ended in divorce and he'd seen too many of his friends, his family, torn apart by the pain it caused.

Kelly nodded. "And wanting you for your body."

She said it calmly, yet he saw the tension in her shoulders, in the way she gripped her mug with both hands, in the defiant thrust of her chin as she put herself out there. Kelly moved quickly away from him and sat down, putting the kitchen table between them. And then the words poured out, as her need to explain herself prevailed.

"I can't deny I find you sexy and I've had, umm," Kelly stumbled a moment, but continued on, "well, dreams, about you. I have no intention of getting married again, but it doesn't mean I'm not interested in sex."

She'd been having dreams about him, too? The vision of his own dream, of Kelly in the huge wood-carved bed of his friend's ski-lodge, filled his mind.

"I think you already know I'm attracted to you, as well," Finn responded, bringing a tinge of pink to Kelly's face. Her sprinkle of freckles seemed to glow. But Kelly took another sip of coffee and seemed to gain her confidence again.

"Yes, well, here's the thing," Kelly continued. "I have two impressionable young girls and I don't want them thinking there is more to us than friendship. You and I are adults and can handle a no-commitment relationship, but I don't want my girls to see us as anything more than friendly neighbors. They don't need to get attached."

Kelly proposed the affair as though it were a

business negotiation, and Finn found it, and her, highly arousing. He moved slowly toward her, stopping when he reached the table.

"So what you are suggesting is a quiet, behind closed doors affair. To protect your children, of course."

Kelly looked up at him and nodded.

"No commitments. Just sex."

Kelly nodded again.

Jumping Beans! Kelly's proposal had him aroused talking about it. Finn circumvented the table and advanced on Kelly. Propping one hand on the table and the other on the back of her chair, he leaned down. Kelly was biting her lip, holding her breath as she waited for his answer.

"I can live with that." And his mouth captured hers to seal the bargain.

Chapter Eleven

Kelly was running on fumes. She should never have had coffee so late at night, or maybe it had been the second cup she'd practically inhaled after Finn left.

Either way, it had to be the caffeine keeping her awake all night. It certainly couldn't be the fact she'd proposed an affair with her neighbor and he'd accepted.

With a kiss.

Goodness, the man could kiss. His mouth had captured hers, confident and sure. He never touched her with his hands, yet, as his mouth worked hers, nibbled, consumed, Kelly's body had filled with a rush of warmth and lust. Thankfully, she'd already been sitting because she had a feeling her knees would have given out before his amazing kiss had ended.

When he'd finally stood back, Finn's voice had been deep and controlled, something she no longer had felt.

"I have to work tomorrow, covering a shift for someone and then I work my regular shift tomorrow night. Why don't I call you Monday to set a date? I'll cook you dinner."

A date. Kelly still reeled from the kiss and her mind refused to work properly. "Ah, my ex-husband is supposed to take the girls next weekend, but is prone to cancel at the last minute. I can arrange a backup plan as well."

He nodded then stole another quick kiss that held a promise of what to come. "I'll talk to you Monday."

And he'd left, with his kiss still tingling on her lips.

So, of course, Kelly hadn't gone to bed. After tucking her girls in, she'd headed down to her office in an attempt to forget her neighbor. That's when she'd poured a second cup.

Big mistake.

She'd paid her house bills, then did a load of laundry. She baked oatmeal-raisin cookies at midnight. At two, when she still wasn't tired, she'd run on the treadmill for nearly an hour.

By the time six AM arrived, the coffee high had worn off and she was ready to crash. But it was time to get ready for her day.

Livvy had a birthday party at eleven to go to, and they still needed to buy a gift. Hannah's friend Noelle arrived at noon and stayed through supper. Knowing a cup of tea would never get her through her exhaustion, Kelly brewed another pot of coffee.

By the time eight-thirty rolled around and her children were in bed for the night, Kelly's nerves were shot and she was beyond tired. She'd existed on coffee the entire day trying to stay awake. She had tried switching to tea shortly after lunch, but felt herself heading toward a crash. With Livvy needing to be picked up at three and Hannah having a playdate, taking a nap wasn't an option. So she had more coffee.

Yet with every cup, and the sudden burst of energy that came with it, came the strange sensation of actually feeling the caffeine running through her body. In a mere twenty-four hours, she'd become a coffee junkie.

She tossed and turned in bed Sunday night needing

to sleep, but it wouldn't come. Her body felt sluggish but her mind wouldn't shut off.

She had a date. She was going to have sex. She needed to call Maddie to see if she'd babysit in case Jeff cancelled. She prepared her deposit slips for her bank run she would do on Monday. Her lawn still needed mowed but at least the toys in her playroom had all been cleaned with disinfectant wipes today. Back to her date. She had no idea what to wear. Should she buy condoms? Would he do that?

Kelly turned onto her side, flipped her pillow over, and adjusted the covers. Still her mind raced, and when her alarm went off at six AM she hadn't slept a minute.

Hating herself for her weakness, Kelly prepared another pot of coffee, adding an extra scoop of the grounds. It would be difficult getting through the day when she hadn't slept the past two nights, if she didn't indulge in the dark brew.

By the time Susan and Heather arrived before the advent of children, Kelly felt energized again and ready to face the day.

At eleven-thirty, before going into the kitchen to make lunches, Kelly heard the phone. When she saw the caller ID with the name S. Finnigan, her heart went into overdrive. Taking a deep breath, Kelly headed into her office, hoping it would give her a little more privacy from her two wonderful, but often matchmaking employees, and picked up the phone.

"Hello?" Oh, darn? Did her voice sound breathless? *Breathe, Kelly.* Act natural.

"Hi, Kelly."

Mmmm. Okay, his voice sounded deeper. Was it too much to hope he was looking forward to this date, too? "How was your weekend?"

Oh, heavens. What was she supposed to say? She hadn't slept a wink in two days? Hardly. They had agreed on a no-attachment arrangement. He could not know his kiss had melted her insides and turned her into a neurotic mess and she'd spent the weekend subsiding on a liquid diet of coffee.

"Fine," Kelly lied. "And you?"

"Slept like a baby." Finn's silky smooth voice caused Kelly's already frazzled nerves to skitter into overdrive. "About this weekend ..."

Oh, no, he was canceling already. Kelly bit her lip as she waited for Shawn to continue.

"I have to take Kate and her boyfriend to the airport on Friday night. They're going to a wedding in Georgia. I work again Saturday, but I'm free in the evening if you'd like to come over around seven?"

He didn't cancel. Kelly refused to dwell on the relief she felt, nor the excitement building for the impending date.

"Sounds good. I'll confirm with Jeff that he's taking the girls. Finn? If you are working all day, would you like me to make dinner?"

"Okay. But next time, I'll cook."

When she hung up, Kelly's heart pounded. Who was she kidding? This wasn't just a date. She was planning a night of sex with a man who turned her insides to mush simply by speaking. And he was already talking about next times.

She picked up the phone a second time. The voice on the other end made Kelly smile and eased her tension immediately.

"Hi, Maddie, it's me."

"Oh, my God, Kel, he is gorgeous!" Maddie's words gushed through the phone lines. "No wonder you are tripping over yourself around him."

Kelly laughed. Her best friend had been polite but reserved at TiTo's as Kelly and Finn retrieved the girls from her and Bryan, but she'd thrown a conspiratorial wink behind Finn's back and held her thumb and pinky to the side of her face as she'd mouthed 'call me' as Kelly left.

Kelly spent a few minutes answering Maddie's questions before she got to the heart of her call.

"Uhm, I was wondering if I could impose on you?"

Maddie, of course, didn't hesitate. "Anything."

Kelly twisted the black cord of the phone as she talked. "Well, I, ah, sorta have a date with Finn on Saturday and …"

"I'll babysit!"

Kelly's laugh was more of an expulsion of pent-up breath. "Wait, Jeff is supposed to have the girls for the weekend, but he has a tendency to cancel at the last minute or bring them home early. I would need you as a backup plan. Overnight."

"Forget Jeff altogether. I'll pick the girls up, either at your place or his, Saturday morning, and we'll have a sleepover. We'll paint nails, do makeovers, and play games."

"You are going to do nails and makeup? Who am I on the phone with? You or Jules," Kelly asked, referring to their friend, Jules Sinclair, whose father owned a fashion magazine. Jules was who they called when they wanted fashion advice.

"Great idea." Maddie answered, "I'll call Jules and ask her if she wants to join in the fun."

With the weekend plans made, Kelly rushed around the kitchen. She made lunches in record time and cleanup went quick. She felt so good afterwards she pulled the soccer net someone had donated to her from beside the shed and set the kids up for a round of running and kicking.

With the coffee kicking around in her veins, Kelly felt pretty good despite the quiver in her body she associated with her lack of sleep and an excessive amount of caffeine.

The phone rang again later in the afternoon and Kelly, who always kept a handheld outside with her, rushed to answer, she didn't bother to check the caller ID when she picked up the line.

"Hello?"

"Hi, Kel." Damn. Jeff. The sound of his voice always sent Kelly into a tailspin. He would probably cancel his visitation, but at least this time Kelly knew the girls wouldn't be too disappointed when they found out about going to Maddie's.

"What do you want, Jeff?" She knew she was being rude, but then, she'd divorced the man for a reason. She didn't have to be nice. But Jeff didn't bite, this time.

"I had a meeting downtown and I know Livvy gets out of school soon. Do you mind if I pick her up and spend a little time with her? I'll have her home for supper."

"You want to take Livvy out?" Kelly stopped in her tracks. First he showed up to take the girls out to breakfast, now he wanted to pick Livvy up from school?

Something was screwy in the Universe. Kelly

could feel it.

"Yes, as a matter of fact, I'm pulling into the school parking lot now. Tell Hannah I'll do something with her next week."

"Uh, huh. Jeff?"

"Yeah, babe?"

Kelly cringed. She'd always hated the endearment, and as much as she wanted to remind him she wasn't his 'babe' anymore, she kept quiet.

"Are you still planning on taking the girls this weekend?" She heard silence through the cell phone as the purr of the car engine cut off.

"Of course," his tone belied the fact he had a history of canceling.

"Well, Maddie invited us over Saturday for a girl's night. You know, hair, makeup, and stuff."

She deliberately included herself in Maddie's invitation. She didn't want Jeff to know about her date. Though she'd been divorced for two years, she didn't know how he'd react. Plus, she didn't want the girls to know she was dating their new friend.

"Well, I was looking forward to having them for the full weekend," and he did manage to sound disappointed, Kelly didn't quite believe him. "But, I have a feeling the girls would have more fun with a girl's night. I suppose I could bring them home early. I've got to go. I'll bring Livvy home in a couple hours."

Chapter Twelve

"Daddy!"

Jeff loved the attention he got as Olivia spotted him and came barreling into his arms outside the school. The school year was almost over, the sun shone bright, and it seemed, to Jeff at least, the perfect day for parents to be outside picking up their kids.

And when his daughter screamed his name and threw her arms around him, he knew they'd drawn attention. He also noticed he was the only father in the crowd.

"I missed you, sweetie," He spoke loud enough to be heard by the group of moms nearby. "I finished a meeting and decided to take the rest of the day off to come get you."

He pretended not to see the approval from the moms. "How would you like a ride in that, sweetie?" He pointed to a red car being admired by children and parents, alike.

"Saaweeet!" Livvy cried. "What kind of car is it?"

Jeff preened. "It's a Lamborghini Gallardo Spyder, six-speed, soft-top convertible." Jeff opened the passenger door of the exotic yellow sports car. "This baby is now available to rent at my shop by my clients as their cars are being fixed for a cool sixteen hundred for eight hours."

And, he prayed, would bring in enough money in a

short time to help pay off his debt.

Jeff eased into the driver's seat and started the engine. "Look at you, Livvy. I bet your friends are jealous of you right now because you are riding in the coolest, most expensive car they've ever seen." Livvy sat up further in her seat as Jeff eased the car into the exiting school traffic and waved to her schoolmates as they drove by.

After taking his daughter for one very fast ride down the highway, a ride that had the sun beating down on them, had Livvy's hair whipping, and the two of them whooping and hollering, Jeff took his daughter out for ice cream.

As they sat at the bench closest to where he'd parked, Jeff eased the conversation to Kelly.

"So, Liv, a friend of mine saw you at TiTo's Saturday night. Did you have a good time?"

Livvy grabbed a sliver of cookie dough and chewed it before answering. "Yep, we went with Mr. Finn."

"And who is Mr. Finn?" Jeff licked at his own Pistachio ice cream while trying to maintain a cool, semi-interested tone.

"He moved into Mr. Belanger's old place behind us." Livvy informed him. "I told you about him. He's like a firefighter and has a really awesome dog."

"Does your mom like him?" The ice cream could have been mud for all Jeff cared about it, but he continued to eat while his daughter talked.

"I guess so. I mean, they're not dating or anything. And it's not like she talks about him all the time like she likes him like a boyfriend, or anything." Livvy ran her tongue around between the base of the ice cream and the top of the cone and worked her way around and around. Jeff waited. He knew his daughter. He'd started the conversation and she loved to talk. She'd continue.

"When Hannah and I were in the game area with Mr. Finn, we saw Maddie and Bryan and then Mr. Finn, like, saw someone talking to Mom. He went rushing over to them, and, like, when the lady left, Mom didn't look happy at all. She wanted to leave. But she still invited Mr. Finn in for coffee afterward."

Coffee. Jeff had to hold back the self-satisfied smile. He had the info he needed. Once Livvy had finished and he'd been certain her hands were completely wiped down using napkins, he drove her back to the shop to change cars. He didn't need super-safe mom freaking out about his racing down the highway with their daughter.

As they pulled in front of Kelly's house, Jeff turned to his oldest daughter. "Pinky swear you won't tell mom about the car?"

Livvy giggled as she locked her pinky with his. "Pinky swear, daddy."

"Come on, I want to see Hannah before I go." Jeff followed his daughter inside the house and trailed after her into the kitchen. It was five-thirty, a time when he knew most of the kids were in the process of being picked up.

"Mom, I'm home." Livvy headed down the steps into the daycare but Jeff stayed behind. He couldn't stand the two women who worked for Kelly. They always gave him dirty looks. Like it was *his* fault his wife walked out on him. He could hear Kelly and listened until he realized she was talking to one of the parents. He had a few minutes.

The site of the half-empty coffee pot on the counter made Jeff's day. He wondered if he'd mixed enough Ritalin in the grounds to have an effect on his ex-wife. He wondered if the new neighbor had felt the effects of the drug after sharing java time with Kelly.

Served him right if he did.

Hannah lumbered up the stairs, her thumb in her mouth. She'd always been a little on the chunky side, which bothered him. No one in either of their families were fat, which meant it had to be what Kelly fed her. Jeff made a mental note to use that when it came to custody.

"No thumb-sucking, Hannah," Jeff admonished as he pulled his little girl into his arms. While Olivia was his buddy, his little informant, Jeff had a hard time connecting with his youngest.

He blamed Kelly. She'd taken his girls away when Hannah was so young, barely old enough for him to really get to know her personality. Legally, he was supposed to take the girls every other weekend, but he had a business to run and his shop was open on Saturdays. Sometimes he'd take them for the day on Sunday. Occasionally, he'd take them overnight. But his parents were dead, and it wasn't like he had a girlfriend he could pawn the girls off on while he worked. Kelly didn't seem to understand.

Jeff unbraided Hannah's hair and watched as the blond curls popped crazily around her face. Kelly's hair was the same. It was one of her best features.

"You have beautiful hair, Hannah, you should leave it down more." Jeff looked up from where he was kneeling with his daughter to see his ex-wife in the doorway to the kitchen. "You, too, Kelly. You should wear your hair down. Maybe you'll find yourself a man to help out around here."

"I don't need a man to help me, Jeff," Kelly climbed the three stairs as Jeff stood and took in her appearance. Kelly looked tired and wired at the same time. Her cheeks were flushed, but there were dark circles under her eyes.

"Really? Because you look beyond exhausted." Jeff slid a chair out from the table. "Why don't you sit down and I'll get you a coffee."

Kelly brushed by him, and Jeff gritted his teeth. "I'm fine, Jeff."

But Jeff caught her around the waist and led her back to the table, almost forcing her to sit. "You don't look good, Kel. And I don't want to leave you alone with the girls if I'm not even sure you can stay awake long enough to feed them.

"Tell you what, why don't I order us all a pizza and you can go take a refreshing shower." The two girls cheered, and Kelly shot a glare his way.

"We had pizza on Saturday. I'm not in the mood for more." Kelly pushed herself away from the table and stood. "Besides, I'm perfectly capable of feeding my girls."

"They're *our* girls," Jeff countered, "and you are swaying on your feet. If you don't want pizza, we can order something else. But I'm staying until *our* children are fed. Go shower."

He would win the battle, eventually. It only took Kelly noticing their daughters looking back and forth between them. Hannah stuck her thumb back in her mouth, and Olivia leaned against the doorjamb to Kelly's office, her face a mix of hope her dad would stay, and fear her parents would start fighting.

Kelly hated fighting in front of the girls. And Jeff knew it. He stood firm, his arms folded across his chest. Kelly relented.

Thirty minutes later, Kelly returned to the kitchen. She'd pulled her wet hair back into a ponytail, which was only a slight improvement from her usual braid, as far as he was concerned.

The jeans and simple blue T-shirt she wore had a lot to be desired, but he didn't comment. When they were married, he made sure Kelly dressed to impress. It was important the wife of a man in his position showed class.

Despite her flaws, he smiled at her and handed her the cup of steaming tea he had prepared once he heard the shower turn off. He'd been tempted to make a fresh pot of coffee, knowing the drugs would enhance Kelly's already frazzled nerves, but he'd controlled the urge.

Tonight was about calming Kelly. Lull her into feeling safe and coddled. Tonight he needed Kelly to relax with him.

Kelly sat down and stared at him as he put napkins, forks, and knives on the table.

"I ordered a chicken, broccoli, and ziti from Italian Express," Jeff told her before he peeked over Olivia's shoulder and checked her spelling homework.

"Why are you being so nice to me?"

Jeff was glad his back was to Kelly when he asked. It gave him the second he needed to prepare the perfect face of surprise when he did turn to her.

"Kelly, you are the mother of my children. Just because we are divorced, doesn't mean I don't care."

He knew she was suspicious. It would take some time, but Jeff knew Kelly. He played the perfect father during dinner, making sure the girls had their milk, ensured they brought their plates to the sink when they were done eating, ordered them upstairs to shower before getting ready for bed.

And after telling his ex-wife to get some much-needed rest, and knowing she would because he had slipped a little something in her tea to help her sleep, Jeff left. Score one for him.

Chapter Thirteen

When Guinness raised his head off the floor, Finn assumed he would hear another rumble of the thunder from the summer storms that had plagued the city for the past two days. But when Guinness stood and whined, Finn knew he was about to have company.

Placing the roller with primer paint onto the tray, he wiped his hands on a rag when the doorbell rang. The bell sent Guinness into a series of loud barks as he lunged toward the door.

"Hush, boy," Finn grabbed the dog's collar and gripped it as he opened the door. And looked down at his ten-year old niece.

"Lisa?" he now struggled with Guinness as the giant dog tried to greet Lisa with his usual jumping and kissing. Lisa laughed and knelt down to give his dog a big hug.

"What are you doing here?" Finn looked at the street, trying to locate whichever parent had brought her. "How did you get here?"

Lisa was still lavishing her love on his dog and refused to look up at him, instead she mumbled her answer into Guinness' fur. "I took the bus."

Finn groaned. Lisa was wet from head to toe and the backpack slung across one shoulder reminded him it was the middle of the week. Not only was Lisa all the way across town from where she lived, she was supposed to be in school.

"Get in here and I'll get you a towel." His resigned words elicited a much too happy grin from the child, which worried him as he disappeared upstairs.

Within a minute he returned with a towel and a T-shirt and ordered the child to change while he silently debated calling his brother or wait to see why Lisa had graced him with the unexpected visit.

Taking a look at his living room with the drop cloths covering the carpet and the one wall he'd managed to prime, he knew he was done for the day. He'd wanted at least this room painted and looking good before Kelly came over Saturday. Shaking his head, he prepared to clean up as Lisa came back into the room.

"Are you painting all the walls white?"

Lisa looked like a waif in his oversized shirt, still wet jeans and long brown hair she'd twisted and dangled over one shoulder. Of all his nieces and nephews, Lisa was the thinnest. She was going to have her father's height and her mother's model thin build. Unfortunately, she was also the one who'd inherited the curse of their Irish stubbornness.

"This is the primer. These walls are going to be brown." He tapped down the lid on the paint can and grabbed the roller and pan, heading to the bathroom to rinse everything else. Lisa followed.

"Eww. Like a chocolate brown?"

"No, more like," Finn tried to think of the best way to describe the color he'd chosen, "more like the color of the nougat in a Three Musketeer's bar."

"Oh, that's cool then."

Lisa stood in the doorway, her hands twisting the

bottom of the shirt into little knots.

"Want to tell me what's going on, squirt?"

She gave a little shrug. "Mom and dad got into another fight."

"Ahh!" The joys of a divorced couple. Finn wasn't sure he wanted to know what his brother and ex-wife were fighting about, but his niece was going to fill him in anyway.

"Dad was two hours late to pick us up last night. Two hours! Mom was supposed to meet some friends for supper at six and ended up missing it. It was the only night they were going to be in town. It was so unfair. Then, when dad did show up, his excuse was work. *As usual.* Mom told him to leave because it was useless for him to take us at that point anyway because he'd just have to have us back in ninety-minutes. It probably didn't even matter to him anyway, 'cause he's probably got some bimbo he's seeing on the side."

Finn cringed. Bethany had vented about Tom. It wasn't true and certainly inappropriate to be saying in front of the kids. No matter what the reason for the divorce, he wasn't thrilled with Bethany for putting such thoughts into the kids' heads.

Now what did he do?

"First of all, Lisa, your dad doesn't have a bim… girlfriend, and even if he eventually does find someone new, I know you and Tommy will always come first. As for your dad being two hours late…"

Finn sighed. It was the age-old story in both the police and fire service. The job was the job.

He'd heard it all over the years from the guys with whom he worked. There was always some event they were missing and their wives were bitching about it.

There was a reason divorce was so high within their professions.

"Listen, kiddo, I can't tell you your dad is going to be on time all the time. It doesn't happen that way with our jobs." Lisa looked down, kicking one foot back and forth across the floor with a soft swish, swish. He knew she'd heard this all before. "What is he supposed to do, tell the bad guy to freeze, pull out his cell phone, call to say he's going to be late, hang up and then tell the bad guy, okay, go?"

Lisa chuckled a little.

"He loves you Lisa, you and Tommy, but your dad doesn't have the type of job where he can put a file aside to be dealt with the next day. Your mother knew that when they married, and unfortunately, that's the life you've had to live with for the past ten years."

Lisa finally looked at him, her brown eyes filled with tears. "I know. But it's harder now with dad not living with us. At least, before, I knew I'd see him at some point at the end of the day, even if it was to give me a kiss when he got in at night."

Her lip trembled as tears coursed down her cheeks. She gave a little hiccup. "I miss him."

Finn took the few steps to Lisa and gathered her into a hug as she sobbed. After a minute, he sat down in the hallway and continued to hold his niece while her pent up emotions about the divorce finally escaped. Guinness whimpered and nudged his nose against them, letting them know he cared, as well.

When Lisa finally stopped crying, Finn looked at his watch. Ten forty-five. Still early in the day.

"Okay, kid. I'd like to be the super-cool uncle and all, but I don't approve of skipping school. So," he helped Lisa to her feet and stood. "Let's get you home to change into dry clothes and get you to school."

"Aww, Uncle Shawn, what if..."

He held his hand out, halting the excuse. "No arguments about it. Let's go."

"Are you going to tell my dad?"

Ahh. Now there was the dilemma. "Don't you think he's going to find out about you skipping school?"

Lisa slung her backpack onto one shoulder. "Maybe not."

"Come on, Guinness, you can come along for the ride," Finn grabbed his keys and opened the door escorting his niece and dog outside. The rain had stopped temporarily but the rumble of thunder continued in the distance. "Lying isn't going to solve anything, sweetheart."

"Guess not," was the mumbled answer.

He put an arm around his niece's shoulder. "Listen, kiddo. I know things are tough right now. You know you can come to me, or Auntie Shannon or even Auntie Kate, if you need to talk. Okay?"

At Lisa's nod, good ole Uncle Shawn had one more thing to say. "Do me a favor. No more skipping."

Finn had no sooner dropped Lisa off at her school when, his cell phone rang. Seeing his brother's name, he prepared himself.

"Hey, Tom. What's up?"

"Are you on duty?"

He grinned. His brother rarely took the time for pleasantries on the phone. Direct and to the point. That was Tom. "Nope."

"Good. Ceci called."

Finn's shoulders slumped as he glanced at the dashboard clock. "It's a little early, isn't it?"

"Guess dad was outside when they opened, already drunk. Must not have gone home."

Finn sighed. "I'll take care of dad. Ah, Tom, while I've got you on the line," Yeah, his brother needed this right now, "I just dropped Lisa off at school."

Silence. *Oookaayyy*! *This was going to be easy.*

"She was really upset about the fight you and Bethany had last night and needed someone to talk to. She came over. We talked. She cried. And I got her to school."

There was a large splat on the windshield as the rain finally moved in again. Another. He turned his wipers on.

"What am I going to do with her?" His brother's voice was tight and Finn heard a click, click, click, like the sound of a pen top.

"Don't be too hard on her, Tom. At least she came to me to talk and wasn't roaming the streets or anything. She misses you." Finn decided to keep the 'bimbo' comment to himself. No need to keep the feud going between him and Bethany.

"Yeah. Okay. Thanks for being there for her. I gotta go, Shawn. Check in on dad."

His brother hung up.

Finn swung his truck into the drive-thru for a coffee and turned to look at his dog panting happily in the back seat. For some reason, his dog loved the rain, even thunder, and had his nose pressed against the window as the rain streamed down.

"Come on, Guinness, duty calls."

****

Finn hesitated before entering the renovated firehouse, now the home of The Halligan Bar and Grille. He ran a hand over the plaque on the outside brick wall, *In Memory of our Fallen Brothers,* before he opened the door to the bar.

"Hiya, Finn," the hostess greeted him. "He's upstairs today."

"Thanks, Tracy."

Both he and his dad had both been assigned to this house during their careers before it closed its doors five years ago. Last year, the doors to the firehouse reopened and Patrick Finnigan had discovered his new favorite watering hole. It didn't take long before each of the bartenders had committed Shawn and Tom's phone numbers to memory.

Finn trotted up the stairs, not at all surprised his father chose the upper level bar. While the first floor's décor maintained an Irish theme, the second floor commemorated the fire service. Bunker gear, helmets, and boots hung from the walls and ceilings, while photos of the city's firehouses adorned the walls.

Walking into the room gave Finn a sense of pride, knowing he was a part of the building's history. It was the reason his father spent more than his fair share at the gleaming bar, regaling customers with stories of his own glory days in the building and within the city.

Finn slid onto the stool to his father's right. The bartender grabbed a mug the moment he entered the room and she filled it with steaming black coffee before he settled into the seat.

"Thanks, Ceci."

"Anytime, Shawn." The short, dark-haired bartender topped off Patrick's mug and walked away.

"Hey, Pops."

"Shawny."

Finn drank his coffee in silence. He could smell the stench of alcohol on his father, but the silence—and cup of coffee, instead of beer in front of him—told Finn his father's drunk was wearing off.

"Know what today is, Shawn?"

"Wednesday, June 11th."

Patrick grunted and checked his watch, seeming surprised at the passage of time. "Yesterday, then."

As Patrick ran his hands over his unwashed hair, Finn noticed a hole in the armpit of his dad's shirt and turned away to stare down at his mug. Once upon a time, his father had been larger than life to him. Now, his dad was worn out by life.

"Yesterday was the anniversary of when I met your mother."

Ah. Of course. How could he have forgotten? They went through this annually.

"We responded to an alarm activation over at the campus dorms. It was four in the morning."

Finn had heard the story hundreds of times, but it was part of the process. He listened as his father continued.

"I spotted her the moment we drove up. She was a tiny little thing with blonde hair and blue eyes and a flirty smile. I was hooked. I was a probie at the time and couldn't think straight to do my job, but the captain kept us in close quarters.

"When we were getting ready to head out, she sashayed by me in her silky little nightgown and walked up to George Hogan and asked him for a pen from the truck. Hell, even Hogan, married eight years,

112

couldn't resist her. He practically ran to do her bidding, then she came to me and wrote her name on my palm. *Faith Shanahan*. What a beautiful name."

Although the memories made Patrick smile, Finn knew the happy thoughts were short-lived. He'd sat through these walks down memory lane too many times.

"Your mother had a way of twisting me in knots. She ran hot then cold, but, man, she was a beauty."

Hot and cold? What an understatement. Finn remembered his mother as an emotional roller coaster. "Yeah, Dad, Mom was beautiful."

"But she hated the job."

Here it comes, Finn thought as rain beat on the over-sized windows. Fond memories are over.

"She knew what she was getting when she married me."

"It's a tough schedule, Pops."

"Did you know she used to think I was cheating on her?" Patrick drained his mug and pushed it aside. "Used to pack you kids up in the middle of the night so she could drive by the station and make sure I was there."

"I remember."

"Faith." Patrick spit the name out. "Hell of a name. She had no faith in me. I loved her but it wasn't enough. It was never enough."

Finn stood and fished money out of his pocket, tossing it on the bar.

"Come on, Dad. I'll take you home now."

"You're the smart one, Shawny." Patrick hauled himself off the stool and placed a heavy hand on Finn's shoulder. "Don't fall in love, son. It's nothing more than the Devil's invention. It'll cause you pain and heartache."

"Okay, Dad."

Finn got his father home and onto the couch, thankful his sister and her family weren't home.

"You need anything, Pops?"

Patrick stared off into space. "I loved her, Shawny."

"I know."

"Why did she have to die?"

Finn walked to the window and turned on the A/C unit, then settled into the recliner.

"Don't fall in love, Shawny."

"I know, Pops. It's the Devil's invention."

Finn sat by his father's side until he nodded off to sleep.

Chapter Fourteen

Having dealt with his family and their various problems the previous day, Finn rose early on Thursday to finish priming and painting his living room. The walls were bare, but at least it no longer looked worn down. Since Shannon had her own furniture, Finn had taken the sofa and chairs from his house. Still, being in his own home, he discovered he didn't have everything he needed. Like a vacuum. So he headed across town and borrowed one from his sister. When he returned it, he snagged a few cleaning supplies and completed his house duties.

After the third trip to Shannon's, this time to ask what color curtains would match his new walls, his sister cornered him.

"Shawn, honey, this sudden need to thoroughly clean your house, does it have anything to do with a certain neighbor?"

Having his older sister question him, even with the silly grin on her face, gave him pause. It was like getting caught sneaking around by their mom.

"I painted the walls and cleaned the house. I've been there a month and realized I didn't have a vacuum, that's it."

Then Shannon hugged him.

"Buy some candles for the table, new sheets for the bed, and remember to use condoms."

"Good God, Shannon!" Damn. He wasn't used to anyone checking in on his love life. Shaking his head at his sister's advice, he headed toward the door.

"And tell Kelly I said hello," his sister yelled after him. It was annoying having a big sister around. But his mouth curved upward.

Finn hadn't seen Kelly since Saturday and their date was still two full days away. He hadn't even heard her sweet voice since their short phone conversation on Monday.

And he wanted to.

No. Kelly had proposed the type of relationship he liked: casual. He didn't need to see her before Saturday.

He took his sister's advice, though, and headed to the store. As he roamed through the aisles, Finn completed his mental to-do list. Bed sheets: check. Candles for the table: check. New box of Trojans: check.

Finn passed by the electronics department and perused the selection of music, looking for something light and romantic. If Kelly was going to cook, he could at least set the mood.

With two new CD's in hand, Finn headed toward the registers. As he passed by the hardware section, he stopped. Considered.

And when he left the store, his excuse for seeing Kelly early was nestled safely in his front pocket.

****

"No sweetheart, I think nine years old is much too young to color your hair." Kelly grabbed a dirty sock off the chair in Olivia's room and put it into the hamper as she answered her daughter.

"What about for my tenth birthday. That's only two

months away. Can I color my hair then?"

Kelly sighed. "Why do you want to color your hair?"

Livvy jumped up and grabbed a teen magazine from her nightstand that also contained a table lamp with flip-flops as the base and seashells along the shade and a beach-chair alarm clock.

Based on how fast Livvy turned to the page she wanted to show, Kelly guessed today wasn't the first day she'd looked at the contents.

"Look at these, mom. It's before and after pictures of celebrities. Look how great *she* looks with black hair."

Kelly cringed. Black? She hoped her daughter wasn't going to get into a Goth stage as she headed into her tween years. How did other parents handle this?

"Yes, she does look good," Kelly acknowledged as she tried to figure a way out of the conversation without totally alienating her child. Taking the magazine from Livvy she stared at the photos. "You know what, though? I don't think it's the color, but the style which makes her look so great."

This could work for her. "What if we looked at getting your hair cut like this, with the choppy layers? I bet it will frame your face nicely and make you look older."

"Really?" Livvy stood on her bed to look over Kelly's shoulder. "You think so? When can we do it?"

Kelly knew once her daughter grabbed hold of an idea there was no stopping her. Patience was a foreign word to Olivia.

"It will have to be after I pick you up from Aunt Maddie's house on Sunday."

"Yay. I'll bring the picture and get Aunt Maddie's thoughts on it, too."

Mental note to self, Kelly thought as she watched her daughter walk to her dresser, prop the magazine and fiddle with her hair at the mirror, *call Maddie and Jules and make sure they agree to the style not the color.*

"Lights out in fifteen minutes, kiddo. Tomorrow is your last day of school before vacation."

"Sure, mom," Livvy mumbled, but she was more concerned with her future haircut.

Kelly peeked in on an already sleeping Hannah. Once she fixed the blankets on her youngest, she headed downstairs.

Ahh. This was her time. With her girls finally in bed, the dishes cleaned and put away, Kelly only had a load of clothes to fold and then she could relax with a cup of tea.

When the phone rang, Kelly was thankful for the reprieve of laundry. And when she saw the name: S. Finnigan, she counted to three to slow her heart rate before picking up.

"Hi, Finn."

"Hi, Kelly." It wasn't fair. How could two words, said over a phone line, curl her toes? "I, ah, well, I was wondering if you'd meet me at the gate?"

Her heart rate accelerated again, perhaps even skipped a beat or two. Hannah was asleep. Olivia, while she was sure hadn't shut out her lights, was consumed in her future make over.

"Umm. Okay. Sure." She hung up the phone and rushed into the downstairs bathroom. She was wearing shorts and a T-shirt. Boring, but at least it had no visible stains. Hair still in braid: check. She smiled.

Nothing in teeth: check. Lip-gloss? She opened the vanity mirror. Not there. Not in the small drawer, either. Fudge. She'd have to go without.

What did Finn want? What did he want to say that couldn't be said over the phone?

"Stop it, Kelly," she admonished her reflection. "Don't make this more than it is. You are the one who told him no attachments. Just sex."

Kelly slipped on a pair of flip-flops and stepped out the sliding doors and into the back yard. June in New Hampshire could be cruel. Today had been hot and humid but as night settled in, so had a coolness causing goose bumps to pebble down her arms. She wasn't turning back for a sweatshirt, though.

It was late enough for the sun to have set, but early enough that the lights from her house and those around her filled the back yard with enough light to guide her to the gate in the fence at the far corner of her yard.

She didn't grab the key to the lock for the gate. She didn't need it. She'd never reattached the lock after the last time Finn had gone through. The gate swung open as she reached for it and there he was, waiting for her on the other side.

Tall, muscular, fit. Dark hair. Deep set eyes, hard to read in the little bit of light they had. Just your normal, average, boy next door—if your boy next door could cause your insides to turn to molten chocolate lava cake without saying a word.

"Hi, again," he said, and Kelly felt the ooey-gooey insides begin to ooze. "Are the girls asleep?"

"Hannah is. Livvy's reading." And her bedroom is in the front of the house, Kelly thought, not without a bit of thankfulness.

"So would it be safe to greet you with a kiss?"

Yes, please. Yes, please. Kelly wanted to scream the words. She'd only been thinking of the way her lips had tingled as he'd said goodbye on Saturday night and wondering if the sensation had been anything more than a dream. She didn't scream the words; instead she nodded and clasped her hands behind her back to keep from reaching out and making the first move.

She expected him to kiss her as he had in her kitchen: quick, but full of promise of what was to come this weekend. Instead, he took his time. First his hands skimmed up her arms and over her shoulders. Then one finger brushed the side of her cheek before moving to tilt her face up. She stared into the dark depths of his eyes for what seemed an eternity before he finally moved to press his mouth against hers.

She couldn't call this kiss an actual kiss. No, it was more of an onslaught of sensation. Deep, penetrating, roaring heat consumed her. Ooh, the man could kiss. Then his tongue explored and the insides of the lava cake exploded in her tummy and caused her to tingle from her scalp to her toenails.

It only got better. Finn's hands moved to her waist and pulled her toward him. He stepped backwards, pulling her with him until they were in his yard. Then he pressed her back against the fence, his body against hers. Heat against heat. She certainly didn't need a sweatshirt now. Finn didn't use his hands to take more of what she was willing to give. They didn't roam. They didn't grab. They held her in place between his body and the fence while his mouth did all the work.

They were both panting when his mouth released hers, but he didn't move away. Even in the dark she saw the pulse in his neck beating rapidly, an echo to her own.

She'd been right in her assessment of this man. He was going to be a fabulous lover.

"I've wanted to do this all week."

Well, zippity-do-da-day! Those were words to warm a woman's heart.

"I've wanted this all week." Kelly whispered. She *had* wanted another kiss, sure. She'd been looking forward to the sex between them on Saturday, sure. But she hadn't expected the volcanic eruption that had occurred. If this was what happened to her when he kissed her, she had better be prepared for the earth to shake and mountains to move.

Finn managed to get in control before she did. At least he was able to string a coherent sentence together. Kelly found thinking logically was difficult while still pressed neatly against his rock hard body. And he was rock hard in *all* the right places.

"I was thinking about Saturday," Finn's breath brushed against her temple as she looked up at him. "So do I get to know what I can expect for dinner?"

Dinner? Oh. Right. She was cooking him dinner. "Do you like eggplant parmesan?"

"Oh, yeah."

Kelly gulped. Good grief. Even that sounded like foreplay to her. Get a grip, Kelly.

"I figured I'd make it earlier in the day and heat it up when I got to your house."

"Sounds perfect. Speaking of my house, sometimes I run a little late at work, so I got you this."

Finn shoved a hand into his pocket, which amazed Kelly, considering how his lower half was still pressed against her and he didn't move even an inch away in order to add the length of his fingers between them.

"It's the key to my house."

Kelly gulped. What was he doing? A key? No way. This was too fast. Sure, they were going to sleep together, but that didn't mean she needed a key.

"Oh, Finn, I don't know. We barely know each other." And considering how intimately Shawn Finnigan was pressed against her, considering he'd turned her insides into a dessert by a single kiss, considering the soft chuckle Finn expelled, Kelly knew she sounded like an idiot.

"Don't worry, Kelly," despite the laugh, his words and tone were serious. "I know the rules. No attachment. No problem. This is mere convenience. I should be home by six-thirty. Then I'll need to take a quick shower and feed Guinness. If you want to come over a little early and put dinner in the oven," his voice got deeper and he leaned down to look directly into her eyes, "we'll have more time to enjoy dessert."

Dessert. Yay! More molten chocolate lava cake. Kelly's heart did a flip and her stomach flooded with the ooey-gooey warmth just thinking about it.

Finn pressed the key into her hand. "I'll let you get back to your girls."

And of course, he kissed her again. This time it was a kiss, what she'd expected before. A taste. A nibble. And he finally pulled away from her.

"Yes. My girls. Should go." Great. Kelly couldn't even speak.

She ran back to her house and slid the door shut with a bang. She threw the key onto the table and stared at it.

Finn gave her keys to his house. Yikes. Kelly paced in the confines of her kitchen, her gaze catching the glint of the key over and over again. What had happened out there? What had happened to her?

She had initiated their agreement. Sex and only sex. That's all Saturday would be about. Had to be about. Neither wanted a commitment and Finn wasn't the marrying kind.

No, he was like Jeff. The more women the better. Neely the Scorned had warned her about all the women. But she had to get control of her emotions here and now.

Okay, she hadn't expected the intensity of feelings out in the yard. Hadn't expected her body to explode. It had been too long since she'd had sex. That was all. Yeah. That was it.

She had been on a man-diet for a long time and now had the opportunity to feast on the sumptuous Finnigan buffet. But she had to prepare herself. This might be a one-night, exclusive party. When it was over, she would have to prepare for starvation again. She'd done it once before. She could do it again.

Chapter Fifteen

When Finn arrived at work on Saturday morning, the kitchen was crowded. Shift change could be chaotic at times, but as soon as he checked in with the lieutenant who'd worked the night before, Finn poured himself a steaming cup of freshly brewed coffee and leaned against the counter.

His mind was on tonight and Kelly. Tonight he would feel her sweet lips again, unbraid her hair, and run his fingers through all those blond curls.

"Morning, Finn."

Finn took a sip of coffee. He needed to change his focus or the next ten hours were going to be very long. Painful even. Time to think about the job. Yeah, right.

First things first. The crew. He looked around the room. Smitty and Bucky rode the truck with their Lieutenant, Corbett. All accounted for. Cosmo sat at the table harassing Probie about his breakfast from McDonald's that left his driver, Jack Rawlings, MIA.

And one other person still in the room. Finn gripped his mug of coffee with two hands as he turned to Kevin Murphy. The man rocked his chair back from the table on two precarious legs as he chatted with the rest of the crew.

"Morning, Murph." Finn greeted. "Did you work overtime last night?"

"Nope."

Not the answer he wanted to hear. He swallowed the lump forming in his throat.

"Rawlings coming in today?" He asked the question but had already guessed Murph's answer.

"Nope. Stomach bug."

Finn slowly put down his cup and reached out to grip the Formica counter. Not today. Please, not today.

But as he looked at Murph leaning in his chair, and Mark Corbett, sitting silently beside him sipping at his cup of coffee, reality punched him in the stomach.

"No. No Effin way. This can NOT be happening." Finn heard the panic in his voice as he stared at Murph and back at Corbett. The knowing looks and the resigned smiles on both faces made him want to howl. Instead, he threw his coffee mug into the sink, shattering it into tiny shards.

Pete Clarkson looked up in amazement, his hash brown forgotten in his hands as he whispered to Bucky. "What's got Lieutenant Finn all riled up?"

"Murphy's Law," Bucky answered with a chuckle as Finn whipped back around to face Murph.

"Who approved this? Everyone knows you and the Shit Magnet over here can't work together."

"Shit Magnet? That's Lieutenant Corbett, right?" Pete whispered. "And why can't they work together?"

Bucky smirked as Finn turned his wrath toward the young recruit.

"January second. That's why. Does anyone want to fill this probie in on what happened the last time these two worked together?"

Smitty, who leaned casually against the kitchen lockers, piped in. "What's the big deal, Finn? You got a date or something?"

Finn glared at him but remained silent.

"He does. Finn's got a date tonight," Smitty announced.

"Have we met her?" Cosmo asked.

"Don't change the subject." Finn gritted his teeth and turned to pick up the pieces of the cup in one hand.

"I still don't know why they can't work together?" Pete looked around at the guys, in obvious bewilderment. Bucky took pity on him and began to explain.

"You've been around here long enough to know Corbett is known as the Shit Magnet. That's because the first day on the job he caught the city's first four-alarm in six years. And since then whatever station he is assigned to ends up the busiest of the day."

Finn rolled his eyes. Yeah, working with Corbett was an adventure. They called him the Shit Magnet because they got the dumb-ass calls such as false alarms or kids getting their heads stuck in railings. It wasn't always dangerous stuff, but mostly calls due to human-stupidity. So no one wanted to work on Mark's shift for fear they'd never get home on time.

"Yeah, I'd heard that before," Pete answered, but being the probie, he hadn't learned to keep his mouth shut, and he continued. "But I heard that's why they paired him up with Father Finn, 'cause it's like he has some sort of angel on his shoulder or something."

Finn raised an eyebrow at the kid while the others in the room laughed. He knew his nickname. Some called him Father Finn because of his aversion to commitment. They claimed he was married to the job and the job only. Other's called him Father Finn because, like the probie had said, an angel sat on his shoulder.

He was the polar opposite of Mark Corbett. When he and Corbett worked together on the same group assignment it was a magic combination. Mark was still a shit magnet, and the station would still get the calls for, oh, say a mother and daughter stuck in a tree, but with Father Finn working with him, the calls usually ended on a happy note.

"So about your date, Finn," Cosmo called out, "is she hot like that red-head, Josie?"

"No, no," Smitty responded. "I liked Monique with the Angelina Jolie lips."

Finn threw a warning look at Smitty and Cosmo when Pete spoke up again, his breakfast all but forgotten.

"I still don't get it. What's the big deal about those two working together?"

Bucky again took pity on the kid. "Murphy's Law, Probie. If you think working with Corbett is busy, it ain't nothing compared to working with Murph. With Corbett, we'll get a call before lunch and not eat until one. With Murph, you can forget lunch all together."

Or worse. The thought alone had Finn cringing. Why today? Why did he have to work with Murph today of all days? He liked Murph. Hell, everyone liked Murph. Murph was the epitome of an Irishman. He talked non-stop, could tell a story or a joke like no other in the department, and could drink like, well, like a firefighter.

Murph took the glare he threw his friend's way in stride as he rocked his chair back on two legs, and sipped his coffee as the crew filled the probie in on working with the man.

"January second," Smitty informed Pete, "Corbett worked an overtime shift on Murph's crew. It started snowing at five-thirty and the roads were as slippery as snot on a doorknob."

"Nice, Smitty, real nice." Cosmo interceded and took over. "With Corbett and Murph working together and the weather bad, it was a recipe for disaster, but this takes the cake. Fifteen minutes into the day the call came in. A gas truck skidded on the highway and pushed a school bus of elementary school kids into a snow bank."

"A bus load of kids?" Pete exclaimed, his eyes wide.

"The kids were fine," Murph defended. "Every one of them."

Finn smirked. "But that wasn't all, was it Murph?"

Pete looked back and forth between Kevin Murphy, Mark Corbett, and Shawn Finnigan. "There's more?"

Corbett chuckled. "Yep. A tractor-trailer swerved to avoid the gas truck, and jack-knifed. Between the bus full of kids, the gas leak and the trailer blocking three lanes, the highway shut down for eight hours."

"Is this for real or are you pulling my leg?" Pete looked around the table. Finn knew his face held a pained expression while Corbett and Murph shrugged in resignation.

"It's the truth, kid," Bucky laughed. "To Hell, if it ain't the truth."

"So, Finn," Cosmo crossed the room to wash out his coffee mug in the sink behind the Lieutenant. "Want to tell us about the date that's not going to happen tonight?"

Finn felt a knot tighten across his back. Kelly was cooking him dinner. He had clean sheets on his bed and a box of condoms on the nightstand. The date had to happen.

"Cosmo, why don't you and Probie help Murph with the truck checks." The terse order was met with knowing grins from his crew and the loud scrape of chairs as the duty crew moved to start their day."

Finn closed his eyes and mumbled softly. "This is not happening. Tell me this is not happening?"

Corbitt leaned against the gleaming kitchen counter beside him. "Don't worry about a thing, Finn. With your angel, we've got it covered."

"Yeah, Finn," Murph piped in as he opened the door leading to the truck bay. "You bring luck to a crew. What could possibly happen?"

****

What could possibly happen? Famous last words. And yet, Finn's luck seemed to be holding. They had one call in the morning, which had been for a minor fender-bender with no injuries. During lunch, Finn held his breath as they'd been called out for an odor of smoke at an assisted living complex that turned out to be nothing more than burnt popcorn.

They returned to the station, finished eating, and cleaned up when the house lights signaled another call.

"Engine Three. Truck Three. Mutual Aid to Portersville, Route 38, at the intersection of Lewis and Greene Streets. Hazardous Materials Response for a large propane leak. Time out: Fourteen twenty-nine."

Finn sent a glare toward Murph. "Son. Of. A. Bitch. I've got a fucking date tonight, Murph. If I'm not home by six..." Finn rattled off seven different ways he'd hurt Murphy as they reached the engine and stepped into their gear.

The worst part, his crew laughed and joked about the call. They didn't understand Kelly made arrangements for a babysitter for tonight. If he missed their first date, what was the likelihood of getting time alone with her again anytime soon?

If she even considered the idea.

The firehouse doors opened and Murphy drove the engine out into the street, lights and sirens on. Finn radioed into fire alarm.

"Station three on, responding. Fourteen thirty-two."

A HazMat call, at two-thirty in the afternoon, in the neighboring town of Portersville. He was fucked. With Murph and Corbett working together, Finn's hope for unwinding that tight braid Kelly always had her hair in, fizzled.

The radio crackled to life again.

"R1 to fire alarm."

R1 was the radio designation for the Division Chief of Training and Safety and that particular position was held by Shawn's best friend, Tony Tedeschi.

"Fire Alarm answering R1."

"R1 clear of the drill yard. On to Portersville with Station Three, hazmat response."

Finn felt a tug of relief. Finn liked working with Tony. T could be a hothead at times, but when it came to the fire ground, the guy knew his stuff. Maybe, with Tony on the scene, his guardian angel would be with him. Hell, it was only two-thirty. They could be done by six.

It took them eighteen minutes to arrive at the scene

and all of one second for Finn to push thoughts of a date out of his mind. To an untrained eye, the scene before him would have seemed haphazard and unorganized. To him, it was a chaotic dance of training and education at work.

Portersville had two engines, a truck, and their heavy rescue already on scene and there were more cops running around than ants on a lollipop.

They were on the street in front of a strip mall consisting of a bank, a Chinese restaurant, and several retail stores, all of which had been evacuated. The Portersville crew had three large hoses pouring water onto a car in the middle of a grassy island separating the entrance and exit to the stores.

There would be no date with Kelly tonight. He would deal with the fall out later. For now, he had a job to do.

Finn stepped out of the engine and met up with Corbett and Tony and the three of them headed toward Portersville's Chief to get an update on the situation.

"Here's the situation," Chief Potter explained. "An elderly couple was traveling south on thirty-eight when they swerved to avoid a squirrel." With a resigned shake of his head, Chief Potter pointed to where the car was sitting. "They managed to avoid both the sign and telephone pole and drove right over the propane tank, shearing off the top and control valves."

"The couple is out of the car?" This from Tony.

"Yep, on their way to the hospital but will be fine. All we need you guys to do is stop the leak."

Finn and Tony took in the car perched over the broken propane tank and the hundreds of gallons of water being poured over it.

In order to stop the leak, the car would have to be moved. Very carefully. One little spark from the undercarriage of the car mixed with the gas and they would be dealing with one very large Kaboom!

Tony grinned at Shawn. "Whaddya think, buddy? A walk in the park, right?"

Finn groaned. Yep. Murphy's Law had struck again.

****

Kelly's hands were moist, evidence of her nervousness. What had she gotten herself into? She had made a date for sex with her neighbor. A man she barely knew.

She'd pawned her girls off with her two best friends so she could indulge in a night of what she hoped would ease the lustful thoughts which had haunted her since Shawn "Finn" Finnigan had moved into the house behind her. Well, maybe as long as when he'd talked her down from the tree, but definitely since he'd become a permanent resident to her neighborhood.

Now she was having second thoughts.

When Maddie and Jules left with Olivia and Hannah, Kelly went to work preparing the meal. Eggplant Parmesan. She'd started the sauce earlier, and gave it a quick stir before grabbing the eggplant to start peeling.

Excitement—or pure nervousness—ran through Kelly's veins. She had slept with exactly four men in her life. Jeff had been her first. It had been prom night. She, Jeff, and three other couples, all friends of Jeff's, had left the prom early and ended up in the rooms above Jeff's father's garage for some drinking and a game of strip poker. The end of the night was hazy, because Kelly had drunk way more than she should have, but at some point, she and Jeff had ended up in another room and had sex.

Kelly barely remembered her first time, but five weeks later, she discovered she was pregnant. Jeff proposed immediately and they planned their September wedding. Of course, once they were engaged and had already indulged once, Jeff expected them to have sex. Often.

With her girls gone for the day, the house was quiet, and thoughts of her past were all consuming. Kelly went upstairs into her grandfather's room and carried his little TV down into the kitchen. A Steve Martin movie was on so she turned the volume up before she started the process of slicing the eggplant. The comical storyline didn't hold her attention long as thoughts of her past intruded again.

She had dated Jeff for over a year before their first sexual encounter, and even though she carried his child, Kelly wondered if she was doing the right thing by marrying young. About a month before her wedding, she had a one-night stand. It had been a disaster.

That night proved one thing to her: her future husband was good at making love. Kelly had still been too naïve to realize Jeff was so good because he'd been practicing since the age of thirteen. That knowledge had come after the wedding, after Olivia had been born. While she'd thought Jeff had not found her attractive during the last three months of her pregnancy and hadn't wanted sex, the truth was he did want sex—all the time—and had gone elsewhere to get it.

Then the post-partum depression set in, along with bouts of anxiety attacks.

Kelly's own mother had been pregnant at seventeen, and married her father right out of high school. They spent seven miserable years together before they divorced. Her mother left Kelly in the care of her grandparents while her mother hopped from boyfriend to boyfriend, husband to husband, not wanting to be saddled with the responsibilities of a kid.

All Kelly had ever wanted was to get married, have babies, and be the complete opposite of her mother. She wanted a family. A true, all-American, family who went on vacations, had picnics in the summer, and attended school plays and open houses. And she'd shared this dream with Jeff many times.

When Kelly found out about Jeff's affair, she'd broken down. Her dreams of the perfect family had been shattered. Jeff had said he loved her—he would never leave her—but her anxiety of ending up like her mother continued to grow until she had a full-blown anxiety attack. Jeff would step up at those times and be the perfect husband again. He took care of her, comforted her. Reassured her.

And when she found out he was sleeping with someone else again, she blamed herself. Why wouldn't Jeff want to be with someone else? She was moody and unstable.

Her grandparents encouraged Kelly to go back to school, get the degree in early childhood education she'd been talking about in high school. They said she needed something to occupy her mind.

Jeff said no, though. He was turning his father's simple mechanics garage into what he planned to be the top foreign auto repair shop north of Boston. All their money went into the renovations. Besides, it was important for Olivia to have her mother around at such a young age.

Then Kelly's grandmother was diagnosed with cancer. Kelly spent more and more time with her grandparents. While driving back and forth to chemo appointments, her grandmother expressed her wish for Kelly to get her degree. Kelly would not deny the woman who had raised her since she was seven, a wish so simple. So Kelly went to college. In secret. With her grandparents paying for every aspect of the education.

Four years later, Kelly earned both her degree and Jeff's wrath at her deception. The week before graduation she discovered two things. One: her grandmother's cancer was back, stronger than ever; and two: she was pregnant again.

Kelly could barely handle the stress. She and Jeff argued all the time. Her grandmother got sicker. And as her stomach got bigger, her husband made no secret about getting his needs filled elsewhere. Her anxiety attacks increased in frequency.

Jeff's family had come from money and Jeff had known a life of luxury his entire life. His grandparents had had staff to clean and cook for them. They were founding members of the city's country club. His grandfather had had enough money to spoil his son on a legal degree from Harvard that went nowhere because Jeff's father preferred to work on cars. Reisland Auto Repair had been started, more because Jeff's grandfather thought a couple years of hard work could only help his son grow as a person, but didn't truly believe it would become a passion and thriving business.

Jeff grew up working side-by-side with his father

at the shop, but preferring to spend as much time being spoiled and coddled by his rich, indulgent grandparents. The only thing Jeff enjoyed about the shop was when he drove the foreign cars being serviced. He wanted to work exclusively with high-end cars, and their high-class owners.

When his parents died tragically the year after Kelly and Jeff were married, Jeff inherited a couple million. He finally had the money to make his dream a reality. By the time Hannah was born, his business had taken off and the money rolled in. The 'clients' who brought their cars to him gave him box seats to the Red Sox or the Patriots. Concert tickets. Dinner cruises along Boston Harbor.

Jeff was well respected by his rich clientele and with that came a responsibility to act and dress accordingly. Which meant his wife as well. Kelly was torn between her need to be with her dying grandmother, and guilt to be the perfect wife to her successful husband, causing even more panic attacks.

Her grandparents worried about her and urged her to get a divorce. But Kelly didn't want to repeat the same mistakes as her mother. She wanted her girls to have a father around. Besides, Jeff knew how to ease her anxieties. When they weren't arguing, he would lavish his attention on her. Back rubs. Bubble baths. Romantic dinners. Waking her with a cup of coffee each morning. Preparing her a soothing drink before bed.

His numerous affairs, though, had been too much. Kelly didn't want to depend on her grandparents forever. Getting a job meant putting her girls into daycare, and meant time not there for her grandmother who was now completely bedridden.

When her grandfather proposed a daycare and showed her how they could renovate the garage, Kelly knew in her heart she could succeed. Despite her fear of leaving Jeff—of putting her own children through the trauma of a divorce, Kelly filed the paperwork and moved in with her grandparents.

With the divorce had gone Kelly's dream of the perfect family: father, mother, two kids, a dog, or two. But she refused to be like her mother, hopping from man to man. At least Kelly knew she could survive on her own. She was independent and proud of it.

Kelly got a stepstool from the stairwell to the basement and used it to look on the top shelf of her pantry for breadcrumbs. She knew she had some. She'd used it a couple weeks ago when making a meatloaf. Five minutes of searching and cursing and thinking she'd have to go to the store, Kelly finally found what she was looking for on the bottom shelf behind a box of Lucky Charms.

The TV station must have been playing a Steve Martin marathon because another began. Kelly had never seen this movie and watched until she realized Steve Martin played a fire chief.

Which reminded her about for whom she was making dinner. She hadn't made a meal for any other man since her divorce. That said a lot. She'd dated a couple of times in the past two years, both times had included sex. Neither time had been earthshattering. Neither man had caused her to dream about them. Neither man's kiss had turned her bones to jelly or left her legs wobbly.

Finn's kiss did, though, and it scared her. Finn

reminded her of Jeff—extremely good-looking, in excellent physical condition, and very popular with the female population. And if Finn's kiss was any indication—and it usually was—he would be no slouch in the sack.

As the eggplant sizzled, Kelly wondered if she was stepping out of the proverbial frying pan and into the fire. Could she handle the affair?

Kelly wasn't concerned about her performance in bed or how she'd compare with previous women in Finn's life. She'd been married to Jeff long enough to learn how to satisfy a man. She wasn't worried about taking off her clothes either. She ran the treadmill for an hour four nights a week. She may be on the short side, but after having two children, her trim and athletic body had curved nicely in the right places.

No, going to bed with Shawn Finnigan didn't make her nervous. What made her nervous was the 'no attachments' deal she'd made with him. It was good in theory. True, she didn't want another husband, but when Finn talked, Kelly's stomach flittered. When Finn looked at her, she couldn't look away. When Finn talked Livvy down from the tree and helped Hannah with her fear of dogs, Kelly felt an unexplainable tug in her heart.

And that was what scared her most.

She had to forget all that. Tonight was about sex and sex only. It was about companionship to ease away the loneliness of being a single mom.

Finn didn't like commitments. She wasn't looking for any. It was the perfect match. She needed to remember that.

Kelly stepped out of the shower around five and

opened the body lotion Jules had given her for Christmas. She had shaved her legs. Her body was lightly scented and smooth. It was time to deal with her hair.

She hated her too thick, ultra-curly hair. It made her look like an electrified poodle. But tonight there would be no unattractive braid. Taming it took lots of hair product and even more time. It took a full hour, but when done, Kelly was pleased.

She'd straightened her hair, using the hot iron, and it fell to flattering lengths past her shoulders with only a slight wave at the ends. Ten minutes later, her makeup had been added. Her eyes were surrounded by dark, full lashes, her lips were pink and moist. Kissable.

Kelly slipped into the dress she'd pulled from the back of her closet. One she hadn't worn for years. It was beige with a purple paisley print, had spaghetti straps which showed off her toned shoulders and arms and fell to slightly above her knees. Though she wore no bra, Kelly's breasts filled the dress with the right amount of cleavage; a purple beaded necklace disappeared beneath the front helping to draw attention to a particular part of her body.

Kelly felt her palms getting sweaty again as she studied herself in the mirror one last time.

"You look great, Kelly. And tonight is going to go fine." Kelly smoothed her hands down the sides of the dress. "There is nothing wrong with two adults who find each other attractive acting on their needs. Tonight you are not a mommy or in charge of a room full of kids. It's about being an adult."

Kelly headed downstairs. She'd left the television on in the kitchen and the six-o'clock news had already started. With half an ear, Kelly heard about a propane leak in a neighboring town before the story changed to a gang fight inside a grocery store. Kelly placed everything she would need to fix the salad into a brown bag. Put the Italian bread on top and balanced the dish with the eggplant in the crook of her arm.

She turned off the television, grabbed the key to her neighbor's house, and headed out her back door with the supper she'd prepared.

Not wanting a repeat of the last time she'd gone to Finn's, Kelly had a firm hold of the meal when Guinness barreled toward her in greeting as she unlocked the back door.

"Hi there, boy." Kelly put everything down on the table, noting with a smile Finn had already set two settings including two long white tapered candles in between. She hadn't expected the romantic gesture.

Guinness nudged her leg and Kelly spent a few minutes petting the dog and giving him the attention he demanded. When he whined at the door, Kelly obliged, letting him out into the fenced back yard.

Finn had said he'd be home between six and six-thirty. Kelly looked at the clock on the stove and saw it was twenty-past the hour. She put the oven on to pre-heat and got to work putting the salad together. Guinness returned within a few minutes and followed Kelly around the kitchen as she looked in drawers for salad tongs and oven mitts.

"So tell me, Guinness, are you used to having a strange woman making themselves at home in your kitchen?" Kelly added the tomato and cucumbers she'd chopped earlier in the day.

"No, don't answer. It's none of my business."

Kelly put the eggplant into the oven, figured out the timer, and turned to her canine companion. "So now what? It's after six-thirty. Finn is running a bit late tonight. Should we wait in the living room?"

Kelly moved into the other room. "Ooh. He painted in here. Doesn't it look nice, Guinness? And such pretty candles. Finn thinks of everything."

Kelly wished she had remembered to put her watch back on and wandered back into the kitchen looking for a clock. The clock she'd used before had been on the stove but now ticked down the minutes until dinner. Kelly located the microwave and saw the time was now six forty-five.

"Well, Guinness, why don't we watch a little television until Finn gets home?" Kelly sat primly on one end of the couch and smoothed her hands down the front of her dress, making sure it didn't ride too far up her legs. She located the remote and hit the power button. The news was once again showing the propane leak in Portersville.

"Route 38 continues to be shut down in both directions tonight as firefighters and the region's Hazardous Materials team work together to contain the leak," the female newscaster informed from her position on the street with several fire trucks behind her. The lights on the emergency vehicles flashed bathing the newscaster in a hazy light as she spoke.

"I did have a chance to talk to Chief Raymond Potter, who told me the car had been successfully removed from the gas tank and what is left now is the tedious job of burning off the propane. He expects this to take several more hours but says the road should be open before morning."

The camera panned the fire trucks and focused on a spray of water in the air behind the vehicles, but it was the smaller red truck, beside the fire engines that caught and held Kelly's attention. A truck with large, white, block lettering: Rocky Point Fire Rescue HazMat Unit. The camera focused on two firefighters chugging down bottles of water and Kelly sat up straight as one grabbed his helmet and headed back toward the fire, walking in front of the camera.

"Well, Guinness, I do believe I shaved my legs for nothing." Kelly refused to dwell on the heavy weight of disappointment that followed her as she went back to the kitchen to turn off the oven.

Chapter Sixteen

Jeff Reisland raised his binoculars and brought it into focus. Kelly's house was located in the middle of a block of well-maintained middle-class homes in an almost perfect square of mapped out streets. The tree streets—Sycamore, Honeysuckle, Willow—were neatly dissected by the berry streets—Raspberry, Huckleberry, Teaberry. The lawns were mowed on a fairly regular basis. For some houses, curb appeal meant gardens while others it was the children's bikes and toys that peppered the grass.

Regardless, it was considered a respectable area of Rocky Point to raise children. It wasn't too close to the inner-city gang-element. No, Kelly's neighborhood almost bordered the literary streets—Shakespeare, Poe, Frost, Bronte—where the more affluent of Rocky Point's society lived. Old money. Where Jeff lived.

The two neighborhoods were in the same section of town and, as kids, he and Kelly had attended the same schools. Jeff had become friends with Ken Lear in middle school. Ken lived on the poorly named Sheepberry Road (who the hell wanted to live on a street that sounded like it was named after animal dung) but was conveniently located on the corner of Huckleberry Street.

Convenient, because looking outside of the back window of Ken's room was a perfect view of the back yards of the resident's of Huckleberry. And look, they did. Beginning their freshman year, with a pair of binoculars and even a telescope, the two boys had set their sights on the yard of twenty-nine Huckleberry, home of Mr. and Mrs. Stanick and their granddaughter, Kelly.

Of course, what hot-blooded, American male of fifteen wouldn't want to look when Kelly and her two best friends, Madison Carlisle and Jules Sinclair, would slather themselves in baby oil and sit themselves out on lounge chairs in nothing but bikinis in the crisping August sun.

Back then, Kelly Stanick was a runner. She was on the relay or sprinting team. Whatever. He hadn't cared really. But it had given the athletic figure enough muscle definition to create a few playboy fantasies.

Her friend Maddie had always seemed fat to Jeff and he'd barely given the mousy girl a second glance in school, but when she'd wear the bikini top and denim shorts (no bikini bottoms for her rounded ass), Jeff's binoculars had focused in more than once on the abundance of breasts that overflowed the material.

Then there had been Jules. Tall. Redhead. Long, perfect legs. Curvy waist. And enough tits to fill out the barely-there bikini she wore even at fifteen. Jules only had to walk into a room to give a guy a boner. Of the three girls, Jules was socially on par with him. They lived two blocks away from each other in the elite section of town. If it weren't for her rich-bitch, ice queen persona, Jeff might have attempted to get a taste of her.

Actually, he'd fantasized, more than once, if he could morph the best of the three women together:

Kelly's blonde wholesomeness, with the legs of one Jules Sinclair and the breasts of Maddie Carlisle, they'd have been perfect.

Jeff sighed as he put down his binoculars, nearly fifteen years later, from his position inside Ken's old bedroom. When Olivia casually informed him Kelly was not going to be at the sleepover at Maddie's house tonight because she had a date, Jeff had seethed and immediately started to plan.

Getting information from Olivia was easy. His little girl loved to talk. He'd discovered Kelly rarely drank coffee anymore, so the Ritalin high he'd seen her on last week had been a rare, one-time occasion. He needed to mess with her head in other ways. And fast.

Ken's parents were on their annual anniversary cruise that made the first part of his plan work nicely. He'd borrowed Ken's house key, a six-pack of beer, and had camped out the moment he'd dropped the girls off this morning. He hadn't seen too much throughout the day. She hadn't ventured into the back yard and her ugly mini-van remained parked in the driveway. Because of the garage—okay, because of the silly-assed garage, turned daycare—there were no side windows into the main house he could watch.

He'd snuck Hannah's favorite dog, the one she slept with every night, out of her overnight bag. He planned to show up after the date arrived, of course, to be the doting, loving father who wants to make sure his baby had the raggedy mutt before bedtime.

It would give him a chance to see the competition and make points as a devoted father.

The sky had turned a Maxfield Parrish blue with little puffs of white wispy clouds. The temperature hung in the low eighties with little humidity and even a bit of a breeze to round out the day. It was a picture-postcard perfect day. Perfect for spying, if there had been anything to spy.

The hours dragged by with nothing to see from Kelly's home. Nothing interesting even from the other houses along the block, either, unless you count watching two brothers beat the crap out of each other over whatever stupid reasons brothers fight about.

His jackpot came several hours later when Kelly entered her bedroom. It had been her grandparent's room when she lived there before. Her room had been on the opposite side of the house, where the two girls slept now. When the old man had moved to Florida, Kelly had taken over the larger room over the garage.

She moved throughout the room, uncaring the shade was up. She didn't undress in the bedroom but took what she needed from her bureau and walked into the master bath, leaving the door wide open.

Jeff opened the window and slid out onto the slanted rooftop. He positioned himself against the dormers, making it much easier to see Kelly's reflection in the bathroom mirror.

She was in the shower, the glass door making her body only a hazy silhouette. But Jeff didn't need to see clearly to know what Kelly's body looked like. Memories of showering with Kelly washed over him.

He'd always been turned on by Kelly's body. She was a tiny woman with perfectly toned arms and legs. Being an athlete, Kelly had also been very flexible. Once Jeff had taught Kelly to loosen up a bit sexually, she'd learned to be a fairly passionate lover, if somewhat a prude as to where she'd do it.

Their bedroom: of course. Back seat of a car: not a problem. Bathroom and shower: she'd been like a pretzel. Pretty much anywhere in their own home was fine, but trying to get a quickie with her at her grandparent's home: not a chance in the world. In the restroom at the country club: no way.

Once she started showing while pregnant with Olivia, Jeff had stopped having sex with Kelly. The protruding stomach thing was too much for him. Her breasts, on the other hand, had turned him on immensely. They grew like little melons he loved to squeeze. At night, Jeff would spoon his wife and, after the requisite tummy rub, would fall asleep with the newer, heavier weight of her breast in his hand.

Fates had been kind to him. After Olivia's birth, Kelly lost the baby weight but kept the lovely, curvier body pregnancy had given her.

The glass doors slid to the side and Kelly stepped out and Jeff got hard looking at her body, dripping from the shower. Her wet blond curls were dark and nearly straight. She grabbed a fluffy blue towel and patted her skin dry then bent at the waist, wrapped the same towel around her hair and stood back up.

She disappeared for a moment from his view but when she returned, still naked but for the towel wrapped around her head, she lifted one foot up to the vanity and began rubbing lotion from her toes slowly upwards to her thigh. Jeff was so hard he wondered if the buttons on his fly would pop.

He watched her hands. Circle. Rub. Smooth. Her leg went down. She lifted the bottle of lotion, tipped it, rubbed it between her hands.

"Wait for it. Wait for it." Jeff hadn't had this much

fun since he was in high school watching Kelly and her friends with their sunscreen. A grin split Jeff's face as Kelly lifted her other leg. With a single touch on the binoculars, Jeff zoomed in to the perfect mirrored reflection of the barely there tuft of blond hair located at the apex of Kelly's legs. The secret garden he'd hoed many times.

It pissed him off when Kelly primped for another man. A man she'd just met, no less. How many had there been in the past two years since she'd left him? When Kelly shimmied into her panties Jeff put down his binoculars and crawled back into the bedroom window.

He needed a drink. Something stronger than the lukewarm beer he'd been drinking. Jeff wandered the house, looking through closets and cabinets until he found what he wanted. He uncorked the Cognac and breathed in the sweet scent permeating around him. He poured the liquid and took a healthy gulp and let the warmth slide down his throat. No, it did nothing to alleviate the thoughts of his wife with another man.

With the bottle and glass in hand, Jeff went back to his original position at the upstairs window. He wanted to see his competition when he showed up at Kelly's for their 'date.'

Shortly after six, Kelly stepped into her backyard and Jeff nearly fell off his chair in his haste to train the binoculars on her. She had straightened her hair the way he loved it.

Damn it all to hell. She was wearing the dress he'd bought her in Bermuda when he'd whisked her away for a romantic four days that had produced Hannah nine months later. How dare she wear that dress for another man!

The heat settling in his stomach no longer had to do with lust. Anger rolled around like a Tsunami ready to strike.

Kelly's hands were full with…what was that? A casserole dish? And a bag with…Jeff zoomed in…bread.

Well, well, well. Kelly was bringing dinner to her date's house. She put down the bag in order to unlatch the gate in her yard. Damn. He'd forgotten Olivia had told him the firefighter lived in the Belanger house.

She walked to a back door and put down the bag again. And used a key to open the door. A key. She had a key to the man's house?

Jeff stood quickly and pushed the chair aside. It flipped over but the rug muffled any satisfying crash. He threw his binoculars but they bounced harmlessly on the bed. He wanted to punch something. He wanted to hurt someone.

Jeff stopped himself short of punching the wall. Instead, he placed both hands against the wall and leaned heavily, forcing himself to breathe.

He needed a new plan.

Ten minutes later, Jeff strolled down Huckleberry. At number twenty-nine he stopped by the mailbox and opened it. No mail. He sauntered to the front door, pulled his key ring from his pocket, and located the copy he'd made many years earlier. He opened the door and walked into Kelly's house as though he belonged there.

Everything in order, as usual. Kelly wasn't obsessive about being clean, but she did like everything in its place. Jeff walked through. He loosened the caps of her salt and pepper shakers in the kitchen. He went into her office and re-filed her bills; those needing to be paid he placed in the already paid to be filed bin. He went into the daycare area and saw the neatly labeled bins. When he finished, dolls filled the bin labeled 'cars' and the one that once held blocks was filled with action figures.

He moved upstairs into Kelly's bedroom. Ick. How could she sleep here? In the bed her grandparents had used? No wonder she went to the neighbor's house instead of having him over.

Jeff left the bedroom alone and went into the bathroom where moisture still clung to the walls. He saw the lotion, placed neatly in the corner of the vanity and picked it up, read the label. Honeysuckle.

He pumped a drip into his hand and rubbed it in before lifting it to his nose. This is what Kelly smells like right now? This is the scent on her legs, on her stomach, on her breasts. Jeff put the bottle in his pocket.

A few minutes later, with enough stuff moved around or missing, Jeff walked out, locking the door behind him. Then he opened the door to the ugly mini-van and popped the hood. Within seconds, Jeff strolled back down Huckleberry toward his car on the sheep's dung road.

Chapter Seventeen

Finn slid his SCBA—self-contained breathing apparatus—off his back, put his helmet on top of the pack and headed over to a row of tables. He helped himself to a slice of pizza from the boxes ordered by the Portersville Fire Department. Cold pepperoni pizza. The cheese tasted like rubber.

It definitely was not eggplant. He'd been looking forward to the hot meal and chilled wine, shared across a candle lit table with soft music in the background.

He'd really been looking forward to a long, quiet evening with his ultra-sexy neighbor that ended with breaking in the new sheets he'd put on his bed this morning.

It had been a long afternoon and it would be hours yet before they were done. And no way or time to call Kelly to explain why he never showed up for their date.

The slice of pizza disappeared without him even tasting it but he found a second piece and bit into it, taking off half the slice in a single bite.

T came up beside him and lifted the box covers to see what was left. "Shit, we do all the work and the fucking blue canaries do nothing but eat our food."

Finn choked on his crust at the reference to blue canaries. Tony was talking about the police officers. Canaries had once been used by coal miners. If the bird died, the miners would know there was poisonous gas in the mines and got out before they suffered a similar fate.

While the firefighters today wore their full protective gear including their face pieces, the cops had been walking around as though they were infallible. Canaries in blue uniforms.

Despite Tony's harsh words, he grinned from ear to ear. They'd been working for five hours now with several more to go. They should have been tired, but this was the job. No two days were ever the same. And neither of them had ever faced a situation quite like this one.

It had taken hours of careful planning and precision to remove the car. They'd slipped large straps around the vehicle and had lifted it straight up into the air using a crane.

While it sounded easy in theory, it had taken hours to get the proper equipment in place and set up. Once the straps had been in place, more water had to be streamed to avoid sparks that could cause a major explosion.

It had been long, tedious, wet work. His men had been standing for hours in clothing when dry weighed a good eighty pounds, and seemed double that when wet.

"I heard Corbett mention something about you missing a date," Tony mentioned casually. Too casually.

Finn shrugged and waited.

"Ran into Tom the other day at Home Depot."

He stared at his friend. Shawn had met Tony shortly after beginning his career as a firefighter in Rocky Point. T had been on the job three years and had taken the probie under his wing when he realized a few of the other firefighters had targeted Finn because of his father. As far as T was concerned, Shawn shouldn't have to suffer because his father had become a drunk and had been forced to retire early.

Finn never forgot and they had remained close friends. Close enough to know the jump in conversation was no coincidence.

"So you saw my brother at the store," he repeated. "And…?"

T grabbed a soda and tossed one to Finn. "He wanted to know if I'd met a certain blue-eyed single mother with whom you'd become recent friends?"

"My siblings need to mind their own business." The warm carbonated beverage quenched his sudden need for liquid.

"Its big news, Finn," T continued. "It's a known fact you stay clear of any woman who even remotely looks like she wants a commitment."

"Who said anything about commitment?" Finn stared longingly across the street to where the Portersville guys took their turn pouring water over the gas. The spray of water, with the backdrop of several spotlights, formed a rainbow.

Damn, the conversation had gotten uncomfortable. Finn wished to be back holding the hose rather than answer his friend. "Neither one of us wants more than casual sex. Nothing more."

"Doesn't she have kids?"

Sweat beaded across Finn's forehead. He didn't need to answer. T already knew.

"How often do you think you are going to be alone with her? To have an opportunity for casual sex?" Tony's tone turned from questioning to a firm warning and he turned to look him in the eyes. "Don't get involved, Finn, if you're not ready to take the next step. You'll want to spend time with her and her kids are part of the package. I've seen you with your nieces and nephews. I've seen you when kids come to the station for tours. You get hooked, Finn. You like kids way too much. And they like you."

His friend was right. Maybe missing his date tonight was a blessing. Every time he heard her voice from over the fence or saw her wide blue eyes, he thought about her for hours.

And her kisses? It was like being teased with a single lick of a lollipop while staring at an entire candy shop. He wanted more. Craved more.

T tossed his empty can into the garbage bag and nodded toward the island. "Come on. It's time to set the Christmas tree on fire."

Finn grabbed his helmet and gear and followed Tony. They were going to set up a piping system which looked like a giant coat rack in the street, connect it to the gas valve and light it on fire to relieve the pressure and get rid of the propane. The piping was called a Christmas tree because, from a distance, that was what it looked like when lit.

Finn worked with his men, but Tony's words haunted him.

Kelly had found a babysitter and made him dinner tonight and because of his job, he'd stood her up. For most women this would be unforgivable. Besides, Tony was right. How often would they have an opportunity to be alone? Alone long enough to act on their urges?

Not often.

It would be best if he forgot about Kelly Reisland

as a potential "friend with benefits" and stuck to being a casual neighbor.

It was the right thing to do. But, damn, the thought depressed him.

Chapter Eighteen

Kelly turned the key in the ignition of her van and got nothing but silence.

"You have got to be kidding me?" Kelly nearly wailed. She turned the key a second time with the same results.

"No. No. No." She punctuated her words by thumping the steering wheel in frustration. "First, no hot water and now this? What more can go wrong today?"

Kelly pulled the button to pop the hood and opened her door. Gray skies hovered overhead threatening the advent of stormy weather, which suited Kelly's mood perfectly.

After laying awake more than half the night, due in large part to thinking about the sex which never happened, Kelly woke early and had tried in vain to exercise her demons with a six-mile run. It hadn't worked. Finn missing their date was not his fault and after having seen the care he'd taken with candles and setting the stage for a romantic evening, Kelly wanted the man more than ever.

When she'd gone to shower, the temperature had been frigid. Not an ounce of hot water. It had only been by chance, while heading toward the laundry room, Kelly spotted the basement door open so she went to the basement to look at the water heater and discovered the valve shut off. Wondering how and when the valve had been shut off had occupied her mind right up until the moment she'd left her house to pick up her girls.

Now her van wouldn't start. Thunder rumbled in the distance and the clouds overhead blocked the sun from reaching the ground as Kelly stared in despair at the engine. "Yep, it looks like an engine to me." Kelly folded her arms and stared at the innards. "I can change a tire. I can pull an engine from a lawn mower and put it back together, but I don't know a darn thing about cars."

"Having a problem?"

The sound of her ex-husband's voice was more threatening than the impending storm. Kelly peeked around the hood to discover the man she despised heading toward her.

"What are you doing here?"

Jeff didn't bat an eye at her tone. Instead he held up a stuffed dog with one hand. "I saw this in the car this morning. I know how much Hannah loves it." He nodded toward the open hood of the van. "Need some help?"

"No, I'll figure it out."

Kelly wanted to doubt Jeff's reason for showing up on a Sunday morning, but she couldn't find the angle. Granted, Jeff was selfish, but he was still a father and maybe he was thinking of his daughter, for once.

"Don't be like that, Kel." Jeff moved closer and put one hand on the car and stood looking down at her. "I'm a mechanic. I can help you out with the car."

Kelly shook off the suspicions and used a hand to reluctantly signal Jeff to go ahead and look. He handed her the stuffed dog and turned his back on her.

"Can you try starting it for me so I can hear?"

Kelly slipped into the driver's seat, thankful to get away from the man who'd shown up unexpectedly. He'd been doing that a lot lately. Throwing her off balance with his sudden interest in the girls. Helping her out. She turned the key.

Jeff came around from behind the hood to stand by the open door. "I know what it is. I'll get my tools out of the truck and be right back."

"Thank you." It was lame, she knew it, but Kelly continued to be stunned at Jeff's new attitude.

"Hey, Kel?" Jeff stopped mid-stride and looked back at her. "Could I ask a favor?"

Kelly braced. Okay, here it comes…

"Would you mind making me some coffee? I'm out at home. I was on my way to the store when I spotted Hannah's dog and detoured here, instead."

Coffee? The man wanted coffee. Not a request to change visitation with the kids as she had expected.

"Coffee. Yes. Sure thing." Kelly slipped the house key off her key ring and practically ran to the house. Jeff being kind and helpful was in direct contrast to the man she'd divorced two years before. Unfortunately, it was exactly like the man she'd dated and then married ten years ago.

When Jeff was good, he was very, very good.

Kelly set up her coffee pot and loaded it with grounds, noting her shaking hands as she poured in the scoops. Jeff made her nervous. She couldn't explain it. It had been that way from the first time he'd asked her out in high school.

The Jeff Reisland had asked her out. Jeff was rich, popular, and the school's star football player. Jeff was tall, lean, and extremely handsome, and he knew it. All the girls wanted to be with Jeff. And he'd chosen her.

Although Kelly knew she'd made a name for herself as an athlete in track, she was still not in the same league as Jeff and his friends. Her parents had divorced and she'd been raised by her grandparents. It was a stigma in his social class and Kelly knew she wasn't the type of girl he'd bring home to his Country Club parents. But he did.

Kelly shook off the memories and retrieved two mugs, sugar and a spoon, and watched as the black coffee began to drip into the pot below. Should she make tea? The last time she had coffee she'd been jumpy for days. Then again, it would be a waste for a full pot of coffee for only Jeff to have one cup. She'd pour herself a half cup. She should be fine. She tapped the spoon against the counter as her thoughts wandered back into her past.

While Jeff's family wasn't quite as rich as her friend, Jules Sinclair and her family, Jeff came from old money. Generations of rich, passed down along with a standard of living. A houseful of servants; proper dress at dinner; knowledge of the correct utensils drilled into the children from the moment they could hold a fork.

Kelly had been overwhelmed while Jeff had been sweet and indulgent, gently guiding her past her many faux pas. She'd quickly and easily fallen in love with the man.

"It's purring like a kitten."

Kelly dropped the spoon to the floor as she whipped around to stare at Jeff as he strolled in from the hallway leading from the front door. She hadn't heard him come in. He was dressed in his usual casual attire: neatly pressed tan pants and a golf shirt with the Reisland Foreign Auto logo on the front. The thin belt showed Jeff had not gained an ounce since their divorce.

Not surprising. Jeff was conscientious of his weight and how he looked. While he liked to indulge in rich foods, he was also a fanatic about working out in the gym in the basement of their—no, *his*—home.

"Oops. Sorry, babe, didn't mean to startle you." He gave her his lopsided grin. The one where only one side of his mouth curled up, but at the same time he would tilt his head the opposite way. It was a quirk that had melted her heart many times. Today, it unsettled her.

"Oh, umm, I didn't hear you come in." Kelly scooped the spoon off the floor and walked across the room to toss it into the sink and get a second spoon out of the drawer. When she turned around, Jeff had moved to the coffee pot.

"This smells great. Thanks for making it." He proceeded to pour the coffee into both mugs, filling them both to the top. "Do you have any cream?" Kelly resolved not to drink more than a few sips of the potent liquid.

"Yes." Kelly got the requested item and finally moved back across the room to stand next to Jeff, handing him the cream then turning to spoon sugar into her mug. Jeff didn't move to the table as she'd expected but continued to stand beside her. The counter made an L where they stood and Jeff turned to lean against one side so he faced Kelly at a forty-five degree angle. While Kelly wanted to move away, she didn't want to reveal how nervous he made her, so instead, she leaned back as well, struggling to find her manners.

"Thank you for fixing the car. Your timing couldn't have been more perfect." See, she could be nice. Kelly congratulated herself as she turned to lean against the counter. Jeff blew at the steam from his mug.

Thunder rumbled loudly overhead. The storm had arrived. The rain started in a light drizzle, barely leaving drops on the window. She took a sip of coffee wishing she'd thought to turn on the overhead lights. With the rain outside, the room filled with shadows.

"How was your date last night?"

Kelly nearly choked on the hot liquid. She managed, barely, to keep the coffee down, as she sputtered and tried to catch her breath again.

"Livvy told me," Jeff continued, blowing the steam off the top of his coffee cup. "I'm happy for you, Kel. It's good you are meeting new people."

Kelly stared at Jeff. *Who was this man?* "You are? It is?"

Jeff nodded. "We married young. I made a lot of mistakes. And I don't blame you for divorcing me. I hope this guy makes you happy."

Jeff put his coffee on the counter and walked around the kitchen as he talked. "I know I was at fault. I guess I wasn't ready to grow up. It was stressful, becoming a dad so soon after high school. Then my parents died and I had the business to take over. I was so focused on changing the auto shop to my dream shop I forgot about my responsibilities at home."

"Jeff." This unsolicited confession from her ex-husband was awkward and Kelly didn't know what she was supposed to say. "Why are you telling me this now? What brought this on?"

Jeff walked to stand in front of her and Kelly felt trapped against the granite counter. He lifted a hand and gently brushed it down her cheek as the sounds of the storm grew in its intensity outside. Kelly nearly jumped, both at the boom of thunder and at the unexpected touch.

"Last week, when you weren't feeling well and I stayed for dinner and helped Livvy with her homework and got the girls ready for bed, it felt good. Having the four of us together as a family felt right. I know I didn't come home often for supper when we were married. I know things were tense and we fought a lot. But I've changed, Kel. I've finally grown up and am ready to accept my responsibilities as a father and husband. And now it's too late."

Jeff took the coffee mug out of Kelly's hands and placed it on the counter behind her and grabbed her hands within his larger ones. Kelly stared at his fingers. As usual, she didn't see a speck of dirt or grease under the fingernails as one would normally expect from a mechanic. Instead they were soft and perfectly manicured. While Jeff knew how to fix cars and claimed to be a mechanic, he rarely worked in the garage himself. He was a manager, an owner. The boss. He had money and liked to live the good life.

"I miss the girls. It's been nice spending more time with them, but most of all, I miss you, Kel."

Kelly gulped at the confession and stared up into Jeff's crystal blue eyes. "Oh, Jeff, I don't… I can't… "

Jeff placed a finger over her lips to silence her. "Shh. I know you are dating this guy, but I need to ask, can we try again? Will you go out on a date with me?"

Date Jeff? The man she divorced two years ago?

The man who'd had several affairs while they'd been married?

"Jeff, I don't know. I mean, I don't want to confuse the girls, and ..."

And then he kissed her. His body pressed her back against the counter, his hands held her face up toward his, and his mouth plundered hers in desperation, seeking a response.

Her body responded. Jeff had been her first love. They had been married for eight years and they knew each other intimately. Everything was familiar. Jeff's hard, lean, muscular body pressed against her softer one. Jeff's strong arm slid around her and bent her further back against the counter, his lips, no longer taking, nibbled, and his tongue entered, re-acquainting itself with her gums and inner cheek.

Then the kiss changed again. Deeper. Hungrier.

Yes, Jeff was familiar. But he was also handsome and a hell of a good kisser. And he still knew how to make Kelly want. And her body wanted. She felt her bones become more pliant. She felt her arms relax and work their way behind Jeff and press him closer. And she heard her own sigh as she gave in to the kiss and gave back as much as he gave.

Jeff pulled away.

"Face it, Kelly. We still feel something for each other. We'll take it slow. We'll date. Let's try again. For us and for our girls."

And he left her standing there. Kelly barely heard the front door close over the sound of the storm raging outside and the one Jeff had started inside.

Kelly turned to stare out the window behind the sink. Rain poured down the glass, giving the outside a hazy, distorted view. But Kelly's thoughts were nearly as unclear.

Oh my goodness! What have I done? Jeff kissed me and I kissed him back. What was I thinking? Kelly lifted her coffee mug in shaking hands and gulped down the tepid liquid.

****

Finn rolled out of bed and hit the shower, hoping the heat would jump-start his day. He'd had all of about three hours of sleep, having returned from the neighboring town after two in the morning. His regular shift started at eight but he wanted a chance to see Kelly and apologize for standing her up. If he timed it right, he could stop by with a cup of tea for her and maybe start his day with a heated kiss. There wouldn't be time for what he really wanted, and he wasn't going to skip out on his duty crew when they were all equally exhausted. They could only pray for a quiet Sunday in the firehouse.

Finn let Guinness out, put food in his bowl and headed to the coffee shop for his first cup of coffee and a Chai tea for Kelly. With a couple croissants for good measure, he turned his truck down Kelly's street in time to see a man exit her house and drive off in a Lincoln Navigator.

He pulled to a stop, grabbed his peace offering, headed to the front door, and rang the bell.

As the door opened, he heard Kelly's sweet voice. "Jeff, I…. Oh!"

"Oh," Finn repeated, as he looked her over from head to toe. He took in the mussed hair, disheveled shirt and the pink staining her cheeks. Her lips had a definite plushness to them that happens when a woman has been kissed … very thoroughly kissed.

"I guess you were going to have sex last night no matter who it was with."

Finn realized he'd said his thoughts out loud the moment Kelly's eyes widened and then her front door slammed in his face.

Chapter Nineteen

Jeff strolled into the store and headed straight to the pharmacy counter. Luck was with him. Ken worked alone and there was no one waiting for a prescription.

"I need something," Jeff leaned over the counter to get his friend's attention.

"Of course you do," Ken smirked, turning from the computer screen. "More Ritalin?"

Jeff shook his head. "No, that's working fine. I've got the bitch all worked up. No, I'm looking for something that will, um, increase her sex drive. A woman's Viagra, if you will."

Ken stared at him. "You mean to say the infamous Jeff Reisland's charm isn't working its usual magic?"

Jeff smiled a knowing smile. After the kiss he'd shared with his beautiful, but stubborn ex-wife, he had no doubts about his plan. "I only want to move things along faster, my friend. Can you help me?"

Ken held up his finger and moved to the other side of the counter where a very pregnant woman had stopped.

"Excuse me, do you know where I can find iron pills?"

Jeff tuned out the conversation while he moved to look over the selection of condoms. Grabbing a couple boxes, for what he hoped would be used soon with Kelly, he met up with Ken at the register.

"You've got her taking Ritalin and also giving her sleeping pills, right?" Ken asked.

Jeff nodded.

"I've got an idea." Ken grabbed a pad of paper and a pen, scribbled for a moment, and handed the top slip to Jeff. "I don't sell it here, but you can get it at the vitamin store over on Tenth Street."

Jeff looked at the words and snickered. "Women's Libido?"

"It's an idea I think will work," Ken continued. "I don't want to mix any more prescriptions, and this is all herbal. Of course, I don't know how you'll get her to take it."

Jeff tucked the paper into the pocket of his shirt, patting it twice. "No worries, my friend. Leave the details to the master."

****

"The girls told me you don't make them take vitamins."

Kelly stared in disbelief as her ex-husband strolled into her house early Monday morning.

"Excuse me?"

Jeff placed two cups of coffee and a plastic bag on the counter. "When the girls were over at my house, I asked if they took vitamins and they said they didn't. I think they should." Jeff dumped the bag's contents onto the counter.

"So you went out and bought vitamins and came to my house?" Kelly glared at the back of Jeff's head. "Jeff, just because you kissed me, doesn't mean we are getting back together. You can't stroll in here like you own the place."

"Remember, you kissed me back," Jeff drawled

then held up one of the bottles. "I bought you some B1 vitamins."

"What? Why?" Kelly crossed her arms.

"Sweetheart," Jeff reached over and pulled her into his arms. Kelly kept her arms crossed, but it didn't dissuade Jeff in any way. "Let's be reasonable. The girls should be taking a multi-vitamin every day, don't you agree?"

"Maybe. I guess it couldn't hurt. Still, you shouldn't have bought vitamins for me. We're not married anymore. You can't tell me what to do."

"Aw, Kel, don't be obstinate."

Kelly cringed at Jeff's tone. It reminded her of a parent talking to a child.

"As parents, we need to set the example. Besides, have you looked in the mirror lately? You are exhausted. Wouldn't you like more energy?"

Kelly refused to answer. She hated—really hated—when Jeff was right. Then he laughed. Kelly's head whipped upward to stare at him. She'd expected him to be frustrated with her, lose his temper at her because she hadn't capitulated. Instead, Jeff was relaxed and didn't seem the least bit put out by her stubbornness. Instead he leaned down and pressed his mouth to hers in a light, friendly kiss.

"Tell you what. Take the vitamins every day for one week and see how you feel. I got a multi for the kids, and a multi and a B1 for you. If after a week, you don't feel a difference, stop taking them. But keep the kids on theirs."

Kelly stared after Jeff as he grabbed one of the coffee cups and sauntered out of her kitchen, whistling a non-descript tune.

Chapter Twenty

"Olivia, if you knocked over my bills tray and tried to put them back, then tell me."

"I didn't do it."

"Well, somebody put the bills in the wrong spot and Hannah is too short to reach the top of the cabinet." Kelly stared down at her daughter who stood with her arms crossed and her chin jutted in defiance. She glanced at Hannah to find her youngest with her thumb back in her mouth. "What about the toys in the daycare? Were you two playing in there this weekend?"

"No."

"Don't lie, Liv." Kelly kept her voice low, despite wanting to yell. She'd brought the girls into the living room, away from the kids in the daycare. "I can tolerate a lot of things, but not lying. A lot of the toys were mixed in together, in the wrong boxes. They weren't like that on Friday when the daycare closed."

"Newsflash, mother," Olivia snapped, not bothering to keep her voice down, "Me and Hannah were with dad on Friday and then at Auntie Maddie's house Saturday and Sunday. We haven't been here to mess with your precious daycare toys, or to go in your office, where we're not allowed to be anyway."

While Kelly heard the words, and knew the girls had been busy, she had no other explanation of how the toys were in the wrong buckets and the bills were misfiled. And Olivia's bratty tone did not help Kelly's mood. She turned to Hannah.

"Get your thumb out of your mouth and tell me the truth. Were you or your sister in my office or the daycare?"

Hannah stuck her hands behind her back and stared up, eyes wide. "No."

Kelly threw her hands up and paced the living room. "I don't know what to do with you two. There is only the three of us living here, so somebody had to mess with the stuff."

"Oh, and *you* couldn't have made a mistake?"

Kelly whipped around at Olivia's sarcastic remark.

"Don't get sassy with me, young lady, or you'll be spending your summer vacation in your bedroom."

Olivia glared at her, anger and resentment radiating from her stance. "Or maybe I'll go live with Dad, at least he would believe me. I hate you."

Kelly stood frozen as Olivia stormed from the room and pounded up the stairs. She hated this. She hated the fighting and the lying. Oh, good grief! If things were this bad now, she could only imagine the teen years.

Hannah came over and wrapped her pudgy arms around her, pressing her nose into her legs. "I love you, mommy."

"I know you do, sweetie."

"And I didn't go into your office or the daycare this weekend. I really didn't."

Kelly squeezed her little girl close as she tried to shake the feeling that the life she'd carefully built since she'd left Jeff was starting to crack.

Maybe Jeff was right. She was exhausted. She

hadn't been sleeping much at all. Ever since she had met Finn, her mind had been focused on how little time she had taken for herself since her divorce. Time for dating. Time for sex. Finn had become a huge distraction, so much so her body was jittery much of the time.

Jeff's bizarre behavior didn't help, either. His unexpected visits had put her off guard and sent her into a mental tailspin.

She had to slow down and take charge again. She was losing focus. At times she even felt she was going crazy. It wasn't just the bills being misfiled, or the water heater turned off, or the toys being mixed up in the daycare. She was losing things, too. Her favorite body lotion was missing. Her lip gloss? Gone. Now she was fighting with her girls.

Her life was in a tailspin, spinning out of control. She hadn't felt this helpless since her divorce and her grandmother's death.

Yet, she couldn't sit still. Her body hummed, as though she could feel the energy, or lack thereof, buzzing through her body. She felt …

She felt like she was going to have another one of her breakdowns, like she used to have when she was married. Back then, when it happened, she would spend a few days in her room, crying and sleeping. Jeff would take care of the kids during those times but he would also spend time with her, making her tea. Holding her. Making love to her. Reassuring her all would be right again.

And it would be. For a while at least.

But as a single mother and a business owner, she didn't have the luxury of a mental breakdown. People depended on her and she had no one to pick up the slack.

Kelly spent the next half hour re-sorting the bills and placing them in the proper bins. She started another load of laundry and told the girls to shower. Hannah complied. Livvy slammed her bedroom door. Kelly slowly counted to ten. She was on the brink of losing it and Livvy's attitude was pushing her closer and closer.

When the doorbell rang at eight o'clock, Kelly threw the sweatshirt she was folding onto the couch. She was SO not in the mood for company.

And when she opened the door to find Jeff standing there, she wanted to burst into tears.

Not now. Please do not lose it now.

"What?"

Jeff raised his hands in surrender. "Whoa, babe. I'm not the enemy." He eased himself inside and closed the door behind him. "Liv called me to say you were wigging out and ..."

"That I am what?" Kelly heard the hysteria in her voice but couldn't control it. "Wigging out? Wigging out? Oh, that child has NOT seen me wig out yet. But if that is what she thinks, she can witness it now."

Jeff grabbed Kelly and pulled her into a steel embrace, refusing to let her go upstairs to confront their daughter.

"You need to calm down, Kel." He spoke softly in her ear, holding her back despite her struggle to be free of his embrace. "We've been through this before. I'm here for you. Let it all out and I'll be here for you."

Kelly didn't want to cry. Especially in front of Jeff. She didn't want his arms around her, holding her as she broke down. There was another man whose arms she wanted to be in. Although she shouldn't still want him. He thought she was a slut.

"I know our marriage wasn't easy, babe, but you know when you needed me, when you fell apart, I was always there. Trust me."

Jeff's words. Finn's betrayal. Livvy's lies. It was all too much.

"I'm sorry, Jeff," even her voice sounded defeated and she felt her body slump as the anger left her and self-pity took its place. "I think I'm tired. I haven't slept well, lately."

"Of course you haven't. You do so much all alone. You are not alone tonight." Jeff pulled her gently toward the couch and settled her into a familiar position. He sat sideways, his legs along the length of the cushions, and she sat between his thighs, her back pressed against his chest. Her head rested back against his shoulder. And he spoke gentle, soothing words while his hands ran up and down her arms for about an hour.

Then, when she was almost asleep, he eased himself up. He returned a few minutes later with a hot mug of chamomile tea. She drank it, letting the heat warm her inside, while her ex-husband stayed quietly by her side until she fell asleep.

The smell of coffee had Kelly stirring, but it was the press of lips against hers—a kiss that screamed "morning after"—which had her eyes popping open.

"Good morning, Babe."

Her mind was thick as fog as she struggled to a sitting position. It was morning. Jeff had kissed her awake. She looked around as she struggled to make her mind work.

Okay, she was in the living room. On the couch. She looked down. Phew! She was fully clothed. She had not had sex with her ex-husband.

"How are you feeling today?" Jeff pressed a steaming mug of sweetened coffee into her hands. Good golly, her mouth felt like she'd been on a bender. She took a sip of the hot liquid and croaked out an answer.

"Okay, I guess."

Jeff ran the back of his hand down her cheek, setting her off balance once again at this recent change of behavior.

"It's early yet, but I wanted to leave before the girls woke. We don't want to confuse them. You know, daddy sleeping over and all."

"Ah, huh." It was all Kelly could manage.

"Drink your coffee. Take a hot shower. Take your vitamins. I will check in with you tonight."

Jeff leaned in and stole another drugging kiss. As his hand slipped away from her face, his knuckles brushed against her breast and her nipple puckered? Had it been an accident on his part? It almost seemed as though it was. Jeff had never been one for subtleties. When he wanted to cop a feel, he'd always been blunt about it.

Not today, though. She didn't even know if he was aware of how quickly her body had responded to his brief, barely-there, touch. His kiss was over and he was gone, leaving her in a muddled mess.

Kelly brought the coffee upstairs with her and into the shower. She sipped the drink while hot water pounded down on her body.

The combination seemed to do the trick to get her

body and mind moving again. She felt the caffeine jolt her system into overdrive and she was ready to start her day.

She headed downstairs and saw her girls exit their rooms. Hannah gave her a huge hug while Livvy barely grunted at her before heading into the bathroom.

And so another day would begin. The coffee pot was on and there was still another half pot waiting. She really didn't need it, or even want it, but had never been one for wasting anything. She poured another cup and noticed Jeff had put out their vitamins. She swallowed both her multi and B vitamins with a gulp of hot coffee and began her morning ritual of making breakfast and preparing for a houseful of preschoolers.

When Jeff had said he would check in, Kelly had expected a phone call, not for him to waltz through her front door at dinner. After his kindness the night before, she could hardly be rude to him. So she let him stay for dinner. Then she allowed him to make her a cup of tea before he settled on the couch with his two girls cuddled against him as they watched the Disney channel for an hour before he sent them to bed.

Then with a brief, non-sexual kiss, he bid her goodnight and left.

Kelly touched her fingers to her lips as she gazed out her sliding glass door to the house beyond her back fence. Jeff oozed kindness. Jeff was checking in on her, soothing her. Jeff was …well, Jeff.

Eight years of marriage had to mean something. So why did her thoughts continue to lean toward a man she barely knew? Why did her lips yearn for the taste of heat instead of familiarity?

Why did she wish it had been Finn who had held

her last night? Who had woken her this morning with a cup of java and molten lava kisses?

Her mind and body were at war with each other. A yawn escaped and Kelly knew she needed sleep, yet there was still an odd energy rush through her veins. She headed upstairs and undressed. She could barely keep her eyes open long enough to pull on a long T-shirt. As she did, the fabric teased over her nipples and sent a surge of electricity through her body. Egads! She was a mess. Her ex-husband wanted her back in his life, and she wanted a man who thought she liked to sleep around.

She dreamed of Finn again. Glimpses of his sardonic smile, violet eyes assuring her she was safe, warm arms catching her as she fell, and lean, hard muscles pressing against her as they kissed.

Kelly woke feeling hung over, yet oddly horny.

She showered and headed down to the kitchen. Jeff had left the bottles of vitamins on the counter as a reminder for her to take them and had even figured out how the timer on the coffee pot worked so a fresh brewed pot waited for her.

Wednesday and Thursday repeated much like the two days before, with Jeff showing up at dinnertime, showering them all with attention. The only difference was each night, after the girls were in bed, Jeff's kisses became deeper, more demanding, but stopped before she felt pressured into saying no to him.

It was all very disconcerting.

As were the dreams of the man next door. Those were also getting hotter and more demanding and having her wake with an urge driving her insane.

Chapter Twenty-One

Jeff's luck had turned. Winning the Spyder for a week had given him ample opportunity to rent it to his elite clientele making enough to get his bookie's goons to back down. He still owed money, but he'd repaid enough to save his knuckles from being vice-gripped.

He ran those knuckles down Alicia's bare back as they rolled across his king-sized bed. "Do you like that, honey?"

He didn't have to ask, he knew what made his lover tick. He uttered the words to make Alicia think he had her on his mind, while he thought of someone else.

His plans were right on schedule. Kelly was putty in his hands. He had her so doped up, she didn't know if she was coming or going. Kelly had always dreamed of having the perfect family. Husband, wife, a couple kids, a picket fence. So, he'd screwed up by sleeping around on her. Hell, that would never change. His mistake was letting her know about it, sometimes even throwing it in her face.

"Hell, babe, you are an emotional wreck half the time. I've got to get it where I can, 'cause you certainly aren't in any mental condition to put out."

Yeah, he had been a bit harsh. He'd do better this time. He could tell Kelly was ready for him to make his next move. Those vitamins Ken had suggested worked like a charm. He barely had to touch Kelly and she was primed. Next he had to get her alone, no kids, for a night of rekindling the old relationship. Which is where Alicia came in. And he knew how to get his way when it came to Alicia. "Hey, baby," he murmured before he sucked a ripe tit into his mouth and suckled. Alicia arched her back and moaned. "Your devious plan for me to get custody of the brats is coming together nicely."

He moved to the other tit, wetting it, then sending a wave of warm breath.

"Ooh, Jeffrey that feels so good."

He reined kisses down her abdomen, moving toward her center. Alicia knew what was coming, knew he would have her screaming his name soon, and she parted her legs to receive him.

And Jeff knew exactly at what point he could ask for a favor and get what he wanted.

He primed her. Then pulled back to talk. "Tomorrow night, I should be able to make my move to push Kelly over the edge. Do you want to go over the edge, honey?" And Jeff nuzzled Alicia more. She was panting.

"But, I need your help, honey. I only trust you." Oh, yeah, she was so there.

"Anything, Jeff. Anything."

He pushed her over the edge, loving how her nails grasped his shoulders as she screamed his name. Then he slipped on a condom. "Great, so you can watch my kids for me tomorrow night while I put my plans in action."

Chapter Twenty-Two

Kelly had a plan. It wasn't the best of plans, but with the way her mind and body were warring with each other, she could barely function during the day, never mind come up with a solid, this-is-bound-to-work, kind of plan.

It was Friday night and Jeff had left with the kids for the weekend. And once again, he'd kissed her and had her body singing for an encore. But her head had gone, once again, to the sexy firefighter next door.

And then it hit her. She had the night to herself. She had been having very erotic dreams about her neighbor. She wasn't looking for a commitment and neither was he.

Sex. That was what they wanted. So what if he thought she was a whore. She was so horny these days thinking about him, maybe she was.

So if he thought she was, why shouldn't she do something about it? Not the best logic, sure, but she couldn't stop the energy rush in her blood. Maybe what she needed was to get laid and to get Finn out of her system.

So she went upstairs and peeked out the window toward his house. Yes, there were lights on.

So how was she going to seduce him? She couldn't knock on the door and say, "Hey, I know you think I sleep around, but let's do it anyway."

Then again…

Kelly took her hair out of its braid and let it fall in thick waves around her face. She stepped out of her clothes and walked to her closet in her bra and panties to find something sexy to wear. She thought about Finn's hot kisses and wanted to taste his lips again.

Not finding anything that grabbed her attention in her closet, Kelly grabbed a silk robe, tied it, and walked barefoot outside and through the fence gate before she could reconsider.

She knocked on the sliders by Finn's kitchen and watched as he turned from the stove, startled by her presence.

"Kelly?"

He opened the glass doors as Kelly dropped the robe to her feet. "I still want you, Finn. Are you game?"

Before he could answer, Kelly pressed against him and locked lips with his.

****

"What the fu…" Finn's words were cut off as Kelly's mouth pressed into his in a deep, mind-boggling kiss.

For the past week, he'd been vacillating between calling her to apologize and waiting for her to call him. He'd been an ass, saying what he had. Shock didn't describe what he felt when she showed up on his doorstep.

Holy shit, could her skin really be this smooth? His hands ran down her back. She was wearing nothing but a skimpy black bra and matching lace panties and she looked hot.

Okay, time to engage brain. He managed to disengage his lips as her hips rolled at just the right location. Zipper don't fail me now.

"Kelly, what…?

She nuzzled his neck while her hands skimmed down his chest. "It's always been about the sex, right? Two consenting adults. No commitments. Has that changed?"

Finn gulped? Had it?

Her hand slid down to feather over the center of his jeans. *Oookaaay, no denying she turns me on.*

"No, I still want you."

"Then what's to stop us from being extra-friendly neighbors?" She nipped at his ear while her fingers worked his T-shirt up his chest.

Finn almost, almost didn't know how to respond. For a week, he'd been kicking himself because he never meant to hurt her.. He'd been beating himself up because while he'd been a total jackass, he'd still wanted to explore his sexy neighbor's body in a hundred different ways.

But to have her show up, unexpectedly and seduce him?

"Kelly, are you sure…"

Again, she didn't let him finish. Instead she threw his shirt over his head, pressed a hot mouth to the center of his chest and groaned, "Oh, yeah."

It's all he needed to hear.

His hand grabbed at her hair and pulled her head up so he could ground his mouth down on hers. From there it was all over. Basic animalistic behavior ensued. They bounced against the counter while they kissed. His clothes disappeared. What was left of hers evaporated.

"Condoms are upstairs." He mumbled as his

erection hit on her soft tuft of blond hair before he pulled his hips back.

"Then let's go." The counter, the table, against the fridge. Their bodies hit nearly every surface as they stumbled together. Finn managed to turn off the stove before he finally swung Kelly into his arms and carried her upstairs.

The shades were still up when he laid Kelly on the bed.

Evening had rolled in, shoving the room into shadows, but not darkness. She flung her arms over her head and arched her back. Finn knelt above her, suddenly wanting to go slow, to learn every pulse point, every inch of her body. Kelly let out a whoop and her legs wrapped around him, pulling him closer. They touched and kissed. They rolled. Kelly's laugh drifted over him and Finn felt something twist inside. He couldn't place it, didn't want to analyze it but as he rolled the condom on, as he looked into Kelly's eye as they joined together, Finn felt a flash of fear this was going to end way too soon.

****

Jeff strolled into Kelly's house with no hesitation. The time had come to re-claim his wife and get his life back on its even track. Ever since she'd left him two years ago, things hadn't gone as expected. His business had taken a bit of a dive financially. Okay, the economy tanking hadn't helped. But other things had seemed to turn, as well.

For one, he loved poker. Always had. And he was good at it. He'd played some major high rollers and walked away with loads of merchandise, but his game had been off since Kelly walked out on him. He'd always had a thing for Kelly, despite the fact she didn't come from money like he did. But she wasn't destitute, either. While her grandparents lived modestly, he knew for a fact they had a very nice nest egg tucked away.

When the grandfather kicked the bucket, and God knows he was old enough to do it, Kelly and the kids would be entitled to a very hefty inheritance. Jeff's recent financial situation had him re-evaluating letting Kelly go so easily. The kids were his, too, and if they were to come into money, then he should have a piece of it as well.

The only way to ensure that was to remarry Kelly. And the only way Kelly would consider marriage would be if she were pregnant. It was how he got her the first time. The promise of a secure and happy family was her dream. He knew, could, would, and had used that to his advantage.

"Kelly? Kel? Where are you?"

Jeff strode upstairs, wondering if Kelly had taken his advice to take a warm bubble bath. He strode into the bedroom and the master bath only to find them both empty. The clothes she had worn earlier were in a puddle on the floor.

Damn. She had gone out. To visit Maddie? Jules? Well, this sucked. He had figured on Kelly being too wiped out from the seesaw of emotions he'd inflicted on her the past couple weeks to consider she might decide to get out of the house.

Should he wait? Alicia was at his house playing babysitter so he could get Kelly back. He knew Kelly had been taking the sex vitamins daily and, his visits throughout the week had shown him they were working like a charm. Kelly was primed for the taking.

Yes, he would stay. He continued to roam the bedroom. He picked up a photo of Kelly and the two girls, noting how Hannah had Kelly's smile, but Olivia had his eyes. This was his family. It was time to have them back with him.

He put the frame down and moved to the window. The days were getting longer and the sun had yet to set. From his vantage at the window, Jeff could see over the fence into the yard behind. The new guy had built a new deck, larger than the rickety one Belanger had there. A pile of brown fabric lay on the wooden planks outside of the glass doors to the home, but the sun had set too far to make out what it was, and frankly, Jeff really didn't care, he was more curious about the firefighter than anything else.

Movement from an upstairs window had him refocusing. The silhouette of two figures in a familiar dance caused Jeff to stop in his tracks.

No way. His fingers pressed into his palms as the two bodies moved around and Jeff took in the thick, curly hair he knew could only belong to one person.

He punched the windowsill, then swore as pain ran up his arm. He'd been priming Kelly all week with the drugs so he…HE… could get her into bed with him.

Jeff turned away from the window and paced the bedroom. This wasn't over. No, it was far from over. He wasn't the type to get mad. He got even. Before he exited Kelly's house, he formulated a plan. He grabbed his cell, found a number he kept on hand and hit dial taking the next step that would send his cheating ex-wife over the edge.

****

Finn rolled to his back, pleasantly spent. Damn, the

woman was incredible.

"Tired?" Kelly kneeled on the bed, looking down at him. Finn reached up to tug on one of her springy curls. He finally got to see her hair down and her hair was as riotous as he'd imagined.

"Aren't you?" They'd been at it straight for over two hours and Kelly showed no signs of slowing down.

"Should be," she admitted, "but I'm not."

Finn ran his palms down her smooth sides and she straddled him. Her skin was unbelievably soft. Even her hands, which she trailed through his chest hair, were like satin. His rough hands probably felt like sandpaper to her delicate skin.

"I can't get enough of you." Her voice was matter-of-fact. No coyness. No flirty smile. It was enough to get him hard again. Before he could react, Kelly swung her leg over and jumped from the bed.

"Are you hungry? I am. Let's raid your fridge?" Then his bare-assed nymph disappeared through the door.

Finn took time to pull on running shorts and grabbed a T-shirt. He grabbed a condom off the nightstand and slipped it into a pocket and headed downstairs.

The sight of naked Kelly in the brightly lit kitchen stopped him in his tracks. She was… It was hard to find words when his head stopped thinking and his body went into immediate reaction.

Kelly Reisland had a compact, fit body. Her hips flared. Her ass was slightly rounded. Her tits were amazing. She looked at him and he knew he had to have her again. Right here and now, with the kitchen lights showing him every emotion on her face as he took her.

He took the condom out of the pocket as he dropped the shorts to the floor. Kelly's eyes widened as she saw his intent and she smiled at him.

They met in the middle of the room. He lifted her onto the table as their mouths met in a hot kiss. He fumbled to roll the condom on as her legs wrapped around him, urging him to enter. Her hands slid to his ass pulling him closer.

"Look at me, Kelly. I want to watch you come."

As their bodies joined, he looked down at his lover. Her blond curls were amazing. Her lips, so full and pink. The sounds she made as he slid in and out. Her eyes … Finn stopped while deep inside and lifted his hand to her face so he could get a good look. While he saw passion in her blue eyes, there was something a little off.

"Don't stop, Finn."

It took a moment. Was it any wonder with his mind a little scrambled as Kelly arched, shifting her body to start their rhythm again.

He had to have imagined it. Kelly's eyes closed as they both panted, release so close for them.

"Now, Finn. Now."

"Open your eyes, Kelly. Look at me." In the bright lights of the kitchen, as Finn watch the orgasm take over he also saw the added glaze to her pupils.

"Shit, Kelly. Are you high?"

Chapter Twenty-Three

Kelly would have cried herself to sleep if she had any energy left to do so. She spent her days with so much excess energy she couldn't sit still, only to crash every night with barely enough time to tuck the kids in before falling asleep, sometimes not even making it upstairs to her bed, falling asleep on the couch.

There had to be a reason she was such a flipping hot mess. Maybe she would call the doctor on Monday. It had been a while since her last physical.

But what if something was wrong with her? Really wrong. Did she want to know? What about her girls? Who would take care of them? Sure, they had a father, but...

Jeff was another issue. Why was he around all the time? Why now? He was suddenly the perfect husband and father. Okay, ex-husband, but he wasn't acting like an ex.

He knew something was wrong with her. Why else would he show up every morning before he went to work to make her coffee and the girls' breakfast? He made sure they took their vitamins daily. Every night, he returned. He played games with the kids. He tucked them in. He helped with dishes and laundry. He made her tea as she struggled to stay awake to pay the bills and do payroll.

If she couldn't focus on those tasks, he would

watch television with her, with his arms around her shoulders.

Then he would kiss her. Every night he kissed her and told her how much he missed her. Sometimes he went as far as touching her breasts, or lying pressed together on the couch. Last night, he'd held her hand against his erection, letting her know she still turned him on.

But no sex. Which was unusual. Jeff loved sex. No, Jeff really *loved* sex but he wasn't pushing her to move forward. The crazy part was she couldn't stop thinking about sex. Even after the fiasco with Finn... okay, the sex part wasn't a fiasco. God, no. That was A-Maze-Ing! It was the jerk comment he made at the end that had finished things abruptly. It had been one week since she'd stormed out of his house and avoided any contact with Finn. As she should. Right?

Still, she caught herself staring at the fence dividing their yards and wishing things were different. Wishing he wasn't so gorgeous or so damn incredible in bed (and on the floor, and on the table). Wishing he didn't have foot-in-mouth disease making her want to slap him upside the head.

Her head told her to forget her neighbor. Her body, though, had other plans. It was like she needed sex. Had she been celibate too long? Was it normal to ache this much and this long between her legs? She wanted Finn, despite not talking to him for a week. Despite his accusing her of doing drugs. Despite his ego the size of the big red truck he rode in. Despite ... oh, hell! All she had to do was look in the man's intense, violet eyes and she melted like butter. Yet, he was all wrong for her.

Jeff, on the other hand, had been there every day,

attentive in so many ways. While he was being a gentleman with his kisses, and while she still thought of another man, her body was telling her to go for it.

Of course, that would depend on if she could keep her eyes open long enough for the act. It was midnight and her eyes wanted to close, but her mind wouldn't stop racing.

By three AM she still hadn't slept, and her body was reacting in a new way. She dragged herself into the bathroom with barely enough time before becoming violently ill. She grabbed a towel, wrapped it around her shoulders, and rested her head on her porcelain companion.

****

Guinness heard them before he did. The dog gave an excited bark, wagged his tail, and pressed his nose against the sliding back door, alerting Finn of visitors seconds before he heard the voices.

"I don't think we should bother him. I can make you lunch."

"You are not allowed to use the stove without Mommy and I want grilled cheese."

Finn slid the door open and looked out at his young neighbors. "Good morning, Livvy and Hannah. What brings you to this side of the fence?"

"Will you make me a grilled cheese sandwich?" Hannah blurted before sticking her thumb in her mouth. Livvy sighed and rolled her eyes at her sibling and put her hand out to pet Guinness as he wagged his tail excitedly.

"I told her I could do it, but technically, I'm not supposed to use the stove without Mom's supervision. Besides, I don't know why she can't have a cold cheese sandwich."

"Where is your mom?"

Hannah removed her digit to speak again. "She's sick. Threw up everywhere."

"I called our Dad, but he said he was out of town this weekend." Livvy informed him, "Besides, he doesn't do sick."

Finn glanced at the house beyond his fence. He hadn't spoken to Kelly in a week. Not a word since their mind-blowing sex fest. The last thing Kelly would want was him in her home.

He looked down at the girls. Hannah hugged Guinness and looked up at him with pleading eyes. Livvy shifted from one foot to the other, obviously pained by having to ask for help. He couldn't leave the girls to fend for themselves. Kelly would have to suffer his existence.

Finn closed the door and followed the girls to their house. Obviously, the girls had managed their own breakfast and had attempted to start lunch. The kitchen was not in its usual immaculate condition. Cereal bowls filled the sink. Spilt milk puddled on the counter. Half glasses of orange juice sat on the table. The bag of bread lay open on the counter, its twist tie on the floor, and slices of cheese were slapped between two slices of bread, ready to be eaten dry.

Within ten minutes, Finn served the girls grilled cheese and chicken noodle soup.

"Let me check on your mom while you eat, then we can clean up." Finn headed upstairs and followed the sound of retching and a flushing toilet to locate the master bathroom. A pale and exhausted Kelly sat propped against the wall. She opened her eyes at his approach and let out a low moan.

"What are you doing here? Go away."

"Your girls asked for my help." Finn noticed the makeshift bed of towels on the floor and knew Kelly had slept on the floor all night. He knelt down and put a hand on Kelly's forehead. Slight fever, nothing worrisome, though.

"Don't want help," she grumbled at him.

Finn snorted. "Tough, independent, divorced mom. Been doing it all on your own. Why ask for help? Especially from a man. You are super woman. I get it. But those girls downstairs need a hand and I'm here to help them. While I am here, I can also help you, because God knows you could use it right now."

That earned him an evil stare, but Finn continued. "I can get the water running for a shower and help you, or you can sit here and pretend you can do it all on your own. What's it going to be?"

Kelly's head tilted back against the wall and her eyes shut as she heaved a heavy sigh. Finn could almost see her mental debate.

"Fine."

Finn stood and started the shower, testing the water before turning back to Kelly. He took her hands and pulled her to her feet, then pulled her against his chest as she swayed.

"Okay?"

At Kelly's nod, Finn pulled her nightshirt over her head and pushed her panties to her feet. The sight of her beautiful, fit, slightly tanned body, reminded him of the hours of fun he'd had the week before, examining every inch and curve.

Finn helped Kelly under the warm spray of water,

got her assurance she could stand on her own, and then quickly pulled the curtain between them.

What did it say about him that he wanted to strip down and join her in the shower? That he wanted to tuck her under the covers of the blanket and hold her naked against him? If the girls weren't downstairs, he probably would do that and use the excuse she needed him.

Kelly was gorgeous. She turned him on. And the sex …

Finn moved into the bedroom and opened drawers, finding clothes for Kelly. The woman was sick. Her girls were downstairs. Get a grip.

He heard the shower shut off and headed back into the bathroom. He grabbed a towel and wrapped it around the petite, wet, body. He was a gentleman as his knuckles brushed across her skin as he tucked the towel between her breasts. He'd hoped to hand Kelly her clothes and leave the room while she dressed, but as she swayed on her feet, he knew she was beyond tired.

With a gulp, Finn took the towel and patted her dry. Memories of their sex swamped him. Her scent. Her soft skin. Her moans. He pulled the shirt over her head then lifted her into his arms and carried her to the bed. Once she was, thankfully, covered, Finn placed a wastebasket by her side and left the room.

First order of business: coffee, and lots of it. He tackled the mess in the kitchen while the coffee brewed, then with a fresh cup of Joe in hand, he spent time with the girls. They played board games, ran around in the back yard, and chased Guinness. He checked on Kelly (lustful thoughts aside—mostly) and cleaned her bathroom. He made dinner, then brewed another pot of coffee. He tucked the girls into bed then checked on Kelly, again, this time earning a thank you.

Finn located an extra pillow and blanket and attempted to settle down for the evening. He couldn't sit still, though. He paced throughout the house, looking at pictures on the walls, picking up knick-knacks and putting them back. There was nothing interesting on TV, instead his thoughts continued to drift to the woman upstairs.

What was it about Kelly Reisland that caused him to think of her so much? Sure the sex was great, but he'd had great sex before. Hell, he couldn't even sit still tonight, knowing she was in a bed upstairs with no panties on because he'd been too horny to have his hands slide up her thighs without wanting to touch her more intimately.

Finn continued to pace throughout the house. He checked on the girls. They were both asleep. He looked in on Kelly. She slept, despite the slight flush to her cheeks.

At midnight, Finn still couldn't sleep. He resisted the urge to stand in Kelly's bedroom and watch her sleep and instead, he flipped through the channels, finally settling on a John Wayne movie.

Sleep continued to elude him. He paced some more, poured the last of the coffee in his mug, and opened the back door to stare out into the night sky.

The stars winked at him while a slight breeze moved through the trees. Kelly and the girls slept upstairs. Maybe that was why he couldn't close his eyes. Today had been ideal. Although Kelly was sick, he'd taken care of her and the kids. It had felt relaxing and perfect. Homey.

A part of him wished he could have this life. A wife, kids, the dog.

Yeah, and a picket fence to make it complete. Get a grip, Finn. The American dream isn't all it's cracked up to be. And the American dream with Kelly? Hell, half the time, you are thinking about sex with her and the other half, you are arguing and saying something so stupid she doesn't talk to you for a week.

Like accusing her of being high. Kelly is so determined to make it on her own, she would never risk her kids, or her daycare by doing drugs.

But she did look strung out. And she couldn't sit still, even after a couple rounds of hot—incredibly hot—sex. She appeared jittery and restless and…

Finn froze. Kelly had acted jittery and restless, much like he did tonight. He could feel an energy running through him that was foreign. He'd been thinking it was lust and want for the woman upstairs.

But what if it was something more?

No, he was being ridiculous.

Finn closed the door and washed out his coffee mug. He emptied the coffee grounds and washed the pot. He went to the couch and lay down. The night dragged on, and Finn watched as dawn peeked through the windows.

The girls were early risers. Finn plied them with pancakes and orange juice and sent them upstairs to get dressed as Kelly shuffled into the kitchen. He was thankful to see she had thrown an old, worn bathrobe over her nightshirt. Had she also put on panties?

Finn pasted on a smile. "Well, good morning. How are you feeling this morning?"

"Better."

"Enough to try a little tea and toast?"

Kelly tilted her head, seemed to consider it, then nodded.

"Sit down. I'll get it." Finn started the tea water, put the bread in the toaster, poured his second cup of coffee of the morning, and turned to find Kelly watching him.

"I owe you a big thank you." Her voice was quiet, but sincere. "You didn't have to help us, especially after..." her voice faded, but Finn knew what she meant.

He grimaced remembering the knee to the members seconds before she ran home naked while he'd been too busy catching his breath to call her back.

Finn buttered the toast and placed a steaming mug of tea in front of Kelly as the girls entered the room.

"We forgot to take our vitamins this morning, Mr. Finn. Oh, hi, Mom." Livvy stopped short. "Are you mad at us for asking Mr. Finn to come over?"

Kelly shook her head. She'd taken her hair out of its thick braid and the curls bounced around her face. "No, you did the right thing."

Livvy turned back to him. "Can we have our vitamins now? They are on the shelf behind you. My daddy says it's important to take care of ourselves and we should take our vitamins every day. He even makes mommy take vitamins, too."

Her comment piqued Finn's interest. "Oh?" He pulled the bottles from the shelf as Livvy talked. Hannah hugged her mom and probably would have crawled onto Kelly's lap, but Kelly whispered something in her ear and the youngest sat down in the chair next to her mom, instead.

"My daddy has been here a lot taking care of us.

He says Mommy is run down and isn't taking care of herself like she should. He said she needs a man around to help out."

"He never said that," Kelly said hotly.

Livvy glared at her mother. "He did to me. He told me you would end up getting sick because you don't eat right and you are an emotional mess. He said you should never have left him because you can't handle stress and no one else would want someone who is as needy as you."

Finn watched as Kelly paled, which was hard to do in her already wan state.

"Here are your vitamins, Livvy. I was wondering if you and Hannah would like to go next door and let Guinness out for me?"

"Sure."

"You can bring him over here like we did yesterday and play with him out back."

He watched as the two girls slipped on flip-flops and headed outside. Kelly sat stiffly, her tea and toast going cold.

Finn wasn't about to broach the topic again with a ten-foot pole, so he gulped down his coffee and turned to Kelly with a smile.

"Eat up. I want to make sure you can keep some solids down. I'll take the girls with me to the store in a little while and get some soup for you for later."

Kelly nodded. With all her hair, she was easily able to hide her face from him, but Finn was almost positive he spotted a tear.

He was torn. Should he leave her alone, which is what he suspected she wanted, or should he pull her into his arms and let her cry it out?

He heard the girls laughing and knew they were occupied. Finn slid Kelly's chair away from the table and lifted her into his arms.

"What the…?" Kelly struggled but Finn swung her around. He sat in her chair and settled her onto his lap.

"Let me go." She pushed back, but Finn tightened his hold.

"Face it, Kelly," Finn whispered, "you are too weak to fight me off. Accept what is."

Kelly stiffened for a moment before she went limp in his arms. Her face nuzzled his neck and she began to cry.

****

"I'm sorry. I shouldn't be doing this." Kelly felt the wall of emotions bursting and knew the dam was about to break. Finn's arms around her were strong, and secure, and felt so right. She wrapped her arms around his body, breathed in his warm, male scent, and wanted him.

Not just sex. She didn't want the no-attachment, sex-only fling she had proposed. No. She wanted companionship, friendship. All that encompassed a relationship between a man and woman who loved each other.

But that wasn't what Shawn Finnigan wanted. Kelly knew it. Besides, she didn't want to admit to him, or any man, she wanted more than what she had in life.

The dam broke and she started to sob.

"I *am* tired. I'm run down, but I don't need a man to take care of me." Yet she curled further into Finn's warmth."

"I have been a mess lately. I can't sleep. I can't eat. And ever since I met you all I think about is sex. But that doesn't mean I can't take care of myself and my children. Okay, so I did get sick, everyone gets sick, right? It doesn't mean I'm weak, just human. So I have a hard time asking for help. Does asking for help now mean I'm weak?"

Kelly pulled back to look at Finn's face—so close to hers. He hadn't showered or shaved yet today. She could see the stubble on his chin.

"Sometimes I think it makes me weak, but I have to get over it, right?" At Finn's nod, she continued her rant. "Jeff isn't right, is he? Am I damaged? Emotionally weak and unlovable?" She didn't wait for an answer.

"I used to have anxiety attacks a lot, but I didn't have them for over two years until I climbed the tree to get Livvy and that's only because I fell from the same tree and broke my arm when I was a kid. I can't stand heights, so I had a good reason to have an anxiety attack, right?

"Then it all started again since then. Maybe Jeff is right. Maybe I can't handle stress. That's why he's been coming over here so often lately. He said I was heading toward another breakdown. He said I've been working too hard and trying to do too much. He could be right."

Kelly knew she was rambling but she couldn't stop.

"I have felt so off my game lately. I can't sleep. Sometimes I can actually feel the blood pulsing through my veins. It's the oddest feeling. Too much energy, then not enough energy. I'm drinking coffee again. All the time. I can't get enough. It's like I need the caffeine rush to get me through the day, then I crash at night and feel sluggish in the morning.

Kelly's rant went down to a near whisper as her gaze went to the fullness of Finn's lips. "And the past few weeks I have thought of nothing but sex, with you, all day, every day. Last week was like a tease. I couldn't get enough. I still want you. The question, though, is do you still want me? After I kneed you? After cleaning up after me? Do you still want me even though I'm on such and emotional roller coaster ride?"

She waited for a response, eyeing him. Then saw his slight nod. "Yes, Kelly, I still want you. As for …"

That was all she needed to hear. For now, at least. Kelly leaned into him and pressed her lips against Finn's. He tasted of male and coffee. He tasted of heat and need. He tasted of home and security.

Kelly twisted in his arms so she could press her chest against his, so she could taste his lips more. She grabbed his head and pulled him into her kiss. She felt his hand on her bare thigh under her robe.

"Why are you kissing my mom? She's getting back together with my dad."

Kelly pulled back in shock to find Olivia glaring at her from the back door.

"Liv, I…."

"You need to leave, Mr. Finn. I don't want you here anymore."

"Olivia, you are being rude." Kelly stood and Finn stood behind her, putting his arm around her waist. "Finn and I have been dating the last few weeks."

"How can you date him when you and daddy have been together?"

Kelly felt the crimson creep up her neck. She had no clue how to answer her child. Of course, she was confused. Jeff had been around almost every day.

"Liv, honey, …"

"I hate you!" Olivia ran past her mother and went upstairs. The slamming of the door made Kelly cringe.

"I'm sorry, Kelly."

She turned to look at Finn. "Why are you apologizing? You came here and took care of us. I cried on your shoulder. I kissed you. And it was my daughter who had a hissy fit. I'm the one who needs to apologize." She leaned against the counter. Her energy level sapped.

"Kelly, we need to talk. About today. About what you said. About the kiss."

Kelly closed her eyes. She wished she could turn back time. She had told the man she was needy and she wanted sex with him. Not the best combination. The floozy at the pizza place had told her Finn did not do commitment. She needed to remember Floozy's advice.

She sensed as Finn moved closer, but she didn't open her eyes. His body pressed hers against the counter and she still didn't look at him. Instead, she pressed the top of her head to his chest.

"Please, Finn, will you forget everything I said today? Ignore it? Chalk it up to my being sick this weekend and not having food in me to keep me sane?"

"Look at me."

Kelly shook her head. Then Finn's hand forced her chin up, but she kept her eyes closed.

"Look at me."

"I can't. I'm tired and embarrassed."

Then his lips were on hers, surprising a gasp from her. The kiss was tender and sweet, coaxing her to respond, which didn't take long. She kissed back, longing in her response. Oh, she needed this. She needed him to erase the entire morning away—all forty minutes of it. She needed him to remind her she was a woman with needs, which did not make her needy. She needed him to kiss those hurtful words Jeff had said about her to their daughter.

She felt a tear escape. Finn released her mouth only to brush his lips against her wet cheek, kissing the tear away.

"It's okay to ask for help and it's human to get sick." He trailed kisses up to her earlobe and whispered, "And I want you as much as you want me and if that is needy, we can be needy together."

Kelly opened her eyes to stare at Finn. She saw it all. Lust, heat, need. Acceptance.

With one child crying upstairs in her room and the other squealing with laughter in the back yard, Kelly went up on her toes and kissed Shawn Finnigan. Her bathrobe parted, his hands skimmed down collarbone, over her breasts, down her stomach, her hips. She arched against him, wishing they could re-enact scene one from last week's play of seduction. She didn't want to stop, but at least one adult had the fortitude to think straight.

Finn broke the kiss and stepped back seconds before Hannah and Guinness charged through the door.

"I'm going home to shower and change, then I'll be back to help with lunch."

Kelly nodded, unable to speak. She stared at Finn, wishing for more. Wanting more.

"Try to eat," he ordered. He scooted out the door, faithful dog by his side.

Chapter Twenty-Four

Finn stood under the warm spray and replayed the past twenty-four hours. Kelly hadn't been thrilled to see him. He couldn't blame her after how things ended last week.

But she had needed him. At least to care for the girls. And, to be honest, he'd wanted to see her again. Maybe not under the current circumstances as he wasn't too keen on picking up puke.

However, there had been one huge advantage: he'd seen Kelly naked again. Even weak, with her hair frizzing around her head, and her face pale, Kelly Reisland was a looker. If her kids hadn't been in the house, he'd have stripped and joined her in the shower with the excuse of her needing his support to stand.

Okay, so she managed to stand on her own two feet and he'd left the room. The image had remained, imprinted on his brain for the rest of the day.

Finn scrubbed his face and his thoughts fast-forwarded to earlier in the day.

Olivia had certainly thrown a zinger on Kelly. Had Kelly's ex-husband really said those things to his daughter? If so, he'd love to have a few words with the scum in a back alley. Some things you don't discuss with your children.

He'd seen Kelly's ex hanging around a lot. Was it to take care of Kelly and the kids? Kelly did admit to feeling run down.

Finn turned the shower off and wrapped a towel around his waist. He'd forgot to turn the exhaust fan on and steam filled the bathroom.

And did the guy actually make Kelly take vitamins every day? What a control freak.

More snippets of Kelly's confession swam in his head as he prepared to shave. She'd had anxiety attacks before. She was drinking lots of coffee. She couldn't stop thinking about sex with him.

Yeah, he'd enjoyed hearing that. He hadn't stopped thinking about her and sex, either.

She'd also mentioned the rush of energy and not being able to sleep. He'd felt the same way last night.

Finn swiped the razor down his face and stopped, frozen in thought.

Like he had felt last night.

He had drunk coffee. Lots of coffee. But that wasn't unusual for him. He could drink coffee at any time and be able to sleep. Years in the firehouse had taught him how to sleep even with a pot of coffee in his system. Not last night, though. He'd assumed it was thoughts of Kelly keeping him awake, but what if…?

He'd felt the energy flowing through his body, like he'd had too much caffeine. He could feel it now, and he'd already had two cups this morning. Kelly had mentioned something similar.

Was there something wrong with her coffee?

Had the ex-husband drugged her? If so, what about the vitamins?

It was a far-fetched idea, but now he was curious.

Finn rushed to change and headed next door.

****

Finn unbuckled Hannah and lifted her out of his truck. While his little helper ran inside, he made quick work of putting her booster seat back in Kelly's van before grabbing the grocery bags.

He still needed to talk to Kelly. If what he feared was true, her ex-husband was dangerous.

The house was quiet when he entered. He could hear Hannah talking to her mom in the kitchen, but it was a heck of a lot quieter than the argument Livvy had been having with Kelly when he'd returned earlier.

Livvy did not like the idea of him and Kelly together. Nope. Olivia Reisland wanted her dad back in the picture. Obviously, the girls coming over to get his help had all been Hannah's idea and Livvy regretted the decision.

Now, Livvy was nowhere to be seen, and Kelly greeted him with a wan smile. At least her color was a bit better.

"How about breakfast for supper?" Finn announced, placing the bags on the counter. "French toast and sausage for the girls and, to keep it lighter for you, scrambled eggs, and toast."

"That sounds lovely. Thank you for everything."

Damn. Her quiet sincerity twisted something inside him. He had a feeling Kelly didn't ask for help often. She was fiercely independent. He lined the food on the counter, including the new can of coffee.

"There's something I want to talk to you about," Finn chatted casually, aware of little ears in the room, "when we have a quiet moment later."

"Sure," Kelly gave him a curious look. "Hannah, go play for a while. We'll call you when supper is ready."

"Okay, Mommy."

She waited until they heard the footsteps disappear up the stairs. "Everything okay?"

Finn nodded as he put on a pot of coffee. How do you tell someone you think they are being drugged?

"Um, yeah. I've been thinking about what you told me this morning. About how you have been feeling and…"

"Thanks for listening," Kelly interrupted. "I'm not usually such a blabbering fool. Or so emotional."

"I figured as much, which is what I wanted to talk to you about."

"Did I scare you off?"

Kelly sat stiffly in her seat. Did she think he was breaking up with her? Now? Just as things were getting good? Damn, he was making a mess of this in a huge way.

"Here, have some coffee." He shoved a cup toward her. "The thing is, I was thinking about what you told me and a weird thought occurred to me. It's going to sound far-fetched, but hear me out, okay?"

"Oh, okay."

"See, it has to do with you not sleeping, and feeling jittery all the time, and…"

"Hel-lo-oo. Anyone home?" A female voice called out from the front door.

"Hold that thought, Finn." Kelly jumped from her seat and moved to the doorway and froze. "Mother?"

Finn heard a whoop from upstairs and knew the girls were on their way down.

"Mother, what are you doing here?"

"Look at you, darling. Jeff told me you've been ill."

"Hello, Jeff."

Finn nearly choked on his coffee. Jeff was here, too? Well, fuck, this should be interesting.

Kelly shot him a look of pure desperation, but he was at a loss as to what to say or do. He was still in the kitchen, and the new arrivals had not made it past the entryway. The girls had used the front stairs and his quiet moment with Kelly was officially over.

"Hi Daddy."

"Hi Grammy."

Kelly finally moved down the hall and Finn took a moment to grab the old, possibly poisoned, coffee can and tossed it in the trash.

"Jeffrey was such a dear to call me and let me know how run down you've become trying to do it all, so I offered to come lend you a hand."

"Oh. Um. How nice of you both, but I'm feeling much better now."

"Really? Well, you look like death warmed over. It will be so much fun to spend time with the girls and maybe help in your little daycare."

Finn keyed in to another conversation going on, as well, between Livvy and her father.

"Daddy, I'm so glad you're here. We like, so have to talk."

Yep, this was going to be awkward.

He wished his coffee were laced with a little bit of Jameson's as he took another sip, and nearly choked on it as a woman entered the kitchen.

This was Kelly's mom?

"Oh, and who is this delicious looking creature? I'm Serena Stanick."

Finn swore the woman purred as she sauntered—

yes, that was the correct word—on her high heels toward him. She wore denim cut-offs that hugged her perfect size two figure and a V-neck tank top that rose above her mid-riff, showing off both her belly-button ring, and the fact she wasn't wearing a bra. Her nipples were dark hues beneath the white fabric and were so perfectly puckered, Finn wondered briefly if she'd pinched them into standing formation, or if the perfect-ex-son-in-law had cranked the air-conditioning in his car.

"Mom, this is Finn. He lives in the old Belanger house. He helped me out this weekend with the girls."

"Oh, that is so sweet of you. Finn? What a strong, handsome name. Is it short for anything?"

"Finnigan. Shawn Finnigan."

"It's truly a pleasure."

Finn didn't know what to make of this Serena, mother of prim and proper Kelly. From her blonde (obviously salon enhanced) hair with more hairspray than a high school prom night, to the freshly applied coral lipstick, to the perfume wafting around the petite woman. It was obvious Serena had been a young mother, but Finn got the feeling she never left her teen years, or at least her twenties. While she still had a body to show off, there came a time, at least in Finn's opinion, you started to dress your age, otherwise...

"Look at the muscles on you." Serena ran a perfectly manicured finger down his arm. "You must work out."

Poor Kelly. He glanced over and saw her look of sheer panic. He also saw Jeff with a possessive hand on Kelly's shoulder. Game on!

"And you must have been a very young mother,

you look no older than your daughter."

"Oh, I was a wild one in high school. Loved to party." She gave a laugh and a swat of her hand as though those times were behind her, but Finn saw her eyes. No, Serena Stanick still partied. And it looked like she'd had a little fortification on her way to visit her daughter.

"I wasn't much of a mother, I confess," Serena crooned, still with her hand on his arm, "but, now, at least, I'm here when my daughter needs me."

"Mom, really."

Jeff whispered something to Kelly and Finn saw her compress her lips.

"Daddy. I saw Finn and mommy kissing."

"Olivia." Kelly admonished."

"And I bet they are sleeping together."

"Olivia!" Kelly's eyes widened. "Enough."

Jeff smirked. "I'm sure they are, Liv, but they are adults and can do that."

"But I saw you and mommy kissing. Are you sleeping together, too?"

Kelly's face paled. Finn put down his coffee cup. He wouldn't be able to swallow the liquid anyway.

Serena giggled. Giggled? Really? Oh, yeah, she was higher than the Empire State building. "Well, isn't this embarrassing. Although, I can't blame you, Kelly. Look at these two men. Absolutely delish."

"Mother, you are not helping. Olivia, go to your room."

"No. I want to visit with Grammy and Daddy."

"I think we should discuss this with her," Jeff added.

"I am not discussing my love life with my nine-year old."

"That's okay, mom, I get it." Olivia taunted, "Basically, once I'm an adult, I can sleep with as many men as I want and its okay."

"Oh, dear, Finn, I do believe this has turned into a family squabble. Why don't I see you out?" Serena pulled him toward the sliding doors and out into the humid night air as Kelly mouthed, "I'm sorry" to him. Jeff, on the other hand, had a look of 'I won this round' as he stepped even closer to Kelly.

"Girls and their moms," Serena shook her head, not one strand of hair moved with the amount of hairspray involved. "You have no idea how vicious it can be at times. Kelly and I had our own share of squabbles."

"I can imagine. I have sisters."

"Do you? So, is it true? Are you sleeping with my daughter?"

"And if I am?"

Serena shrugged. "I can't blame you, or her, of course, but Livvy wasn't lying when she said Kelly and Jeff are back together. It's good to see, actually. They married too young, much like I did. They've both matured, though. Jeff was too busy building his business to be much of a husband or father, but now? Well, he's at a point where he knows what he lost. They'll get back together."

"I see. And what about what Kelly wants?"

"Oh, she'll come around. Running a daycare? Please. With Jeff, she'll have a nanny. It will be back to social clubs and dinners with the Mayor.

"I'm so sorry about all the drama today, but, well, every family has them." Serena opened the fence and nearly pushed him through. "Thank you for helping

Kelly while she was sick. That was sweet."

With a click, the gate was closed and he heard the lock engage. What the hell had happened? One minute he'd been about to talk to Kelly about...

Shit! He never told her his suspicions and now she was alone with Jeff and her psycho whore of a mother.

Chapter Twenty-Five

"Here you go, sweetheart. Eat up."

Kelly stared at the tea and toast and the vitamins her mother placed on the table and sighed. She was in Hell. Serena Stanick as a doting mother? Puh-leeze!

She took an obligatory bite of toast, washed it down with tepid tea, ignored the vitamins, and headed down the stairs to the daycare. Her charges would be arriving shortly.

"How can I help you today?"

Kelly turned back to her mother and looked her up and down. While the weather did predict a scorcher today, her mother's attire of shorts and tank top were too skimpy to wear in front of her young children. But how do you tell your mother she dresses like a slut? She had to say something, though.

"Um, Mom, if you want to help today, can I ask a favor?"

"Anything."

Kelly bit her lip and charged through. "Can you put on a bra?"

Her mother flounced upstairs while muttering under her breath, but Kelly didn't care. She barely had her strength back. Dealing with her mother's antics was not high on her priorities.

She looked forward to the young kids' arrivals, so she could keep busy and not deal with the repeat of drama that had occurred yesterday.

After Finn left—well, been forced out—Jeff and her mother had joined forces to take over her home. She'd been relegated as useless. *"You poor sick child. You lay down and I'll take care of everything. It's not often I get a chance to take care of my child and grandchildren."*

Jeff and Serena had been thick as thieves, whispering as they made dinner, kept the kids busy, made her tea and toast, tucked the girls into bed, and prepared more tea for her.

At least, she had slept well.

Her mother made it to ten-thirty before the noise and activity of the daycare sent her scampering with a headache. Kelly's day improved from there.

By the time the last child went home, Kelly should have been exhausted. Instead, she felt better than she had in weeks.

She headed up the stairs into the house to discover her mother herding her children out the door and Jeff sitting in her living room.

"What's going on?"

"Your mother is taking the girls out to eat tonight."

"What? She should have asked me first."

Jeff lounged back. "She asked me. I am their father. I do have the right to make decisions for them."

Kelly turned on him. "I have physical custody. They live with me during the week and during that time I make the decisions for them. When they are with you on your weekends, then you can decide when and with whom they go out to eat."

Jeff stood and moved casually toward her, but Kelly saw the steel in his eyes and knew she'd royally pissed off her ex-husband. She stood her ground as he stood before her.

"Kelly, do you really want to have this battle with me?"

Oh, yeah, he was pissed. She hated confrontation. Actually she was bad at it. Especially with Jeff.

"I don't want the girls going anywhere with my mother. She drinks. She smokes pot. She could be high right now and you let the kids go in a car with her?"

"They'll be fine." Jeff continued to advance until she stepped back and bumped into the wall. "Besides, I wanted time alone with you." Jeff's arms pressed the wall on either side of her, trapping her in place.

"Why?"

"So, did you sleep with him?"

Anger snapped her back to attention. "That is none of your business." She pushed at his chest but Jeff refused to move.

"It is my business. Our daughters are impressionable and don't need to see a parade of lovers coming through their home."

"And what about the numerous lovers you had *while we were married?* You're such a hypocrite, Jeff. Step back."

She didn't really expect him to move away at her demand, and he didn't. Jeff didn't respond to orders. He would move when he was ready. Instead he pressed his body against hers. He placed both hands on her face and lifted it, forcing her to look him in the eyes.

"I want you back, Kel, and I will do whatever it takes to make it happen. I have the resources, and the connections to make it happen."

Then he kissed her. It was a hard, demanding kiss.

When he was done and had stepped back, Kelly raised her hand and slapped him.

Jeff smiled at her. His look of victory scared her more than if he had retaliated.

"I will see you tomorrow, Kel."

When the door closed behind him, Kelly sank to the floor, knowing she had lost that round.

****

Finn pressed the number on his phone and waited impatiently for an answer.

"It's four in the morning. What's wrong?"

"I'm outside. Open up."

After a crazy long five seconds, the door swung open and his brother stood there in shorts and nothing else. Finn stepped past him and let himself inside.

"I need a favor, bro."

His brother wiped his hands across his face as he suppressed a yawn. "This should be good."

"Can you have this tested for drugs?" He shoved a plastic bag toward his brother who opened it.

"A can of coffee?"

Finn paced the living room of his brother's apartment. "I'm pretty sure he is drugging her, and I think he put it in the coffee. I'm not sure, though, it could be the vitamins, which I don't have."

"Whoa. Hold up. Can you start at the beginning and maybe tell me why you are here at four in the morning?"

Finn took a deep breath and dropped into an armchair. "I think Kelly's ex-husband is drugging her. I don't know why, exactly, but she hasn't been feeling well, and this past weekend, she was sick, so I went over and took care of the girls. Anyway, I drank her coffee and felt jittery. It's not a normal reaction. She also mentioned vitamins her ex-husband insists she take daily. So, those could be laced, too. I don't know."

Tom sat down on the sofa and placed the coffee can on the table between them. "I guess I can look into it. How did you get this? Or do I want to know?"

"Well, Sunday, I bought her a new can of coffee and threw this one out, but before I could talk to her about my suspicions, her ex-husband, and her mother showed up. So I went through her trash tonight before the garbage trucks arrived."

Tom shook his head at his covert operations, but Shawn knew his brother was taking him seriously.

"Tell me about this ex-husband of hers. Who is he?"

"His name is Jeff Reisland. I don't know what he does, but Kelly's mother implied he had money."

"I know who he is. Shit! Jeff Reisland is on a watch list. He is suspected of several crimes but nothing has been proven yet." Now it was Tom's turn to stand and pace, which didn't help Finn's nerves at all.

"You do realize, Shawn, even if I find something in this coffee, it probably will not trace back to the ex-husband in any way."

He nodded. "Yeah, but I can at least tell Kelly what he's doing. Right now, she thinks she is going crazy. She is an emotional mess right now."

"Watch your back, Shawn. This man is dangerous."

"That's what I'm afraid of."

Chapter Twenty-Six

When Finn was not working, he spent his time spying on his neighbor. He'd even gone so far as to buy binoculars. The windows only allowed him limited access to Kelly's movements inside.

He was worried. Other than when Kelly was out in the back yard with her daycare children, he didn't think she left the house. Either Serena or Jeff did the grocery shopping. One of her employees did the banking (yes, he'd followed her). Most of all, though, Kelly was never, ever left alone.

He tried calling. Twice. Serena answered and told him Kelly didn't want to speak with him. That made him more determined to figure out a way to get to her, if he could find a way to get her alone.

The closest he'd come was a few days before when he'd spotted Hannah in his yard. The young girl had opened the gate and was sitting with his dog, chatting with him like an old friend.

"Hey, squirt. What are you doing?"

"Guinness and me are playing tea party. Wanna join us?"

Finn joined his unexpected guest on the grass and played along as she handed him an invisible cup.

"Remember to sit up straight, Mr. Finn."

"Oh, sorry. Am I doing better now?"

Hannah giggled as he straightened his back and put

a pinky out as he sipped from his pretend cup. Guinness lie down and put his head on his paws.

"I guess my dog doesn't know his manners." Finn sighed.

"Oh, no, Mr. Finn, Guinness is fine. My mommy gets tired after drinking her tea, too."

"Hannah? Hannah, where are you?"

Finn looked up as Serena walked through the gate entrance.

"Hi, Grammy. We're having a tea party."

"It's time to clean up. Run along, dear."

Hannah crawled over to the dog and gave Guinness a huge squeeze around the neck before standing up. "See ya, Mr. Finn."

"See you later, squirt." Finn stood as the young girl skipped into her yard but Kelly's mom stayed.

"Such a sweet thing."

Finn kept silent as Serena walked toward him. Her clothes were subtle today. Khaki shorts, tank top, with bra, hair pulled back into a large barrette. It wasn't the clothes that put Finn on high alert, though. Serena oozed sexuality and, at the moment, she was looking him up and down. Finn crossed his arms and waited. Guinness sat up and looked back and forth between him and their newest intruder.

"I heard you're a firefighter." Serena ran a finger down his bicep. "Such muscles. So strong. My daughter does have good taste in men."

Finn looked down at the woman, but didn't move. "How is Kelly feeling?"

Serena waved a hand in dismissal. "Oh, she's fine. We're taking good care of her."

Interesting choice of words.

"Jeffrey is so good to her and the girls."

Finn kept himself from rolling his eyes. Serena hadn't moved her hand from his arm. He waited silently, and Serena started to talk, as he'd hoped.

"I know you and my daughter had a little fling, but you do realize it is over now, don't you?"

Serena stroked his arm. "My daughter has been lost without her husband by her side. It's so nice to see the family back together and the girls are doing so well with their father in their lives."

"It looked to me like Kelly was doing quite well before. She has a thriving business and the girls are happy and healthy."

Serena laughed as she patted him on the arm. "Appearances can be deceiving. Kelly needs Jeff. My daughter can be a bit emotional and Jeff has a way of keeping things together."

"I see."

Serena smiled at him. "I'm sure you do." She turned and walked away. When the gate was latched, Finn heard the click of the padlock. Guinness gave a low yowl. They both knew the gate had been officially closed off to passage... from either side.

Since that encounter, he'd only had his vantage from the upstairs window to see what happened next door.

Guinness gave an excited yelp before heading downstairs. Finn knew someone had arrived but at that moment he spotted Kelly standing by her sliding glass doors. He lifted the binoculars as his brother's voice wafted through the house.

He was too focused to respond. He'd discovered the window from the spare bedroom gave him the best view of the kitchen. Tom would find him.

Jeff was back. They were all sitting down to dinner. The table was perfectly set, Emily Post approved. The girls must have been told to sit still because they stopped shuffling in their seats and sat up straight. They gently placed cloth napkins on their laps.

He could see Jeff giving the girls a lesson in holding their silverware properly. He had a clear view of Jeff and only a profile view of Kelly, who sat next to him on his right. The two girls were on Jeff's left. Serena was there, too, but he couldn't see her from his angle. Occasionally, he would see her hand reach out toward one of the girls.

"You've got it bad, bro."

"I haven't been able to reach her in a week. They have her secluded."

Tom walked around and looked out the window. "Looks like dinner."

"More like Stepford training." Kelly lifted a glass of red wine and took a sip, but he hadn't seen her lift her fork yet. Damn, she needed to eat.

Tom leaned against the wall as he observed the scene across the fence. "I should cite you for being a peeping Tom, except I came here to tell you the coffee was laced."

Finn dropped the binoculars to his lap. "So I'm not paranoid. What is he drugging her with?"

"Methylfenidate. Also known as Ritalin."

"Shit. Okay, so now I know. What do I do about it? I can't get close to her to warn her. Maybe I should confront the bastard when he leaves, beat his ass to a pulp."

Tom snorted. "You said that to a cop, like I'm

going to agree."

"I said it to my brother, not the cop. Want to join me?"

Tom pushed away from the wall and stood in front of the window, blocking Finn's view. "Dad may be a drunk, Shawn, but he taught us a few things growing up. One was not to let emotions get in the way of reasonable action."

"She needs help, Tom."

"I didn't say otherwise. I mentioned before her ex-husband is being watched. I put a few calls in. Mr. Jeffrey Alan Reisland is going to see some added police attention over the next couple of days."

Finn glanced up at his older brother. "You have piqued my interest."

Chapter Twenty-Seven

Jeff was drugging her. Kelly knew it. Her mother was probably in on it, as well. How she managed to get through a day with her daycare kids without one of her employees or a parent commenting was beyond her understanding. Why wasn't it obvious to anyone but herself?

She'd stopped taking the vitamins three days ago. Well, she'd figured out how to cheek them under Jeff's eagle eyes. She believed those were a cause for her sexual drive because now her skin wasn't quite so electric whenever Jeff touched her. And he touched her all the time. A hand on her back. A touch to the cheek. And the kisses at night were becoming more prolonged and aggressive.

He started staying the night, too. On the couch. Still, he had wormed his way back in to their lives. This was *her* house, though. She wanted him out, but she couldn't get her mind clear enough for a battle of wills.

Her mother was upstairs reading to the children. She hadn't been allowed to do that since her mother arrived. She hadn't been allowed to do anything since the invasion of her parent and ex-husband. She didn't cook, do the dishes, laundry, or put her children to bed. All of her food and drinks were prepared for her.

She knew he was doing it. She couldn't prove it and didn't know how to stop it. But it had to stop.

Jeff joined her on the living room sofa, her evening cup of tea in his hand. More than likely it was drugged, too. Last night she had decided not to drink the tea, but when Jeff's hands had started to roam, Kelly had picked up the tea as a way to keep occupied.

If she didn't take the cup tonight, was she in for another dose of amorous Jeff? Kelly reached to take it, like the doting wife he wanted and knocked the cup of hot liquid onto his leg.

"Ow! Shit, shit, shit."

Jeff jumped up and Kelly reached for a towel from the laundry basket her mother had folded an hour before. "I'm so sorry. I'm so clumsy lately. I didn't mean it. Why don't you go take a shower and wash it off and I'll clean the mess here. Grandpa Joe has clothes in the closet upstairs."

While Kelly mopped up the spill on the couch she saw Jeff's hand clench. She looked up and saw Jeff's face and she knew he forced himself to push his anger aside as he reached out and caressed her face.

"Shh. It's okay, baby. You can't help it." Kelly closed her eyes, not wanting him to see her disgust with him. "I'll be right back."

Kelly made quick work of cleaning the spill then rushed to the kitchen to make her own cup of tea as Jeff returned to the living room.

In nothing but his boxers.

Oh, no. Total backfire.

"I put my clothes in the washer. I'm sure the stain will come out."

Kelly gulped. "Um, yeah. Sorry about that. Like I said, Grandpa Joe has clothes here. You are more than welcome to wear them." *Please.*

Jeff smiled. "This can't bother you. We were married and I walked around with less than this."

True. Jeff had never had a problem with body image. He'd slept in the nude and walked around their bedroom suite sans clothes every night.

Kelly chose to ignore his comment and instead pointed to her freshly filled cup on the counter. "I made more tea. Would you like some?"

Jeff continued to walk toward her. He was in predator mode. She knew the look. She knew the walk. Jeff had made his decision and Kelly searched for a way to distract him.

"I really should go check on the girls. I didn't get to say goodnight to them."

"Serena is taking care of them."

Jeff had reached the edge of the counter, only two steps to her now. Kelly instinctively backed up, which brought her back to the edge of the counter.

"Jeff, I…"

"No, Kelly. I've been patient with you." He put his hands on the counter, trapping her between his arms. Kelly stared at his lean, muscular chest. Jeff was fanatic about taking care of his body. He worked out. He ate healthy. Her ex-husband still made heads turn.

But he didn't compare to Shawn Finnigan. Finn's muscles came from working a job that required real strength. Finn's chest was broad. Finn's hands were large and calloused and manly, not like Jeff's moisturized and manicured ones.

Kelly wanted Finn. Instead, it was Jeff who leaned in. Kelly ducked and maneuvered her way around his body and quickly walked to the other side of the room.

"We need to talk, Jeff."

Jeff turned around to face her and Kelly knew he wasn't mad. No, quite the opposite. He was turned on, like this was a game of cat and mouse and he had laid the perfect trap.

"There's nothing to talk about, babe. You. Me. We've known each other forever. Sure we got married young, but we've always had passion. Our bodies know each other so well."

With every step Jeff took toward her, Kelly moved back. He was playing her. The stairs were behind her. Should she run? No, the bedrooms were up there and the last thing she wanted was Jeff and her near any kind of bed.

The living room? No, the couch was too accessible. Her mother and the girls were upstairs, and Jeff knew she would never make a scene with them in the house.

"I don't want this."

"Your body tells me otherwise. When I touch you, you come alive. I've seen it. I've felt it."

Of course, it had. He'd been drugging her to make sure of it. Kelly felt as helpless as a lab rat in a maze. Jeff knew he had her cornered as he moved closer and closer.

"Baby, you need me. The girls need their father. We had a good life together and we can have it all again." Kelly stepped back. She was running out of options. Stairs two steps behind to her left. Living room immediately to her left. Bathroom with laundry immediately to her right. Or the wall behind. One more step and Jeff would be close enough to reach her. She needed to react, but she felt frozen. For the past few weeks, almost all decision-making had been taken from her. She'd been a puppet and now she didn't know how to break from those strings.

The doorbell rang and Jeff stopped in his tracks. He was in his underwear and that meant Kelly would be able to answer the door to her own home.

Kelly bolted to the left and darted through the living room to the front door and swung it open before Jeff could stop her.

"Shannon?" Finn's sister stood on her doorstep. Kelly wanted to grab her, and ply her with questions about Finn, but she knew Jeff listened from down the hall.

"I was in the neighborhood and saw your lights on. I hope you don't mind." Kelly smiled at Shannon's natural exuberance.

"No, of course not," Kelly wished she could invite Shannon inside. Instead, she stood, holding the door closely, blocking Shannon from entering. "How... how are you?"

"The family is going to be attending the festivities on July Fourth down at the park and the kids wanted to know if you and the girls could join us?"

"Oh, ah..." Kelly didn't know how to respond. She desperately wanted to say yes, but Jeff and her mother were always around and how would she manage to get away?

Away? Oh, hell. She would not be a victim. No. Jeff did not control her life. She pasted on a smile.

"The girls and I would love to join you. Why don't we talk later this week and finalize all the details."

Shannon reached out and took Kelly's hand in hers, slipping a piece of paper into her palm. "Thatta girl!" she whispered.

At that point, Kelly knew Shannon had been sent

here on a mission. "Tell your family I am looking forward to spending time with them. It's been too long." Kelly responded, casual enough for the listening ears, but Shannon grinned before she turned and headed down the walkway.

Jeff wrapped his arms around her waist as he came up behind her. "Who was that?"

Kelly closed the door and forced his arms off of her. "A friend. Her husband is in the military and they recently moved back to the area. Her kids and the girls have played together."

Not a lie.

Jeff grunted.

"I'm going upstairs. Your clothes are probably ready to go into the dryer." Kelly headed upstairs and made sure to engage the lock on her door.

She opened the note.

You are being drugged. Don't drink the coffee.

Kelly knew she needed to take her life back. Between her mother and her ex-husband, she'd been tag-teamed into submission. Not anymore.

She shredded the note and flushed it down the toilet.

She'd had a small victory tonight. But one battle was not the war and her opponent played dirty.

****

Jeff closed his office door and threw his keys across the room. He had just received a ticket for speeding. From a fucking woman cop.

His family name, money, and longstanding membership at the country club gave him plenty of connections throughout the city. Unfortunately, not many cops ran in the same circles as he did, or drove the high-end cars that came through his shop. He would have to pay the fine, but, damn, the woman cop pissed him off.

Actually, Kelly pissed him off this morning. He'd made her coffee this morning, with her usual dose of Ritalin. She'd dumped it down the drain and said she was having water only. Then he caught her pocketing the 'vitamin' he'd handed to her when he gave the girls theirs.

His wife had caught on.

"Hey, baby, what's wrong with you today?"

Alicia strolled in, closing the office door behind her. As usual, her large breasts strained the buttons on her purple shirt/dress and her black leggings accentuated her luscious curves. Jeff got hard.

"I need a new plan. Fast."

Alicia sat on his desk and swung her legs back and forth as he paced the room.

"The cash flow isn't coming in fast enough for what I owe. I thought I had Kelly under control, but, well, things are taking longer than I thought."

"So you need access to her money and getting re-hitched isn't happening?"

Alicia had always been quick.

"Not fast enough. It will happen though. I always get my way."

"What about the mother?"

Jeff waved his hand. "No, her father shut her off years ago. She's got nothing."

"But is she the type you can persuade to do your bidding over her daughter's?"

Jeff turned at the devious voice and saw the manipulative brain working in high gear. Oh, this would be good. He crossed the room toward her.

"A little white powder and she's all mine. What are you thinking?"

"It's highly illegal."

"When has that ever stopped me?"

He didn't like to leave Kelly alone. When she was alone, she tended to visit her neighbor and he wasn't going to allow it. When he wasn't there, Serena was.

But now he needed Serena alone. Which meant leaving Kelly unsupervised. He figured the best time to get her by herself would be during a weekday when Kelly was busy with all the brats.

He'd instructed Serena to meet him at eleven at his house. Her hair and makeup were flawless, as usual. Why didn't her daughter understand how important those things were to a man? Serena had listened and wore a sundress. It was a bit faded, but it would do.

He greeted her with a glass of whiskey, which Serena threw back with a natural grace. He refilled the glass.

"I assume there is a reason you asked me to meet you here."

Jeff nodded as they strode toward the living room. He gestured for her to take a seat on the sofa. Two highly polished silver trays graced the table. Cheese and crackers adorned one and the other held the white lines of coke.

"When I called you back to Rocky Point, I told you I needed your help to get Kelly back."

He saw the tremble in Serena's hands as she placed her glass on a coaster. Her eyes kept glancing to the candy as she tried to focus on him.

"And I've done everything you've asked. You and

my baby belong together."

"And the girls need their father," Jeff added. "Kelly is a stubborn woman. Her little business provides her a modest income but she could have so much more with me."

Serena's eyes looked over at the silver tray again.

"Please, help yourself. That's why it's there."

Serena shook her head and instead lifted her glass. The liquid disappeared. Jeff smirked.

"Anyway, I need leverage and the only way I'm going to have it is if I take the daycare away."

Serena nibbled on cheese. "How would you do that?"

"I need to own the house."

Serena gulped. "My father signed the house over to Kelly before he moved to Florida. It's hers, free and clear."

Jeff let out a forced sigh. "I know. And I don't think she would sign it over willingly. We'll have to go around her."

Serena wrung her hands together.

Ah, yes, his dear mother-in-law was nervous. He pressed his lips together to hide a smirk as Serena scooted to the edge of the sofa, closer to the table.

Jeff took one of her hands in his. "In order for me to give Kelly a good life, I need to have her back with me. Look around, Serena. Look at this house. It's so much bigger than Kelly's. Look at the artwork, the silver. These heirlooms will be passed down to my daughters.

"My girls should be spending their summers swimming in the pool out back with their mother lavishing all her attention on them, not on other people's children. I had to teach the girls how to set a proper table. I knew how to do that when I was four."

Jeff stroked Serena's manicured nails. "Kelly and the girls should be having spa days on a regular basis. Have you seen Kelly's hands?"

Serena sighed. "I agree. I want all of that for my daughter."

Jeff let go and reached for the silver tray.

"What I am going to ask of you is not exactly legal."

Serena stared at the white lines until she couldn't deny the craving. She leaned down.

Jeff let her have her moment. Let Serena take in her powdered fortitude. He waited patiently.

"What do we need to do?"

Jeff held in a smile. "Here is a fake ID I had made for you with Kelly's name. I already found the deed to the property in Kelly's office last night while everyone slept. We'll leave now to meet with a lawyer outside of town, who doesn't know you or Kelly. All you need to do is sign the house over to me."

"Won't she hate you?"

"I'll handle Kelly." Jeff sat back as his mother-in-law snorted another line. He let her have a little courage now. Once their mission was accomplished, he'd let his mother-in-law have full access.

****

Kelly saw her mother leave the house and her mind started to race. This was the first time her mother left when Jeff was not here. Would Jeff be arriving shortly? He rarely left his shop during the workday, though.

The rain outside meant being indoors with all the children and Sue had left to make a bank run for her.

She couldn't leave. She couldn't slip outside and sneak over to Finn's house. But she could call.

She checked if Heather was all set with their charges and walked upstairs into the kitchen. She grabbed the phone from the charger and made her way into the bathroom and closed the door.

Her hands shook as she dialed Finn's number. Oh, hell, she really was a victim afraid of getting caught calling for help. As the phone rang, Kelly tried to put a coherent thought together. What would she tell Finn? What did she want?

"You've reached Finn's voicemail. You know what to do."

Damn! Damn! And Double Damn!

"Um, Finn, it's me, Kelly. Ah… well, I got your note. Thank you. I'm working on a plan." Well, not really, because she hadn't come up with one yet, but at least it sounded hopeful. "Um, well, I guess I'll try to call you again when I can." She sounded pathetic. Kelly sighed as she hit the off button.

****

Jeff padded across his bedroom to get to his ringing phone out of his pants pocket. The blond in his bed never stirred. He looked at the caller ID. Alicia.

"Hey, baby, what's up?" he drawled.

"Mr. Reisland," Oh, no. Alicia was using her 'business' voice. "I have Rocky Point P.D. here to do a follow up on the vehicle that went missing last month."

Fu—uh-uk!

"Thank you, Alicia. Tell them I will be there in five." Jeff slipped on his pants and looked over at the bed. Serena never had the inhibitions her daughter did and they'd had fun the last couple hours. He pulled his black polo shirt over his head and walked over to hit the off button of his little insurance policy.

Serena was in his pocket now. Much like her daughter, Serena longed for her family. Jeff knew his mother-in-law had wanted any excuse to be part of her daughter and granddaughters' lives again. He'd provided that to her. This video could tear it all away in a moment.

He left Serena to sleep off her high. He only had an hour to deal with the police and get to Kelly's before she was left completely alone. Who knew what she would do if left to her own devices. He also had to come up with a plan to get the drugs back into her system.

His shop was located on his family property so the ride was a short one. He plastered a smile on his face as he entered his office and greeted the recent bane of his existence. He wasn't worried. He'd talked himself out of worse situations plenty of times.

Chapter Twenty-Eight

Kelly groaned as Jeff's Audi pulled into her driveway as the last two children were leaving. Sue had left at three and Heather would be leaving within a few minutes. No time to herself. It was a rainy Friday night and her vacation week had officially started. She always closed her daycare the week of July Fourth. She'd hoped to take her two children out to dinner, to get out of the house and enjoy a night of freedom. She should have known it wouldn't happen.

Her head had cleared enough now to start formulating a plan. She'd considered talking to Sue and Heather today while the kids napped. But what could she tell them? That she suspected her ex-husband was drugging her? They'd want to go to the police and then what? Drugs and a daycare full of children were not a good match. So she kept silent.

She heard Jeff in the house chatting with the girls, telling them to go wash up. She locked the door after Heather left and looked around.

She put a few stray toys away, but they had a system down to keep things organized and there wasn't much to do to keep her occupied. She took a last look around and walked up the steps into her kitchen as the girls went into the bathroom to wash. Jeff had brought dinner.

Smelled like Chinese. Everything was still in the

large paper bag with the top folded down and stapled shut. Okay, should be harmless.

"You shouldn't be here, Jeff. You are giving the girls the wrong impression we are getting back together."

Jeff pulled on the paper bag and a staple flew to the floor. Kelly squatted down to pick up the staple and was startled when Jeff followed her.

His hair and shirt were damp from the dash inside from his car. He smelled of rain and his Hermes cologne.

"We *are* getting back together. Why can't you see that? Why do you want to deny our girls a family?"

"Give me a break, Jeff. You're the one who cheated in our marriage. You didn't want a family. The girls and I are fine without you."

Kelly saw the flicker in Jeff's brown eyes and knew she'd said the wrong thing. Jeff had a mean streak and her words had ignited a stick of dynamite.

Liv and Hannah entered the room again and Kelly knew her reprieve would be short lived as Jeff stood up. Kelly's legs were rubbery as she got glasses of milk for the girls. She set the table as Jeff took out the Styrofoam containers of Chinese food dinners. Jeff would never eat directly from the containers so each meal had to be transferred to a plate before being placed on the table.

He'd gone to the Purple Dragon, which had been a favorite of theirs when they were married. She'd always ordered the same dinner special and Jeff, of course, remembered. Jeff had become friends with the owners during her first pregnancy when she'd craved Chinese for an entire trimester.

Her mother hadn't returned and she noticed Jeff had only bought enough for the four of them. Something was up.

"Do you know where my mother is?"

Jeff shrugged. "No. Why?"

"She left before noon and hasn't returned."

"I'm sure she'll show up."

Kelly poured Duck Sauce over her chicken fingers. She'd already pushed Jeff's buttons a few minutes ago, did she dare push the issue?

"I figure you must have spoken to her to know she wouldn't be here for dinner tonight. You only bought enough dinners for four."

Jeff placed his fork on his plate and sat back in his chair to look at her. Yep. Buttons pushed. Red light on.

"I bought four because I figured the two girls would share one."

Lie. She could tell. She really should leave well enough alone.

"And yet you gave them each a full dinner serving."

Jeff stared at her for an endless moment, before his eyes flickered to his daughters before returning to stare her down. Kelly watched as he took a sip from his glass of wine, his eyes never leaving her.

She gulped and tried not to fidget in her seat. She got his message, loud and clear. She lowered her eyes and silently ate while Jeff asked the girls about their day.

As soon as dinner was over, Jeff sent the girls upstairs for showers and offered to help with the cleanup. When Kelly stood from the table her body felt heavy and sluggish.

How had he done it? How had he managed to drug her again? She'd watched him take the food from the container. She'd been the one to open the bottle of wine and pour it into the glasses. How?

"Hello, Darlings. Sorry I'm late." Serena strolled, her silk blouse mis-buttoned, her hair a mess. But it was her eyes Kelly looked at for confirmation.

Kelly lifted her wine glass and threw it across the room, getting the attention of her mother and ex-husband. "This is it. I'm through with the both of you. Mother, pack your bags and leave this minute. I will NOT have my children around a drug addict. And you," she whirled to point a finger at Jeff. The room spun, but she managed to continue her tirade. "I know you are drugging me. I don't know what your game is but it is over. You need to leave. Now!"

She saw Jeff walking toward her a moment before the world went black.

****

Finn paced while Tom and Shannon discussed strategies to get to Kelly. He'd listened to Kelly's voicemail over and over throughout the day. He'd been at work when she'd called, working an MVC, a single car rollover on the highway due to excessive speed in the rain. There had been no way he could take a call.

He'd met his siblings at the family homestead. Shannon sent her children upstairs while his father and brother-in-law yelled at a Red Sox game on TV.

"Do you hear her voice?" Shawn asked after playing the voicemail for Tom and Shannon. "She needs help. She wants help. What can we do?"

"The Fourth of July is Saturday. She said she would come to the park with us for the picnic and games." Finn could tell his sister wanted to sound encouraging.

Tom continued for her. "There is no way Reisland is going to let her go alone, not if he's been playing the doting family man the last few weeks. We'll have to figure out a way to separate Kelly and the girls from him."

"I could always play the part of the jealous lover and punch the guy's lights out." Finn offered gaining a snort from his brother.

"Not a far stretch, bro, but you will risk losing your job. No, we'll figure out a different way. And stop pacing. You're driving me mad."

Finn flipped a chair around and straddled it. His hands gripped the back and his fingers began an incessant tapping. His brother and sister exchanged glances and he forced himself to stop.

"Before we go further," Finn received a determined look from his brother, "I need to know something."

Finn nodded.

"Why are you doing this? You haven't known this Kelly for long."

"What the hell does it matter?"

Tom and Shannon exchanged glances but Tom continued. "I get you see she's in trouble and needs help. That's who you are. Anyone in this family needs something they go to you. Kathleen needs a ride to the airport she calls you. Shannon needs help with anything around the house she calls you. Dad…"

"Yeah, so?"

Shannon reached over and put her hands on his, silencing the fingers tapping again.

"What he means is you are a fixer. You see

something is wrong and you want to fix it. There's nothing wrong with that, but we want to know your motives for helping your neighbor."

Tom leaned back. "Shawn, her ex is bad news. What we do next could have lasting effects. Are you ready for that? Is she worth it?"

Finn froze. True, he had only met Kelly a couple months ago and they hadn't spent more than a few hours together here and there. So why was he doing this?

Did he need to 'fix' her problem? Or was there something more?

Was it the sex? There certainly was heat between them and he wanted a repeat of their night that had ended abruptly.

It wasn't it, though. It was the sound of her laugh and the way her eyes lit up when she smiled. Then there was the way her face softened when she was with her children. She was fiercely independent even when she grudgingly accepted help when she was sick.

When he'd been watching her house for the past week, he'd been crazy with wanting to help. But not due to lust. There had been something more, something underlying.

Finn looked up to find Tom and Shannon staring at him.

"You love her." Shannon stated softly and Finn nodded.

"Aw, for the love of Pete," Patrick's voice boomed as he entered the kitchen. "Didn't I teach you anything, boy?" He grabbed a beer from the fridge and slammed the door shut. "I told you love will bring you nothing but heartache.

"Look at Tom. Divorced. Look at Shannon. Her husband's leg gets blown off and she's stuck with an invalid and having to work extra hours to make ends meet. They fight all the time."

"I know what you said, Pops. Love is the Devil's invention."

"Enough!" Shannon yelled as she stood up. She crossed the room and poked a finger at their father's chest. "How dare you? How could you fill your own son's head up with crap like that? And don't you go judging my marriage."

She looked over at her husband as he hobbled in on crutches. "Yes, we've hit a difficult patch, every marriage does." Her voice softened. "But I wouldn't trade a moment of it. Devon and I have been through other difficult times. He has always been there, especially during my pregnancies when I went off my bi-polar meds."

"You're bi-polar?" Tom asked.

Shannon nodded. "So was Mom. That's why she and I fought so much. The best thing I did was move out. I was lucky, Devon's mom is a nurse, and she recognized the signs. I got help. Mom didn't want help. She didn't think she needed it."

She swung around again to their dad. "You loved Mom, but didn't understand her and what was happening. I get it. Most people don't want to discuss mental illness. But don't fill Shawn's head up about love being evil.

"Hey, do I get a say about anything here?" Finn interceded.

Shannon spun around and placed her hands on her hips. "What?"

"Thanks for defending me, Big Sis, but I never took those words to be more than drunken ramblings. I love Kelly and I'm good with it."

"Oh." Shannon seemed to deflate a bit. "Well, then, I guess we need to figure out a plan to get you two together."

****

Kelly stirred. Her mouth felt like cotton and her head pounded. She pushed herself to a sitting position, her arms nothing but spaghetti.

It only took a few seconds for her to realize she was in bed, but not her own. At least, it hadn't been hers for over two years.

What the hell was she doing at Jeff's house?

"Hello, baby."

Jeff sat in a chair in the attached sitting area, a magazine in his hand. A tray containing fruit and yogurt, along with a pot of coffee sat on the table beside him.

Oh, hell's bells, it was morning.

He wore only his boxers and Kelly gripped the sheet closer as she realized she didn't have much more than that on either.

"Why am I here? What did you do to me? If you raped me, by God I will…."

"Relax. I didn't touch you," Jeff sneered. "I'm not so hard up I'd have sex with you while you were unconscious."

"Drugged to oblivion, you mean."

Jeff didn't deny it. "You need some food in your system." He pointed to the tray. "Come eat, you'll feel better."

"I'll eat at home. Where are my clothes?"

"I have those as collateral. It's time we talked."

"Talked? You drugged me. You kidnapped me. You stripped me naked," okay, he'd left her panties on, but still... "and you expect me to sit and have a chat with you? Not happening. I want my clothes and then I am going home."

Jeff crossed one ankle across his knee and leaned back as he took a long sip from his steaming coffee.

"Then go find them."

Kelly narrowed her eyes. Oh, the conniving bastard. He was counting on her strutting around the room, naked, while she searched for her clothes, while he had the central air set to frigid.

"No?" Jeff stood and poured a second cup of coffee and strolled toward her and placed the liquid on a coaster on the nightstand then sat down on the bed beside her.

"Where are the girls?"

Jeff sighed. "At home, with your mother."

Kelly clenched her teeth. "My *mother* was high as a kite last night and you left my girls with her?"

"*Our* girls," Jeff stressed the words. "And your mother is under strict orders not to leave the house with them."

"Now my mother is taking orders from you?" Kelly felt the rolls of panic settling in. "Move. I want to leave. I need to get home."

"This is your home, Kelly. This is where you belong. We are getting married again and you will move back here so we can be a family."

"That's not going to happen. Did you think drugging me would make me want you again?"

Jeff smiled and reached out to push her hair from

241

her face. "No, I drugged you for an entirely different reason." Kelly felt herself tremble as she waited for Jeff to continue. His hand moved from her hair to cup her face, and she knew she would not like what he had to say next.

"You will agree to get remarried and move back here, because if you don't, I will let it slip in the news you are under the influence of drugs while caring for all those young children."

Kelly took an audible gasp.

"You've had drugs in your system for nearly a month. They'll do a drug test on you. And while you lose your business from the accusations, you will also lose your children, because they'll certainly be removed from your care, especially when your coke-head mother is also living with you."

Kelly didn't bother saying, 'you wouldn't dare' because she knew he would. She would lose everything.

"Why?"

Jeff smiled and leaned in to steal a kiss, and Kelly held back the tears.

"Because I don't like to lose."

Kelly knew it was the truth. He'd won. "I want to see my girls." It came out as a near whisper.

"We'll get married Saturday night, at the park, before the fireworks. I know a Justice of the Peace who will perform the ceremony."

Of course he did. And he probably had connections with the media so it would make the eleven o'clock news as well.

"We can start packing your things and have you moved into the house by then."

Kelly snapped her head up. "Wait. I have a

business."

"Close it."

Kelly slapped Jeff's hand away from her face. "I can't just close it. It's not so simple. I have families who count on me for daycare. I have employees who count on me."

Jeff shrugged. "Fine. Give them one month. August first the house is going on the market."

"No, it is not. That was my grandparents' house. It is not going on the market." Kelly felt her fight coming back.

Jeff stood and walked away. Kelly watched him as he opened the door to his walk-in closet and spun the dial on the safe in the wall. A few seconds later he dropped a piece of paper on the bed.

"What is this?" Kelly reached for the paper.

"It is the deed to the house on 29 Huckleberry Street. I own it."

"How did…? I didn'…This is not my signature."

Jeff smirked. "Darling, according to what I would say to a judge, you signed it over to me during one of your highs. You must have blacked out. Yet another reason the kids should be removed. You don't even remember going to the bank."

"You bastard!" Kelly scrambled to her knees and lunged at Jeff. He laughed as he grabbed her arms and pinned them behind her back. He put a little space between their bodies and gave a long perusal of her breasts.

"I always did love your body, sweetheart. You've put a few pounds on since the divorce but nothing a few months back at the gym won't take care of."

Kelly struggled to get out of his hold, but Jeff was

too strong. "Saturday is the wedding. Your mother can keep the girls at night and we can have this house to ourselves." Jeff released her arms and gave a tsk as he saw her clench her fists.

"I dare you. Remember, all I need to do is make a phone call and you lose everything. I don't mind adding an assault charge to the accusations."

Jeff walked away again. "Your clothes are hanging in your closet. I'll see you downstairs."

Kelly jumped from the bed and swung open her side of the master closet and turned on the light. She closed the door behind her and sank to the floor.

He'd won. Once again, Jeff Reisland held all the cards and there wasn't a damn thing Kelly could do about it.

Chapter Twenty-Nine

Finn sat in the guest bedroom with his binoculars. Shannon would be arriving at Kelly's house shortly under the guise of finalizing plans for the Fourth of July festivities. His sister must have rung the doorbell because he saw the two girls run through the kitchen with Kelly's mother following behind. He didn't see Kelly, nor did he notice any movement in the upstairs windows. When he saw Liv and Hannah return to their breakfast, Finn finally lowered the binoculars and expelled the breath he'd not realized he'd been holding.

The guest bedroom didn't have any furniture in it yet, except for the folding metal chair he'd been occupying more than any normal man should. He slumped back in it and rubbed his chest with the heel of his hand. He knew the heavy weight was due to stress.

He had always been a man of action. After his mother's death—aw, hell, who was he kidding? She'd committed suicide. After his mother's suicide, he'd thrown himself into his new job as a firefighter, continued going to school and became a paramedic and been big brother, father and mother to Kathleen. Sitting back and doing nothing was foreign to him. These past weeks, watching as the woman he cared about become a prisoner in her own home...

Cared about? No, it was so much more. From the moment she'd placed her icy hand into his, his heart had melted. Kelly Reisland was an enigma: strong and fiercely independent, yet all soft smiles and forgiving.

He'd been attracted to Kelly when he rescued her. He'd been intrigued with her when Shannon had invited her and her girl's over for a barbeque. But somewhere after that, somewhere between a slice of pizza, incredible sex, false accusations and pancakes, he'd fallen for her.

He heard Shannon downstairs. Finn stood and sprinted out of the room. He felt a renewed sense of urgency to help Kelly.

"Well? What did she say?" He sounded like a kid in middle school waiting to hear if the girl he liked, liked him back. Then his sister's expression stopped him short. "What's wrong?"

Shannon hadn't moved from her position with her back against the front door. "She wasn't home."

As unusual as that was, given how little freedom Kelly had these days, Finn braced himself. "Oookaaay?"

His sister cocked her head to the side and shrugged her shoulders. "Shawn, I'm sorry, but, Kelly's getting married."

"Excuse me?"

"Her mother said she wasn't home because she was off getting her marriage license. She and her ex-husband are getting re-married. On July Fourth."

The ache in Finn's chest returned. "Oh."

Shannon crossed the room and put her arms around him, but he didn't respond. "I'm sorry, honey. I know you care about her."

"How...? Why?" He couldn't get his thoughts together.

"Come on, Shawn, I'll make you coffee."

He followed his sister into the kitchen and leaned against the counter as Shannon dumped what remained in the coffee pot and started a fresh pot.

"He's been drugging her, Shannon. He put Ritalin in her coffee and God only knows what else he's been doing to her. How could she agree to marry him?"

"I don't know, Shawn. They have a history and he is the father of her children." She placed a steaming mug into his hands. "You haven't known her long. Maybe she still loves what's his name?"

"Jeff. His name is Jeff." Shawn bit out the name. "No.'

Shawn put his coffee on the counter and stood straight. "I'm not accepting it. I need to hear it from Kelly directly."

"Shawn, honey, maybe you shouldn't interfere."

"Maybe not. But I'm going to."

He waited until he saw all the lights go out at Kelly's house then waited an additional hour. With a stepladder and bolt cutters, he made swift work of reaching over the fence and disposing of the lock then opened the gate. The next morning, he watched from his perch until he saw the girls get ready to go outside and he let Guinness out. The good dog made straight for the open gate and headed into Kelly's yard, yipping and yapping as the girls chased him.

He hoped Kelly would be the one to come outside and waited at the gate when she exited her home.

She looked tired and had lost weight, if that was even possible, and she barely looked at him. He wanted to drink in the sight of her. He wanted to touch her, to hold her.

"I need to talk to you."

Kelly glanced back at the house. "We shouldn't be doing this?"

"What? Talking? Being neighborly? My dog got into your yard and the girls are having a great time. We're just exchanging pleasantries."

"Please, call Guinness home."

"You're afraid of him." Kelly's anxious glance to the house confirmed it.

"I heard you were getting married. Why? What does he have on you?"

"Finn, you have to go." She placed a hand on his chest to push him back through the gate and he took the opportunity to grab it and hold tight.

"Kelly, all you have to do is say the word and I will help you. Whatever it takes."

She finally looked at him and he saw the fear in her eyes, he saw the desperation. For a brief moment, he thought she'd say yes.

Instead, she pulled her hand from his and stepped away. "I have to do this." She took another step away as Jeff slid open the sliders off the kitchen. "Call him home, please."

Finn whistled for Guinness and his obedient dog ran passed them through the gate. He stepped back as Kelly closed the gate between them. He knew, without a doubt, a new lock would be in place before the day was over.

But he was far from done. Kelly may not have asked for help, but he'd received the confirmation he needed. Kelly didn't want to marry Jeff. She was being forced.

Shannon said Kelly was getting married on July

Fourth. That gave him two days.

Finn pulled out his phone and called work to request vacation time. He had a few ideas, some of which he would be better off not discussing with his brother. If he managed to save Kelly, a few minor legal infractions would be worth it.

****

Kelly avoided answering the phone all week. With her daycare closed for the week, she didn't need to make an effort to put a smile on her face for her employees or the children and their parents. But she had received messages from her two best friends. Jules called to plan their annual Boston weekend getaway, then Maddie called to say her boyfriend, Bryan, had made it official and asked her to marry him.

Normally, she would have responded immediately to both her friends, especially with Maddie's exciting but unsurprising news. But the last thing she wanted to discuss right now was upcoming nuptials.

If either Maddie or Jules got wind of her and Jeff re-tying the knot, they would both be on her doorstep to talk her out of it. But if she didn't marry Jeff, she would lose her girls.

She knew Jeff still drugged her, although not in an excessive amount to make her feel jittery or sluggish, but enough to keep drugs in her system in case she tried to back out.

Jeff still slept on the couch, keeping an eye on her. However, with her daycare closed for the week, he came back from work at lunch daily. She knew it was to keep tabs on her.

He strolled into the laundry room at twelve fifteen, where she was folding laundry, and gave her a possessive kiss. She knew it didn't matter to him if she didn't kiss him back. They would be married in two days and she knew her husband would have sex with her in order to get her pregnant. But she also knew he would be getting what he really wanted from someone else.

She would be his trophy, his arm candy to parade around the Country Club. When she got pregnant, he would dote on her in front of his friends, lavishing her with gifts. But it was all show. For Jeff, success included a wife and family along with a thriving business.

Kelly had defied Jeff two years ago when she had left him. Their divorce had been a slap in the face and had ripped an important status from him. She wasn't sure why it had taken him two years to force her to come back, but when Jeff put his mind to something, he didn't back down.

"What's for lunch, babe?" Kelly turned back to the laundry. "I guess it's whatever you find to make yourself. I already fed the girls and cleaned up."

Jeff pressed himself from behind and locked his hands around her wrists, stopping her from her task. This was one of the times she hated being short. Jeff seemed so much larger and stronger. Her heart leaped into overdrive, but Kelly tried hard not to let her fear show.

But instead of being angry, Jeff became amorous. "The girls are outside. How about I lock this door and we can feast on each other?"

"How about I send you back to work with a bloody nose?"

Jeff laughed at her but he stepped away. "I love it

when you're feisty. I came home to tell you to be ready for four o'clock. I'm taking you and the girls to Bella Bridal to choose your dresses."

Kelly stared at him. "Why? It's not like I'm walking down the aisle. We're having an outdoor wedding in the park surrounded by strangers."

"Did you think you would show up wearing something like that?" He gestured toward her denim shorts, which frayed at the hem and her tattered Pink Floyd tee. "Make sure you change before I get home."

Kelly didn't know how long she stood still after Jeff left, but she had twisted the shirt she'd been folding into a wrinkled mess.

She couldn't do this. She didn't want to marry Jeff again and be under his control. But how? She glanced out the window toward her neighbor's house.

Finn had offered help. But if she went to him, would it put him in danger? If she defied Jeff, he said he would ensure the girls would be taken from her and her life would be ruined with accusations.

But her life would be ruined if she married Jeff.

Kelly placed the wrinkled shirt into the dryer and walked out of the laundry room. She heard her mother singing to herself upstairs. The girls said hi as they came inside and went into the daycare, which they used as their personal playroom.

She stepped outside, being sure to close the sliding glass door quietly. Within seconds she was through the gate and knocking at Finn's door. The moment he spotted her through the glass, he rushed to unlock it.

"I need help."

The moment she said it, the emotions overwhelmed her. Finn grabbed her and pulled her into his arms and held her as the tears fell.

"I don't want to marry Jeff, but I have to. I'll lose my kids if I don't." She told Finn everything through her sobs. When she was done, she realized they were sitting in his living room, with her on his lap, his strong arms wrapped around her. His blue t-shirt wet at the shoulder from her tears.

"I'll help you. We'll figure it out together."

"Make love to me?"

She knew she'd shocked Finn at her request, but she wanted to be with him, wanted to feel safe and secure in his arms.

"Now?"

"I need you. Please, Shawn."

He brushed a tear from her cheek and looked at her for a long moment before he slowly brought his lips to hers. His mouth was tender, as he tasted her. His hands moved slowly as they moved to press her closer.

Kelly didn't understand the feelings that filled her as she opened her mouth to let her tongue tangle with his. She knew Finn took it slow, making sure this was what she truly wanted.

Her hands roamed over his broad chest. His biceps bulged as she felt him lift her from his lap. In a quick maneuver, they both lay lengthwise on the sofa, giving each other more access to explore each other. Hands slid under shirts, legs intertwined, as their mouths continued their own journey. Their tees disappeared and Kelly suckled at Shawn's nipple, eliciting a moan that melted her insides. Finn wasn't to be outdone, his fingers made quick work of disposing of her bra before he slid down to lavish her breasts with his hot mouth.

As she nibbled on his ear and made a trail down his

neck, Finn rolled onto his back and they both dumped to the floor. Their slow, easy pace picked up and they rushed to slide off the rest of their clothes.

Kelly reached down and stroked him while his hands and mouth feasted on her breasts. Then Kelly grasped his shoulders as Finn's kisses made their way down her abdomen and lower. His mouth worked magic as Kelly tightened in release. When he moved to slide into her, she was ready and met his thrusts in an equal rhythm.

"I love you, Kelly."

Kelly heard the words and cried. She wanted to say the words back, but she couldn't. She had been selfish in coming here. Shawn Finnigan loved her and by doing this, she had put him in danger. Jeff would find out. He always did.

She had come here to ask for help, but it had been an excuse. She'd wanted, needed this last moment with Shawn. She had to marry Jeff, because it was the only way to keep her daughters with her, and to keep Finn from any repercussions Jeff would dish out.

She left by the front door and walked the long way around the block to her home. Jeff's car was in the driveway, which meant her mother had called him to say she wasn't home.

The moment the front door closed he appeared from the living room.

"Where have you been?" She hated that Jeff never yelled.

"I went for a walk." She tried to push past him but he put an arm out to trap her against the door. Kelly looked at the arm, and while Jeff worked out regularly, his biceps didn't quite bulge like Shawn's did.

"For ninety minutes?"

Kelly shrugged. "I don't have a watch on. Is that how long I've been gone?"

"Where have you been?"

"A walk. Around." If she didn't give him more details, he would ask about Finn and she wasn't having that. "I walked down to the high school and ran the track, and then I sat for a while."

Kelly held her breath and prayed he would believe her lie. Jeff examined her clothes. She knew she was disheveled. Her hair had come out of the braid in a curly mess. It wasn't a far-fetched lie. She'd often run the track after they were married, but that stopped after having Hannah, and now she only had time to run on the treadmill.

"You didn't tell anyone where you were going. We were worried." His voice had dipped from demanding to controlling. She knew what needed to be said.

"I'm sorry. It won't happen again."

For a moment, Kelly thought Jeff was going to lean in to kiss her, but then he seemed to think better of it, probably thinking of her sweat from her run, and he stepped back.

"Go shower and we'll start our shopping early."

Kelly stepped into the hot spray and closed her eyes. She couldn't stop thinking about Finn. About his soft, tender kisses, his large hands cupping her breasts, his tongue dipping inside her.

Kelly felt the heat rise as her thoughts continued to her lover. And oh how the man was built. He was a powerhouse of muscles, large and firm in all the right places. Mostly, though, she thought of his beautiful, violet-colored eyes, as they'd deepened when he'd told her he loved her.

If she let herself, she could love him back, but she couldn't allow herself that emotion. Not now. Now, she had to do what was necessary to keep her girls, whatever the consequences.

Chapter Thirty

I C THEM. AT REVIEWING STAND.

Finn read the text from Kathleen and felt a mix of emotions. A part of him figured with the impending wedding, Kelly and the girls would not attend the parade and the plans he and his siblings had concocted would be for nothing.

ON IT.

The responding text from Shannon meant the first part of the plan was happening. His older sister and her kids would set up their chairs by Kelly and chat her up during the parade and ensure Kelly agreed to go to the park for the numerous activities set up for the kids. Finn allowed a touch of a smile. Very few could resist Shannon's powerhouse personality.

Finn paced inside Station One where he stayed out of sight. While this wasn't the house he was assigned to, this station adjoined the park where Phase Two would happen. Fingers crossed.

The crew and apparatus had emptied the station several minutes before, heading toward the parade line, leaving Finn alone in the cavernous tub room with too many thoughts.

What if Shannon couldn't convince Kelly back to the park? If she did, would they be able to separate Kelly from the crazy bastard of an ex? Could he actually stop her wedding from happening?

Finn looked at his watch. The parade started at the other end of Main Street and would meander its way past the firehouse and end at the park. If he listened closely he could hear drums in the distance.

The side door opened and Tony Tedeschi strolled in. Finn needed the distraction.

"Hey, brother, you doing okay?"

The two clasped hands and moved in for a quick brotherly hug. "Yeah, plans are moving forward."

He'd filled Tony in on his plans Tuesday night and by Wednesday they had a few other firefighters willing to participate in his hair-brained scheme. Tom had rallied a couple of his friends on the cop force to also lend a hand.

"You know I think you're crazy as hell to be doing this, right?"

"There's no doubt I've lost my mind, T. You don't need to be a part of this, though."

Tony laughed, the sound echoing in the empty room. "Are you kidding me? Shawn Finnigan in love? I wouldn't miss this for the world. I get to watch the fall of Father Finn."

"Fuck you." Finn chuckled but his stomach twisted in knots. The woman he loved was scheduled to marry another man in ten hours. A man who drugged her and manipulated her, but had money, political connections and the power to take Kelly's children away from her. Did he really think he would be able to convince Kelly to walk away?

"Seriously, bro, from what you told me, you need to watch your back."

Finn nodded as he watched a family set up lawn chairs on the sidewalk outside.

"She has to want to walk away, Finn. If she's not ready, it won't matter how hard you try to save her."

Finn turned back to his friend. "I know, but I have to try."

The next two hours were torture as he hid out in the firehouse. He was a fool, banking on a plan with more holes than Swiss cheese. The sound of the school marching bands moved closer, their music, keeping pace with the riotous beat of his thoughts.

Tony was right. Kelly needed to be the one to walk away, but if he could convince her she wasn't alone; that he would help her, maybe she would trust him.

So he waited until the next text.

GOOD TO GO.

That was his cue. Finn stepped out into the blazing sun, adjusted his Red Sox ball cap, slipped his shades on and headed toward the park. He and Tom had roped off a section of the park in the early hours. They had contacted their friends—cohorts—who'd arrived before the parade to set up grills and start the burgers and dogs cooking.

The cordoned off section was filled with firefighters and cops and their families, but Kelly and the dipshit she was with wouldn't know it until they were settled and being introduced.

The entire plan consisted of the guys keeping Dipshit talking about cars, Shannon would keep Mother Dearest occupied with all the kids at the public activities and he would sneak Kelly away. And, if Dipshit should spot them and try to intervene, it would be handy to be surrounded by police and firefighters who had his back. Yeah, the entire plan rested on strength of numbers. Cops and firefighters against one manipulative asshole.

When he spotted Kelly, Finn stopped in his tracks. She was beautiful. She wore a red sundress with wide straps, which plunged into a v-neckline where her sunglasses hung. A white floppy hat and red, white, and blue flip-flops completed the patriotic look.

Kathleen stood beside Kelly with her phone in hand. Shawn guessed his sister was showing off photos of her wedding dress and discussing her upcoming day. Probably not the best choice of topics today, but his siblings had succeeded in separating all the parties.

Finn caught a nod from Tony and watched as his crew shifted positions to block Dipshit's view as Finn made his way to Kelly. He slipped his hand into hers, clasped her fingers, and whispered. "Come with me."

He saw the smile light her eyes before fear settled back in.

"I can't."

Finn placed a finger to her mouth to shush her and tugged her. While she followed, Finn knew she kept glancing back as they made their way into the tree line. He pulled her deeper and deeper into the woods, until he felt certain they wouldn't be seen and then Finn tossed his hat to the ground and pulled Kelly in for a heated kiss full of want and need.

He heard her moan as she answered him. He tasted her fruity lip-gloss as his tongue found entrance. Their bodies melded together. Finn skimmed his hands up Kelly's bare arms, across her clavicle and to her face where he slowed his kisses.

No longer demanding, Finn gave his heart to Kelly with each touch, each breath. Kelly's hands moved down his back and slipped under his shirt, her fingernails scraped his bare skin and she grasped him, pulling him closer. The fly of his shorts strained as he pressed into her.

He wished they were completely alone, somewhere other than behind a few trees in a public park filled with families. He wanted nothing more right now than to wrap her naked legs around his waist and stake his claim.

He tasted her tears and moved to kiss the salty trail from her cheeks.

"Don't marry him."

She hiccupped on a sob.

"I have to."

Shawn weaved a finger through a wayward curl that had escaped Kelly's tight, thick braid. Her white hat lay at their feet by his ball cap.

"Press charges against him for drugging you. We already have a coffee can laced with Ritalin."

He felt Kelly's fingers curl into a fist at his waist, but still she shook her head. "It won't work. He knows too many lawyers and judges from the country club and from his shop."

"The cops know who he is. My brother said they've been watching him for a while."

Kelly pulled away and leaned back against a tree trunk. She looked tired. He could see the dark circles under her eyes, despite the attempt to conceal it with makeup.

Makeup. That's what was different about her today. He'd never seen her wear it before. His kisses had wiped away the pink of her lip-gloss, but he noticed the eye shadow, the thickness of her eyelashes, the hint of color on her cheeks that had nothing to do with their encounter. He brought her hand up to inspect it and found perfectly manicured nails.

"Your dress is beautiful, did you pick it out, or did he?" Finn tried to hold back the venom, but knew Kelly heard it when she let out a deep sigh and released his hand. She walked a few paces away. "He is controlling you. You know what he is doing and yet you won't let me help."

She whipped around, facing him again. "Jeff has always gotten what he wanted. He doesn't take no for an answer. For some reason he has decided he wants me and the girls back and he has made it impossible for me to say no."

Kelly wrapped her arms around her middle and pleaded with him. "If I don't marry him tonight I will lose my girls, my home, and everything I have worked toward with my business. My girls come first, can't you understand?"

"But at what cost, Kelly? You'll become a slave to his demands. You will lose yourself and how does that help Olivia and Hannah?" Finn moved to close the space between them. "I love you, Kelly. I'll do whatever it takes to protect you and the girls, give me the chance. Trust in me." He reached out his hand, hoping Kelly would take it.

But she didn't. She stood still, her arms around her waist. She had closed herself off to him. "I wish it were easy. I can't do this, Shawn. I know Jeff too well. I know the wrath that will follow if I defy him. Even now, being here with you ..."

"You're living in fear. It's not healthy. Think about your girls. Think about their life under Jeff's dictatorship."

He watched as she fought back tears. "I am, Shawn." It came out as a whisper, but he heard it. "He has the power to take Liv and Hannah from me, and if I defy him now, I won't be there to protect them."

She stepped back. "I have to go. Please, Shawn, if you care about me, you'll understand why I have to do this."

"Kelly…" She turned from him and walked away, her shoulders down. "I love you," he whispered, knowing she didn't hear him.

Kelly freshened up as best she could in the restroom. She used her sunglasses to hide her red eyes then stepped outside and walked slowly back to the picnic area. She saw Jeff's scowl immediately, before he pasted a grin on for the men around him. "There's my woman now." He moved toward her and planted a possessive kiss as he wrapped his arms around her waist. "I hate to cut this short, gentleman, but we have a wedding to attend this evening."

Kelly barely had a moment to say her goodbyes before Jeff herded the family toward his car. "Where were you?" He had a strong grip on her hand, keeping her close to his side.

"I went to the restroom."

Jeff snorted. "Don't lie. You were gone a long time."

"I ran into parents of my daycare children before I made it there. I stopped to chat."

"Where's your hat?"

Kelly lifted her free hand to her head, remembering her hat being knocked to the ground while Finn kissed her. "I—I must have forgotten it in the bathroom."

Jeff took his keys out of his pocket and pressed the

release button. He opened the rear door and Livvy scurried in to sit in the middle while Serena buckled Hannah into her car seat. She saw Jeff wince as he looked at the car seat. He had insisted they take his car because her van was an ancient death trap he wouldn't be caught dead in. However, that meant moving Hannah's car seat into his Lexus LS with all leather interior. He'd used a towel to try to protect the seat, but Kelly knew the indentations on the leather were silently killing Jeff. It made her smile.

"What's the smirk for?"

"Oh, for goodness sake, Jeff, stop being so paranoid." Kelly reached for the handle of the car but Jeff squeezed her other hand and stopped her.

"Did you forget everything I taught you?" Jeff reached out and opened the door for her and waited until she was settled. As he closed the door, she heard his name called and looked out the window to see the Mayor and his wife approach. Kelly sighed. The gentlemanly act was all for show to the public. She overheard as Jeff invited the couple to the gazebo that evening to watch the ceremony. Yes, it would figure he would want as many prominent members of Rocky Point society to attend as he could muster in such a short time.

Moments later Jeff slid into the driver's seat and started the ignition. It was obvious his encounter with the Mayor had turned his mood around. He turned to look at the three in the backseat. "So my little bridesmaids, let's go get pretty for tonight's wedding."

Livvy squealed in joy while Hannah said a gleeful, "Yay!" before she stuck her thumb in her mouth. Serena quickly chided the youngster and Jeff turned his attention back to her in the front seat.

Instead of reaching for the gears in the center, his hand reached over to skim across her bare knee. "Let's get remarried, wifey."

Kelly pushed his hand away and adjusted the hem of her dress to cover her legs before she stared out at the passing scenery.

She took deep breaths to stop the tears. Livvy and Hannah. This was for them. She could endure anything if it meant keeping them with her.

All their wedding clothes were at Jeff's house. He had insisted they get ready there because his home had more bathrooms. His cook, an elderly woman by the name of Gracie, had prepared sandwiches for them and had everything laying out when they arrived.

Kelly moved on autopilot as everyone ate, and then headed to take showers. Serena took charge of getting the girls ready while Kelly sat in the master bathroom at the vanity to apply her make up. Instead, she stared into the mirror.

Her hair had been washed, dried, and straightened, the sides pulled to the back and secured with a white clip. She'd lost weight over the past month and her face seemed shallow, her cheeks a bit more prominent. She added a bit more concealer under her eyes that looked back at her with an emptiness she felt to her soul.

She saw the outline of Jeff behind the glass blocks of the open shower. How many years had she sat in this same seat preparing for an evening out at the country club, or a night in Boston, or to go to an event Jeff insisted they attend?

How many times had she used makeup to hide the ravages of tears before she played the part of dutiful wife knowing her husband would have sex with the babysitter when he drove her home? And how many times had she allowed it because she knew he would be leaving her alone because he was getting his kicks elsewhere?

The water stopped and Kelly watched through the mirror as Jeff walked out as bare as the day he'd been born. In seconds he had wiped the moisture from his body and dropped the damp towel into a hamper before sauntering to her.

Once upon a time, Jeff's body had excited her. His confidence in himself to stroll naked had intrigued Kelly, who'd never thought herself a prude, but she had been raised by her grandparents and they'd always made sure she had dressed and behaved conservatively.

Jeff had awakened her sexual side in high school. They started dating middle of their Junior year and Jeff had taught her everything she knew about sex. She had kept it at a slow pace, though, which she knew frustrated the hell out of him. Over the next year she allowed more than a few kisses and him touching her breasts. He'd taught her how to perform oral sex but she had retained her virginity until prom night her senior year.

Jeff placed his hand on her robed shoulders and stared back at her in the bathroom mirror. "Finish up. We only have a half hour before we need to head back to the park."

Kelly nodded and picked up her lipstick as Jeff exited the bathroom.

She didn't remember much of the prom. Well, the early hours she did. She remembered the laughing and dancing with her friends, Maddie and Jules. The live band Jules' rich dad had arranged for the night. She remembered the slow dances with her boyfriend and his promises to make it a night to remember. Then they left in the limo he'd rented and the bottle of champagne they'd shared.

She remembered waking up naked on the mattress in the room above his father's garage the next day and the satisfied smile Jeff had on his face as he greeted her. By graduation she'd discovered she was pregnant and on the Fourth of July they had been married at the country club.

She'd been scared then, too, but for a different reason. She had done the one thing she had vowed not to do, which was to repeat her mother's mistake of becoming a teen mother. But at eighteen, she'd also been in love and believed she could make it work. Besides, she wasn't a drug addict like her mother, and that of course, was the biggest difference.

Kelly stood and turned her back on her memories and walked with a heavy heart into the bedroom. Jeff adjusted the cufflinks on his tuxedo. She assumed it was by some famous designer and Jeff would probably sneer at her for not knowing, but she didn't care.

The wedding dress he'd chosen for her was also by a famous designer, which in her mind didn't make the dress any better, just more expensive. But Jeff had insisted. Besides, when the wedding photo was posted in the morning paper, the designers' names would be listed as well. All part of the image, of course.

Jeff had insisted on a white dress, despite it being a second wedding, however Kelly had won when she'd asked for a short dress versus a long gown.

The dress was barely more than a sheath with a

lace overlay and a red ribbon at the waist. It was strapless, so Kelly dropped the robe and slipped the gown over her white thong. She knew Jeff watched, but it didn't bother her. Nothing did right now. She was numb to any emotion.

Olivia and Hannah became her mantra as she sat on the bed while Jeff slid strappy sandals on her feet, then she followed her soon-to-be husband downstairs.

She told her girls how beautiful they looked in their matching blue and white dresses. She applied pink lip-gloss to their lips. Then watched as her mother packed the girls into the Lexus and Jeff escorted her to a waiting limousine.

"Would you like a drink?" Jeff offered.

Kelly saw the bottle of champagne chilling and wanted to choke. "No."

"Suit yourself." Jeff slid open a door and grabbed a bottle of cognac and poured a glass.

Kelly looked at Jeff and saw past the polished exterior. Jeff was devious, a manipulator. He had been a spoiled rich kid of parents who'd had him late in life and didn't know how to say no. Jeff had done well in school but had excelled in football where he'd been the center of attention. His privileges had given him access to drugs and women and Jeff had indulged in both with complete abandon.

On her twenty-first birthday, Jeff had brought her to Foxwoods and introduced her to gambling. At first he'd stayed with her while she dabbled in the slots, then he'd joined a poker game and she saw a different side of him. The stakes were high and she watched her husband drink and throw money into the pot. At first it was exhilarating watching him win, then lose, then win big again. He would kiss her, tell her she was his good luck charm, then he would drop ten thousand dollars. She'd gone to their room for a while but eventually returned to check on her husband, only to find a scantily clad blonde pressed to his side. She watched from a distance as Jeff won another round, pulled the pot toward him, and then grabbed the bimbo for a heated kiss.

"You've been quiet."

"What do you want me to say, Jeff?" Kelly looked out the window. "I don't want to marry you, but I will because it's the only way to keep my children. Isn't that enough?"

"Our children, Kelly. Say it."

"Fine. Our children." Kelly nearly spat the words out.

"You took our children from me, Kelly, and I have lost out. Hannah barely knows me."

Kelly scoffed. "Hannah barely knows you because you've cancelled visitation after visitation. You're as much to blame on that score."

"Don't push me, Kel." Jeff's tone turned icy, but Kelly disregarded the warning. "Or what, Jeff? What more can you do? You've already threatened to take my children away from me. You've stolen my house and want to sell it. You're forcing me to close my business and to play the dutiful wife while you continue to have affairs. There's nothing more you can do."

Kelly laid it all out to Jeff calmly. There was no heat, no passion. Only complete defeat. She was done fighting. Jeff had won.

Jeff tossed back another drink before speaking. "Hate me, if you want, but you should be thanking me.

You sink all your money into taking care of other people's children while your own are just part of the crowd."

"They most certainly are not," Kelly spat back at him.

"Shut up and listen," Jeff demanded. "You drive them around in a vehicle that should be in the scrap yard. They have no clue about place settings and proper behavior at a restaurant and the only clothes they own are suitable for playing only. And Hannah sucks her thumb. Why in the world do you allow such behavior?"

"There is nothing wrong with how I raise my children. They are..."

"OUR children, Kelly. They are my children, too. They are Reisland's and the Reisland's have a long standing in Rocky Point."

"And I suppose you want them groomed to become wives of the doctors and lawyers who are members of the country club, too."

"With money comes a certain responsibility, Kelly. We discussed this many times when we first got married. It is our duty to teach Olivia and Hannah early so they don't bring embarrassment to our family name."

The limo stopped on the side road by the park. Kelly looked out at all the families gathered with their lawn chairs and blankets as they waited for the fireworks to start.

"Stay here. The driver will let you know when to get out." Jeff exited the vehicle. He walked to his Lexus and Kelly watched as he led Serena and the two girls to the gazebo. He shook hands with a man Kelly assumed was the Justice of the Peace.

The door opened and the driver reached out a hand

and Kelly stepped out.

People were starting to notice the bride, her, and the ceremony that was about to take place. Kelly took a step and stumbled on the rocky terrain.

"Are you okay, Miss?"

Kelly looked at the driver and noticed he was about the age of her grandfather. He had a kind, weathered face, and a paunch stomach beneath his suit.

"I think I want to throw up."

The man smiled gently. "Wedding nerves. You'll be fine, dear." He reached into the car and then stood back up to hand her a bouquet of flowers. Kelly took them, thankful for something to hold in her slick hands.

Music began to play. The Wedding March. Kelly took a step forward, then a second. The music grated on her. They should be playing something more haunting, like the death march.

She took another step and felt the crowds closing in. This was wrong. She shouldn't be here. She had escaped Jeff's hold on her once, if she went back, could she survive?

Marrying Jeff was like committing a long, drawn out suicide. Shawn had offered her a way out. He had said he would help her. Why hadn't she taken him up on his offer?

Shawn loved her. He loved her girls. He was kind, giving, helpful, and forgiving. She loved how he interacted with her girls and she'd seen him with his family. Shawn Finnigan was everything good. If she put her trust and her heart in Shawn, she knew he would protect both with his life.

If only she'd said yes to him earlier. Instead she had sent him away and ruined all chances of a fulfilling life.

She'd made her choice. But had it been the right one?

No, not the right choice. She'd made the choice she felt trapped into taking.

She took another step closer to the gazebo. It had been covered in tiny white lights and sparkled as the sun settled behind the trees. Olivia and Hannah both fidgeted, excitement evident in their participation in their parent's wedding. Jeff put out a hand to tell them to stop. She mentally heard him scolding them for acting out in public.

Another step forward. She averted her eyes, blinking back the tears, and spotted him in the crowd. Shawn was here. She blinked again, afraid she'd only imagined him.

No, it was him. There was only about ten feet until she reached the gazebo. Ten feet until Jeff would take her hand in marriage, again.

****

Shawn couldn't help himself. He had to see Kelly again, even if it meant watching her marry another man. She was a vision in white. The strapless dress did amazing things to accentuate Kelly's breasts and the red satin seemed to show how incredibly skinny she was.

Tony put a hand on his shoulder. "Don't do this to yourself, Finn."

"Look at her, T, she doesn't want this. Look at her face. She's scared shitless."

"But she made her choice. She's got her reasons." Tony tightened his hold on his shoulder. "Come on, Finn, I'll take you home. Don't watch this."

His friend was right. This was torture. Every step

Kelly took toward her ex-husband was a knife-jab to the heart.

Jesus, Mary, and Joseph, his father had been right all along. Love was the Devil's invention. He dangled something so good and pure in front of him, then snatched it away, leaving nothing but pain and heartache in its wake.

He should walk away right now. But where would he go? Home? And stare at the white fence separating his yard from Kelly's? Not likely. To a bar? He'd already had several beers today, but if he walked into a bar he'd most likely start drinking and never stop. Hell, maybe he could get a stool next to his dad's. They could toast the Devil as they tossed a few back.

Finn couldn't tear his eyes away, though. His feet were planted like cement as he watched Kelly take one slow, agonizing step after another. Then she turned her head toward him and his heart gave an extra beat.

There was a glimmer of tears in her eyes and he felt her pain. She looked away but only for a moment and then she looked back at him and he knew this was the moment.

"Trust me." He said the words softly and knew she couldn't actually hear them, but prayed she could read his lips enough in the fading sunlight to know what he said.

She looked forward but she stopped moving. He saw her shoulders straighten and calmness ease her features. She looked at him and simply said, "Yes." Then she turned and ran.

Shawn pushed through the crowd, trying to catch up with her. He heard Jeff shouting Kelly's name, but he didn't dare look back to see if the man gave chase.

The crowd tittered with the gossip but he heard a large group cheer for him and knew his family and friends were there to witness Kelly's escape. He spotted the bride heading toward the street. He broke through the crowd and met up with her as she reached the sidewalk.

He felt a hand grab his arm and swung, ready for a fight with the abandoned groom, only to find Tony shoving his truck keys at him.

"It's over there. Go." Tony pointed five cars down and Shawn nodded as he and Kelly raced to safety.

He pulled out into the main street, careful of pedestrians as they headed to watch fireworks. Finn glanced over at Kelly to find her staring ahead, her face ashen.

"I did it. I ran away. Oh, my, goodness, what did I do? My girls, I left my girls behind. He's going to take them from me."

Finn reached over to take Kelly's hand. As soon as he could safely do so, he'd find a place to stop, but for now, at least, he had Kelly with him and that was all that mattered.

****

Kelly watched as they drove past street after street, taking her further from her two girls. What had she done? She had made the wrong choice. What kind of mother was she to abandon her children and leave them behind while she ran away with a man she'd only met a couple months ago?

"Pull over. Pull over." Kelly released the seat belt she didn't remember putting on in the first place, and reached for the door handle. She had to get out. Now.

"Whoa. Kelly. Stop."

She felt a hand grabbing her arm, pulling her back

and she desperately tried to get free.

"…Got … to … go…. Girls."

The truck came to a stop and Kelly stumbled out onto the sidewalk. She didn't know where she was. Tears streamed down her cheeks as she clutched her chest and sank to the ground.

"You need to breathe, love." Finn's gentle voice penetrated through the loud roar in her ears. His hands were warm as they lifted her face to look at him.

"That's it. Look at me. I'm going to put your hands over your mouth. I want you to breath into your hands. Slow breaths. Relax."

She didn't know how long he talked to her. A minute? Five? It seemed like forever, but eventually she calmed down enough to realize they both sat on the sidewalk. She lowered her hands and took a steadying breath.

As she looked around, Finn slid his fingers over her wrist, taking her pulse as she stared up into the darkening sky.

"I need to find my girls."

"We will." Finn's voice was calm and steady and she believed him.

Kelly rubbed at the tightness in her chest with the heel of her hand and then gave a nearly hysterical laugh.

"You probably think I'm weak and stupid. Every time we get together, I'm either having a panic attack, or I'm sick, or crying. Jeff is right. I am a mess. I … "

"Stop. Just stop." Finn swung her into his arms on the ground and held her tight. "Don't think about that asshole and don't lump me in with him."

Fresh tears welled. "I'm sorry. I didn't mean …"

"Shhh. Let's get something clear. I love you. I think you are beautiful and amazing. You love your children more than anything and were willing to marry a man who… Oh, I can't say what I really want to in mixed company, but suffice it to say, you were extremely brave to run from him today."

"You don't understand, Finn. I ran, but because I ran I will lose everything. He's going to take my girls from me. And my house. And business. He's been drugging me to use as proof I'm an unfit mother."

Another wave of panic was building but she didn't know how to stop it. She pulled from Finn's embrace and stood quickly but a wave of dizziness had her grabbing for him as he stood up beside her.

"Steady." Finn pulled her against his chest and Kelly breathed in his scent. Goodness, how could someone actually smell of strength? And security? She let herself melt into his arms. She could hear his heartbeat. Steady and sure.

"Your oxygen levels are still off from hyperventilating, you'll be fine in a moment. Let's get you back into the truck."

Kelly let Finn settle her into the seat. He pulled the seat belt around and, leaning over her, he fastened it. Then, he locked his lips to hers, giving her a deep, deep kiss, taking her breath away again.

When he pulled away, he gave a slight grin. "There. Now you have color back in your face."

Kelly stared at him in silence as he closed the door and walked around to the driver's side and slid in beside her.

"Feeling better?"

"Um. Yes. A bit." Actually, she felt disoriented,

but now she wasn't sure if it was from the earlier attack or the toe-curling kiss.

"Good. Now, let's go find your children."

"I'm scared. You don't know what Jeff is capable of."

Finn snorted. "I've watched as he has kept you secluded, drugged your coffee, and brought your mother in to help him. I'm not letting anything else happen to you."

"I did stop drinking the coffee, and taking the vitamins, but Jeff kept finding ways to get the drug into me. He said if I didn't marry him, he was going to say I was a drug addict and use that to take the girls."

"Well, if it's any consolation, Tom said the police have already been watching him. He wouldn't tell me for what, but I don't think you have anything to worry about."

"He has the deed to my home. I don't know how, but my signature was forged turning the house over to him."

"Holy shit, the man is conniving. How did you ever end up with him in the first place? Never mind, I don't want to think about it."

"I often wondered if Jeff drugged me at our Prom, because I don't remember having sex with him. We drank. I remember drinking. And I woke up next to him in the morning. Six weeks later, we were planning our quickie wedding."

"Bastard. I'd like to put my hands around his neck and squeeze until his eyes pop out."

They turned the corner and Kelly could see her home ahead. The Lexus was in the driveway. The knot tightened in her chest again.

"I have to do this, Shawn. I need to be strong, but I am so scared."

"We will do this together, Kelly. You are not alone."

Kelly looked at Shawn Finnigan and knew she loved him. He was the man she had dreamed of all her life. A man she could depend on in a time of crisis. He would love her children like his own. Hell, he'd love her girls more than their father ever could, as Jeff loved himself first, and his stature in the community a close second.

She wiped her clammy hands on the white dress. Despite the warmth of the July evening, a chill settled in her bones.

Running away from her wedding had been the right thing to do. She'd won a small battle in her fight for her life back, but she had a much bigger war to settle.

Finn parked the truck in the driveway. She was done being a victim. It was time to kick her ex-husband from her home and to protect her children from the man they called their father, but who was nothing more than a narcissistic son of a bitch.

Before Finn could come around, she'd already opened the door and jumped out of the truck. "Let's do this."

Finn smiled at her and took her hand in his as they walked into her home, together.

Chapter Thirty-One

"Well, well, well, look who decided to come home."

Kelly took a steadying breath as Jeff greeted her at the door, a scotch in his hand. He had unbuttoned his tux jacket and his bow tie hung loosely around his neck.

A disheveled Jeff was a pissed off Jeff.

"And it is MY home. Thank you for dropping off the children. You can go now." Kelly gave herself kudos for the calm delivery and major points for being able to stop Jeff in his tracks for once.

Jeff took a menacing step toward her and Finn stepped between. "Don't."

Height-wise, the men weren't far apart. Physically, they both worked out. But Jeff worked out in order to keep his appearance. Finn used his strength at his job daily. There was no doubt, in Kelly's mind at least, who would be the victor if it came down to it.

Jeff took another sip of his drink then sauntered into the kitchen. "I didn't drop off the kids, dear. Serena is helping them pack. They're coming home with me."

Kelly forced herself to stay calm. "I don't think so. I was awarded physical custody of the children. They stay here."

"You abandoned your children at a park in front of a crowd of hundreds so you could run away with your lover. I think any judge would grant me custody."

"I didn't abandon anyone. My children were left in the care of my mother. They arrived with her and they left with her."

"Your mother is a junkie and you have drugs in your system. Neither of you are fit to watch those children."

"Drugs you forced on me."

Jeff shrugged. "Can't be proved."

Damn him. He still believed he had the upper hand. Kelly glanced at Finn as he stood by her side. She knew Finn wanted to intervene, and would if things got physical, but this was her battle and she had to do this.

"The children stay but it is time you left my house."

Jeff leaned back against the counter and crossed one ankle over the other.

He was enjoying this. The more she argued, the more he believed he won. The man was a freaking sociopath.

"Sorry, Kelly, but I have a deed to this house which says it belongs to me. I am not going anywhere."

"Let's face it, Jeff. I left you standing at the altar, in front of a crowd including the Mayor and reporters. Your name will be plastered on the news tonight and in the papers tomorrow. If I call the police now, they will see you as nothing more than a jilted groom causing trouble."

She caught the slight tightening of his fingers into a fist and knew she'd touched a nerve. He tossed back the rest of the scotch and gently placed the glass on the counter.

"Have another one, Jeff. When the police show up, they'll see you've been drinking, too."

She caught Finn in her peripheral vision. He still stood back, but she could see he was ready to step in if Jeff lost his cool.

"You won't call the police."

Kelly crossed her arms and raised an eyebrow, waiting to hear more. Instead of answering her immediately she noticed his gaze had gone to her chest.

Crossing her arms while wearing a strapless gown had pushed her breasts together, and the bastard was turned on. Finn took a step closer and Kelly uncrossed her arms in order to put a hand out to stop Finn from stepping in.

"Why won't I call the police?"

"What do you think will happen with the girls while we end up in a custody battle that includes a drug charge?"

Kelly drew in a sharp breath and knew Jeff caught it.

"That's right. Olivia and Hannah will end up in the system and your daycare will be shut down immediately."

"Are we being sent away?"

Kelly jumped at the sound of Olivia's voice as she stepped down the stairs.

"No, of course not." Kelly rushed to assure her daughter.

"Well, actually, Olivia, that's not true. If your mother continues with her current course of actions, the police might come and take you and your sister away."

"Enough!" Finn stepped forward.

"Jeffrey!" Kelly spun toward her daughter, saw her trembling, and went to reach for her. Olivia stepped back and rushed back upstairs.

"You bastard. You son of a bitch."

Finn pulled her to his side before she could swing her arm and hit her ex-husband. She struggled but Finn whispered in her ear.

"If you hit him, he'll use an assault charge. Be calm."

Serena came down the stairs and looked around. "What did you say to Livvy? She's hysterical."

"Are the girls finished packing, Serena?" Jeff never stopped looking at Kelly as he spoke to her mother. His expression held a look of victory.

"Mother," Kelly looked away from Jeff and down the hall toward Serena. "Did you forge my name on the deed to the house?"

Ah, the guilty glance to Jeff said it all. She didn't need to see Serena's hands clasp and unclasp and she tried to find the right words.

"Was it the day you came back here high as a kite?" Serena gave a barely noticeable nod. "What did Jeff give you, Mom? What was your drug of choice? Cocaine?"

"Shawn, I think I will call the police. Let's start with your brother, because I bet my smug ex-husband still has a stash of drugs in his house, perhaps in the wall safe in his master closet?"

The lack of movement from Jeff proved she was on the right track. And the smug look he'd been sporting disappeared.

"Mother, if we had to go to court, whose side would you be on? Would you testify against Jeff?"

Kelly caught another glance between her mother and her ex-husband. Fear from one, a smirk from another.

"Oh, mom, he's blackmailing you, isn't he?"

"I'm sorry, Kelly." Her mother hung her head. "I am so sorry. I was high. I didn't know what I was doing. He has pictures of… of…"

"Shawn, call your brother. I want this bastard out of my house, and out of my life."

"Are you sure?" Finn, reached into his pocket and pulled out his phone.

"I'm sure. If he is ruthless enough to drug me, and give cocaine to my mother and whatever other vile thing he did, what will he do to my girls, as they get older? I will fight whatever battle I have to with the courts to get full custody. And if that means the battle starts now, then so be it."

As Shawn called his brother, Kelly walked over to Jeff. "I suggest you leave now. Maybe you will have time to get rid of your stash of drugs before the cops show up at your house."

"I'll leave, for now, but this is not over between you and me."

"There is no 'you and me', Jeff. There hasn't been in a long time."

"What? You think what you have with lover boy is going to last? It's nothing more than a flash in the pan. I was your first, babe, and I am the father of your children, we will always be connected. I'm not going anywhere."

Kelly thought of one last thing. She lifted her hand and removed the diamond, shoving it at Jeff.

"Tom is on the way along with a sector car." Finn moved behind Kelly and put a hand on her shoulder. She stepped back and pressed her back against his chest.

Jeff gave a snort then walked past Serena who avoided eye contact with him.

When the door closed behind him, Serena burst into tears. "I am sorry, Kelly. I messed up. Please, forgive me."

Kelly sighed. "Mom, I have a feeling there is a lot more to this than what I know. We'll talk later. But first, I need to check on Olivia and Hannah before the police show up here."

"I'll do it." Serena wiped her tears. "It's the least I can do."

Kelly turned and wrapped her arms around Finn and welcomed the feel of his strong arms as they pressed her closer.

"Thank you."

"For what? I didn't do anything."

"Yes, you did. You let me fight this battle. I saw how much you wanted to step in but you didn't. I needed to do it myself. I needed Jeff to know he couldn't manipulate me anymore."

"It's not over, Kelly. We're getting the police involved and there are going to be a lot of questions and a court battle."

"You said you love me."

Kelly could tell her change of topic surprised Finn.

"I did. More than once."

"I haven't said the words back, because I was scared. I couldn't say them when I felt trapped in a relationship I couldn't escape."

Finn ran a hand over her hair then moved to settle along her cheek. Kelly moved her head to rub into its warmth.

"And now?"

Kelly looked up at Finn, into his violet eyes, the color of a summer storm, and took refuge.

"Now? I'm still scared. The feelings I have for you are different from any I have felt in the past. When I am with you, I feel safe and secure. There is a part of me that becomes more self-confident. There is this peace within me. Well, when I'm not lusting after your body."

Finn laughed and Kelly squeezed him close, slightly embarrassed she'd let those words out. "Good, because I certainly lust after yours, too."

Kelly kissed Finn. Perhaps she intended it to be a brief touching of lips in the middle of expressing her heart, but brevity wasn't meant to be at that moment.

The stress of the day melted away as the kiss heated. Finn's arms wrapped around her, lifting her off her feet. He maneuvered them out of the kitchen and into her office, closing the door behind them, but his mouth never left hers.

Kelly's hands swept under Finn's shirt, and her fingers explored the hair on his chest. Finn's hands moved up her waist and she felt his fingers run along her skin, following the fabric of her strapless dress. His lower half pushed her against the wall.

Oh, yes, the lust was quite obvious. His mouth released hers to travel down her neck then to follow the path of his fingers across the crest of her breasts.

He rocked his pelvis and Kelly wanted nothing more than to slide her dress up and wrap her legs around Finn's waist. But the hum of an engine and a car door closing ended their fast and furious make-out session.

Finn stepped away and gave her one last light kiss. "To be continued."

Kelly let out a sigh and straightened her dress. She put her hands to her cheeks, knowing they would be red, and her lips swollen. She gave Shawn a shaky laugh as he took her hand as they went to greet the police officers who had arrived with his brother.

Chapter Thirty-Two

Jeff arrived at home only to find a black Lincoln waiting in his driveway.

Shit. Bad news.

The two bouncers who stepped out of the front seat put more of a fear into him than the thought of police arriving to search his home for cocaine. The rear door of the vehicle opened and a short, balding man got out.

In a fist-fight, Jeff would beat the weasel looking runt in a single pop—which was why the man never went anywhere without his bodyguards.

But Jeff never showed fear. He pulled the Lexus to a stop and got out to greet his visitors.

"Hello, gentlemen."

"I'm not here for pleasantries, Riessland."

"I didn't think you were, Santoro." Jeff moved to stand in front of his car but didn't move any closer to the trio.

"I understand your wedding didn't work out so well today."

Jeff shrugged. "Not exactly."

Santoro lit a cigarette and took a long drag. "I was under the impression your wife would help pay your debt? Now, what's the plan?"

"You can have this." Jeff pulled Kelly's diamond ring from his pocket."

"Do I look like a fucking pawn broker?" Santoro

gave a nod to Goon One who stepped forward and sent one fist deep into his rib cage.

Jeff struggled to catch his breath.

"I'm done waiting, Reisland. Just because your payday left you at the altar, doesn't change anything. I want the remaining thirty thousand in one week."

Jeff went inside. Hatred filled his body. This was all that bitch's fault. She would pay for ditching him today. She would pay for making him look like a fool.

****

Kelly remained calm as she spoke with the officers. The moment they walked in, Olivia stormed down the back stairs and out the slider to the back yard, screaming they weren't going to take her away.

It broke Kelly's heart to have to wait to talk to her daughter, to reassure her, to hold her. She'd also sent Hannah outside, hoping to spare her from overhearing as she sat at the table, describing her ordeal with her ex-husband to the police.

Finn explained how he stole the coffee and Tom used a favor to have it analyzed at the police lab, discovering the Ritalin.

"What about the vitamins?" Finn asked, and Kelly stood to get those from the cabinet. "I don't think those are multi-vitamins. I bought a bottle to check and they look nothing alike."

"I'm not sure what else he may have been using," Kelly explained, handing over the bottle. "But I believe there is more."

"There is." Serena stood and walked over to the fridge, taking down a cookie jar from the top. She removed a bag from inside. "He had me crush these into your tea at night. He said they would help you relax."

"What was your part in this, Ma'am?" The officer gave Serena a stern look.

"Jeff called me and told me Kelly was run down and getting sick. He said he'd made a mistake and should never have let her leave. They belonged together. He asked me to come and help him win her back.

"She was sick when we arrived. I believed Jeff. I thought he was helping her by giving her sleeping pills. I didn't know he was also drugging her during the day. And then…"

Serena stopped.

"And then?" The officer probed? But Serena refused to go on.

"He gave my mother cocaine and blackmailed her into forging my name on the deed to this house and turning the house over to Jeff. There's more, but she won't discuss it."

Hannah came to the door. "Mommy?"

"Yes?"

"Olivia climbed the tree again. She said she is never coming down and she's crying."

Kelly sent a pleading look to the officers while Finn stood, giving her a reassuring squeeze on the shoulder. "I'll check on her."

"Mrs. Riessland," the officer started.

"Kelly. Please call me Kelly." She seriously needed to consider changing her name back to Stanick.

"Kelly. I suggest you go to court Monday and file a restraining order and contact your attorney to start the process for a custody hearing."

"Yes, I will."

"Since your ex-husband has left the premises, taking the report is all we can do tonight. If he shows up again, give us a call."

"Okay. Thank you." Kelly watched as Tom exited the house with the two officers then she went outside to check on Olivia.

A feeling of déjà vu flowed through her as she spotted her daughter high on the limbs of the oak tree. Dusk had turned to darkness and Kelly shivered in the chill of the night air.

The last time Olivia climbed the tree Kelly had been wearing jeans and had climbed up after her. The short, white, wedding dress she wore now was a far cry from the jeans. Besides, her previous rescue had not been completely successful.

Finn stood below and spoke gently to her daughter, and love swelled in her heart. She still hadn't said those words to him, yet. She'd meant to earlier, but they'd become distracted.

"Dad said if mom called the police they would take us away. I don't want to go away." Olivia said to Finn through a deep sob.

"The police are gone and you are still here. You are not going anywhere." Finn explained.

"But mom called them. She was trying to send us away."

"Liv, honey," Kelly stepped forward to look up at her daughter's shadowy figure above her. Finn put his arm around her waist, and Kelly felt like they were one unit. "There is a lot of grown-up things going on right now, and I know it is very confusing to you. I did call the police but it had nothing, nothing, to do with sending you and Hannah away.

289

"I will sit down with you and Hannah and explain what I can, but before I can, I need you to come down from the tree so I know you are safe. I want to sit with you, and talk with you, and hug you, but you have to come down here first."

There was a long silence from above. She heard a sniffle.

"Do you pinky-swear promise you are not sending us away?"

"I pinky-swear promise and any other kind of promise you want me to make. Please, Livvy, come down."

Again, Kelly waited during another long silence. "Mom?"

"Yes, Olivia?"

"It's too dark. I'm scared to come down."

Finn let out a chuckle. "Well, guess what I own? A ladder. Give me a minute, Liv, and we can have a repeat of the day we met."

When Olivia was once again on the ground, Kelly wrapped her daughter in a huge hug and pulled her to sit as she rocked her back and forth on her lap.

"I love you so much, Olivia." Her little girl curled into her and cried.

****

Finn stood looking at mother and daughter for a few minutes before he looked around the yard. Serena stood by the sliders, still wringing her hands. That woman had a lot to account for, but he had a feeling she wasn't going to stick around for long, hoping for her daughter's forgiveness. She was the type to run.

"Where'd Hannah go?"

Kelly's head snapped up and did a search around

the yard as well. With Olivia still on her lap, he motioned for them to stay. "I'll find her."

He walked toward the house. "Did Hannah go inside?"

Serena shook her head. "I don't think so. I didn't see her come in."

Finn brushed passed Serena and called for Hannah as he searched the house. Daycare area. First floor. Upstairs to the bedrooms. A glow out the window had him brushing away the curtains.

"Shit!"

Finn grabbed his phone and called the Rocky Point Fire Alarm office.

"Sealy, this is Finn. I got a working fire. My home."

"Okay, Finn. Working fire. The guys are on the way."

Kelly and Olivia were running toward the house as he exited. "Your house is on fire."

"I know." He stopped and calmly looked at Kelly. "I didn't find Hannah. I need you to look for her here. I'll go let Guinness out and see if she is with him."

He saw the fear in Kelly's eyes but she nodded before he sprinted toward the gate he'd left open when getting the ladder. He slowed down long enough to assess the fire. It wasn't coming from the roof, or from one window, or one area. No, the fire circled the perimeter of the house, and trailed the fence line out the front gate.

God Damn Son of a Bitch had set his house on fire. Finn opened the back door to the garage and entered, calling out for Guinness. Finn's spare set of turnout gear sat in a corner. He grabbed the coat, slipping it on as well as his helmet. He flipped on the attached flashlight and entered the house. He called out again for his dog, and then yelled for Hannah as he systematically searched the first floor. He heard sirens approaching.

The smoke was getting thicker, like black cotton candy. He knew he should get out of the house, but not knowing if Hannah was inside kept him moving up the stairs.

Again, he called out for Guinness, surprised he didn't hear his dog at all. The flashing lights out front let him know the crew had arrived. Two more rooms to search. He coughed. It was getting harder to breathe. He wished for his breathing apparatus.

If he went outside now, he'd be ordered to stay out. Where was that curly-haired, miniature of Kelly? He'd finished searching the last bedroom and sank to his knees as he went back into the hallway.

He hadn't found Hannah. After everything Kelly had gone through, he failed her when she needed him most. He made it to the stairs and rolled down before the smoke overtook him.

****

Kelly and Olivia stood at the open gate between their yard and Finn's, watching as the flames climbed the walls. Kelly had already searched her home and didn't find Hannah. Could she have gone into Finn's home? Had she seen the fire and went to search for the dog on her own?

The moment the firefighters arrived, Kelly ran forward and told them Finn was inside looking for her daughter.

Then she was ordered to get on the other side of the

fence and stay there.

It was the hardest thing she had ever done, and it had been a hell of a day to begin with, as she stood, not knowing if her daughter and the man she loved were inside the flaming inferno of a house.

Kelly spotted a shadow at the far end of the yard. Guinness's doghouse. Was the dog outside? In his house?

"Stay here, Liv," Kelly ordered and started across the yard. The heat coming from the house was intense and Kelly stayed as close to the fence as she could.

"Hey, what are you doing?"

A firefighter moved to block her path.

"The dog. I think he's over there." Kelly tried to get by, but the firefighter stopped her.

"Get behind the fence. I'll get the dog."

"But ..."

"This is not up for debate. Move back."

Kelly did what she was told, but watched as the firefighter went to check on the dog. Sure enough, with some coaxing, Guinness came out but refused to move away from the shelter.

The firefighter leaned into the doghouse and a second later, he stood back up with Hannah in his arms. Kelly once again stepped across the fence line and ran to get her daughter and pull her into her arms.

As the firefighter handed Hannah to her, he spoke again. "Listen, they took Finn by ambulance, I thought you'd want to know."

Kelly nodded. "Thank you." She walked the girls back to their house and gathered them to her in a huge hug.

"It's been a long day. I need to go see Finn at the

hospital. Will you stay here with Gram?"

Hannah clung to her neck and refused to let go. Serena stepped forward. "I don't think they want to be away from you right now. I'll go with you and help with the girls."

Kelly looked at Olivia's tear-streaked face, and Hannah's ashen features. "Okay. Can you grab me a sweatshirt? I haven't had a chance to change."

Kelly managed to get to the hospital without being stopped for her speeding. Hannah refused to walk, so Kelly carried her youngest with her into the emergency room, the young girl's arms practically strangling her neck. Olivia was surprisingly quiet as she walked beside her mom.

She spotted Tom, Shannon, and Kate and went to check in with them.

"Shawn is fine, Kelly," Tom said as she got closer. While she heard the words, she didn't think she would believe it until she saw Finn for herself. "A bit of smoke inhalation."

"Can I see him?"

Tom nodded. "Dad's in with him right now, but when he comes out you can go in."

Shannon reached for Hannah. "Hi, sweetheart, do you want to sit with me so your mom can visit Shawn?"

Hannah shook her head and burrowed deeper into Kelly's neck.

"She won't leave me. She hid in Guinness's doghouse while Finn's house was on fire. She hasn't said much either."

Tom motioned toward the chairs. "Have a seat, will you?"

He waited until they were all seated and then he

started talking to Hannah softly.

"I've seen you with Guinness. He's a great dog, isn't he?"

Hannah nodded.

"Did you know Guinness was outside when you went to Shawn's house?"

Hannah shook her head and put her thumb in her mouth.

"No? What made you go next door?"

Hannah looked at her mom and Kelly gave her a reassuring squeeze.

"Finn left the gate open when he got the ladder. I wanted to see Guinness and he was already outside. He brought a ball to me and I threw it and then we ran around the yard."

"Did you see how the house got on fire?"

Hannah nodded and put her thumb back in her mouth.

Tom smiled. "You are not in any trouble, Hannah. I promise you."

"I hid when I saw him come into the yard. Guinness barked at him and he kicked him hard. He poured something around the house and then it was on fire."

Kelly bit her lip. She felt so bad for her little girl. The poor darling was so scared. She wanted to say something but didn't want her to be distracted from Tom. She gave a little more squeeze.

"Did you get a good look at the man in the yard?"

Hannah nodded and put her thumb back in her mouth.

"Do you think you could describe him for me?"

Hannah curled around and put her face back into

Kelly's neck. She mumbled something but between her thumb and her position, Kelly couldn't understand her.

"Shh. It's okay, sweetie. You can help Tom catch the bad guy who set Finn's house on fire. You are doing such a great job." She gently pulled Hannah's hand away from her mouth.

"He'll be mad at me."

"Who'll be mad? Finn?" Kelly pulled Hannah away far enough to look at her face. "Finn won't be mad at you."

Hannah shook her head. "Not Finn."

Tom leaned closer. "I won't be mad. Who do you think will be mad at you?"

Hannah looked at Tom and whispered. "I was going to say hi to him but when he kicked Guinness I hid."

Kelly gave a sharp look at Tom, and knew he had the same thought she did. He shook his head, letting her know not to say anything.

"Hannah, you are doing the right thing by talking to us." Tom continued. "When someone does something wrong, even if we know who it is, sometimes you have to tell a grown up."

"But I don't want Daddy to be mad at me." Hannah gave a hiccup. "I saw him kick Guinness and then the fire started."

"Hannah, you were such a brave girl to stay hiding. We are all very proud of you." Kelly kissed the top of her daughter's head, and closed her eyes as she tried unsuccessfully to keep the tears from dripping.

A large, gray-haired man came into the room and Shannon went to talk with him.

"There's my dad," Tom nodded toward them. "Do

you want to go see Shawn now?"

Kelly nodded. "Hannah. Oh, my sweet girl. I love you. Will you do mommy a favor and stay with Tom and Shannon and Liv and Grammy?"

Hannah agreed and slid over into Tom's arms and Kelly stood. "Thank you," she mouthed to Shawn's brother.

She zipped the sweatshirt over the white dress and knew she looked ridiculous in a short, white wedding dress, gray sweatshirt, and flip-flops. With her fingers she brushed her hair behind her ears, took a deep breath and went in to see Finn.

He looked better than she expected. He was sitting up in bed, playing with the IV bag attached to his arm.

"Hey there, hero."

Finn's eyes lit up as he spotted her. "Hey, there. Did you find Hannah?" His voice was raspy but Kelly didn't care. Finn really was okay.

She nodded. "She was hiding in the doghouse with Guinness. She saw Jeff set the house on fire and got scared."

"Son of a bitch."

"Shh. Don't talk. It sounds painful."

"I'm fine. I want to go home. See the damage. Check on Guinness."

"They'll be plenty of time for everything. What was the doctor's recommendation?" Kelly sat on the edge of the bed and took Finn's hand in hers.

"Night of observation," he mumbled.

"Guinness is at my house. Water out for him. I can pick up food for him first thing in the morning. Then you can come home with me and I will play Florence Nightingale for you this time."

"Sounds like fun. Will you wear a nurse's dress?"

Kelly laughed. "When was the last time you saw a nurse in a dress?"

Finn began to cough and Kelly reached over to get his glass of water. "Here you are." When he was done she put the glass back and grabbed his hand. "You scared the hell out of me. I was waiting for you to come back outside and you never did."

"I wanted to find Hannah. I couldn't leave without her."

Kelly's heart swelled with more emotion than she could handle.

"When they said you were at the hospital, I didn't know what to think. I only knew I had to see you."

"See, I'm fine. Good to go." And he concluded with another bout of coughing.

Kelly laughed. "Such a man. Stop talking for a moment and let me have my say."

"I'd rather you have your way." Finn raised his eyebrows and Kelly punched his arm gently.

"Stop, I'm trying to be serious here."

Finn brought her hand to his lips and kissed her fingers. "Go on."

"You saved me today." Kelly continued. "You made me realize I couldn't marry Jeff and the real way to save my children was to save myself, first. You gave me strength."

Finn shook his head. "You've always been strong. You were scared, and you had every right to be."

Kelly put two fingers over his lips. "Shhh. You're supposed to be quiet." Finn nodded, but then sucked a finger into his mouth. Kelly looked around furtively; making sure no one could see them. "Finn."

She tried pulling her finger out, but Finn grabbed her wrist and held it in place as his mouth toyed with her fingers.

"You must be feeling better. Enough already, someone will walk in."

Finn released her hand and placed it under his on his chest and shrugged. "You were saying something?"

"Oh, yes, I was. What was it?" Kelly stared at his long fingers, at the coarse chest hair, at his broad shoulders. "Damn it, Finn, you distracted me. I forget what I was saying."

"I believe you were going to tell me you love me."

"I was going … What? No, well, yes!"

Finn pulled at her hand again until Kelly was leaning over him. "No? Yes?" His arm moved again and wrapped around her to pull her across his chest so he could reach her for a kiss.

Kelly shifted quickly into a more accessible position and kissed him back. She loved kissing Finn. She loved being with him, loved watching him with her children.

"I wuv oo." She mumbled against his mouth."

Finn laughed as he pulled his mouth away. "Again, sweetheart."

"You know what I said." Kelly grinned down into his beautiful eyes and sighed.

"Do you know what I am going to do tomorrow?" Finn asked.

Kelly shook her head.

"I am going to put you up into the oak tree behind your house and I am going to wait until you say those three words before I come up and rescue you again."

"Really? Are you trying to scare me because it's

not going to work?"

"No? How about tickle you? Are you ticklish?" He tried to reach around but Kelly evaded his hands.

"Stop, before the nurse comes in and we get in trouble."

Finn tried to laugh but a cough came out instead. Kelly tried to move to get him water, but he held her tight beside him. "Stay."

A nurse walked in and Finn released Kelly as she moved to allow the nurse to take vitals. "They are preparing a room for you for the night. It won't be long now."

"Thank you." Finn nodded and waited until the nurse left before reaching a hand for Kelly to come back to his side. "Don't leave me. I hate hospitals. I'm afraid."

Kelly's eyes narrowed as she watched a slight tug at the corner of Finn's mouth.

"No fair. You are playing with my motherly instincts now."

His grin widened. "It was worth a shot."

Kelly shook her head. "I have the girls with me and I need to get them home to bed. I will come back in the morning to bring you home."

Finn nodded.

Kelly leaned over and kissed him again, keeping a slight distance because she knew if she didn't she'd end up back in his arms. As she pulled back she whispered in his ear.

"And I DO love you."

Epilogue

Kelly stared through the darkness to the snow covered mountains around them. The swish of the wipers whispered along with the radio as large flakes of snow battered the windows.

"You're quiet. Missing the girls, already?"

Kelly turned to Finn and smiled. He clasped his right hand around her left and lifted it to kiss the gold band circling her finger.

"No. Well, maybe. I'm thinking of the day."

"Mmmm, that's nice, because I'm thinking of tonight." Kelly rolled her eyes at her new husband.

"Actually, I was thinking your father looked good. He didn't have a single drink the entire wedding."

Finn nodded. "His AA meetings are going well. He's come a long way in six months."

Kelly sighed. "I wish I could say the same about my mother. I don't think she'll ever change."

"Maybe not." Finn squeezed her hand. "At least she came. With Jeff's impending trial next week, I actually thought she would stay far away."

Finn took a right into a driveway and pulled the truck to a stop outside a rustic cabin.

Kelly sighed. The next week would be difficult. Jeff's trial started on Tuesday. That meant their honeymoon would only be the weekend.

"It was nice of Tony to let us use his cabin. New

Year's is a popular skiing week."

Finn nodded. "He's a good friend. He said he came up yesterday and made sure it was presentable. Come on, let's go inside and I'll come back for the luggage in a few minutes."

Kelly followed Finn to the cabin door and waited while he unlocked it.

He turned back and swung her into his arms and walked through the door.

A small lamp glowed in the living room and Kelly saw a giant stone fireplace set with wood, waiting to be lit. Leather furniture adorned the room with a large blanket thrown over the back.

"It's beautiful."

Finn gave her a long kiss before setting her down. "I'll get the bags. Don't go anywhere."

Kelly took the time to roam the cabin, noting the galley kitchen to the left and followed a hallway to a set of rooms along the back. She entered the largest room and gasped.

She'd seen this room before. The large, four post bed, the dark walls, and the many candles waiting to be lit.

Finn came up behind her.

"Do you like it?" At her nod, he continued. "I had a dream about you once, of you and me in this room. I always hoped we could make it come true."

She would have told him she had also dreamed of them in this room, but he turned her around and kissed her. "I love you, Mrs. Finnigan."

Kelly wrapped her arms around him as he lifted her and carried her to the bed. "How about we light these candles then start a fire of our own?"

"I do like how you think."
Kelly laughed, as her own dreams became reality.

A word about the author...

Gina Leuci started reading romance at the age of thirteen and never stopped. She met her soul mate on a blind date and married him—not once, but twice. They live in Southern New Hampshire with their son, who makes them laugh every day, and two dogs who vie for control as Queen of the residence.